A TURN IN FORTUNE

Jon Pepper

To Dee, my co-conspirator

Cover design by Diane Pepper
Cover art by Michael Mullen

Jon Pepper
View my website at www.jonpepperbooks.com

Printed in the United States of America

First Printing: August 2018
Second Printing: October 2020
Third Printing: February 2022

Hardcover Edition: November 2021

ISBN: 9781719810852

PART ONE

1. COVER STORY

Nothing had ever beat the after-dinner swirly he got from the boys at the Porcellian Club during his sophomore year at Harvard, and hopefully, nothing ever would. But if the latest cover of *Fortune Magazine* was not the worst humiliation in Robbie Crowe's life, it was certainly in the top two. There, beneath its iconic type, was a portrait of Walker B. Hope the savior of Robbie's company and his personal nemesis—with the headline: "*The Best CEO in America?*" Robbie felt like he was turned upside down once again, his head in the toilet, water churning around him as he gurgled and gasped for air, while people from other storied families held him by the ankles and laughed uproariously.

Now this! Robbie picked up the magazine from his desk and stared at it, slack-jawed. *How was this even possible?* He studied every agonizing detail: Walker, dressed in his customary paean to all the ordinary office slugs across America—a Jos. A Bank two-for-one suit, an Oxford cloth shirt and a rep tie. His hair was expertly colored to just the right shade of anthracite coal with wisps of fly ash at the temples, and meticulously parted, apparently with tweezers. He wore a broad grin with teeth as white as Chiclets, as a panoramic backdrop of Lower Manhattan with a view of the Statue of Liberty and New York Harbor glistening behind him. Walker looked like a man whose world had revolved in just the right way to deposit him on top, where it seemed he might reside permanently. With his arms folded casually across his chest, his chiseled face smiled smugly up at Robbie, taunting him. *You can't touch me.*

To which Robbie could only shake his head and mutter, "*Tuh.*" With his breath coming in heaves, he turned with trepidation to the story, "Why There's Room for Hope at Crowe Power," by Sarah Hudson, Senior Writer.

> Until four years ago, the Crowe Power Co. was Wall Street's poster child for chronic underachievement. Founded in 1914 by the legendary Homer Crowe and built into a worldwide industrial colossus, the company stumbled for decades under the leadership of successive generations of the Crowe family until it nearly went bankrupt in its centennial year.
>
> That's when the death of Chairman and CEO Lester Crowe II precipitated a sudden change in direction. Under pressure from activist investor Maurice Klinger, the Crowes finally looked outside their nest to find a leader to do something they couldn't: Run the company. They bypassed heir apparent L. Robertson "Robbie" Crowe III, kicking him upstairs to Chairman, and recruited the highly-regarded turnaround specialist Walker B. Hope as Chief Executive Officer. It didn't take long for Hope to instill long-needed rigor and discipline into the company—providing a welcome jolt to company shares, which have soared.

Robbie slapped his forehead and ran his palm down the side of his face. *God!* As if he couldn't run the company? He *chose* not to. Where do they get this crap?

> Hope, the son of a Detroit steelworker, brought both a track record and results,

2

turning around Crowe by streamlining its energy-generating operations, cutting underperforming subsidiaries and revamping the management team. He retired all of the late Lester Crowe's cronies (save his son-in-law, Digby Pierrepont, the General Counsel), subdued the company's notoriously toxic culture of rivalry and back-stabbing, and brought in key members of the team that helped him turn around BFC Energy and Goliath Industries. Bottom line: Crowe has been restored to health and profitability and its once-dim future now looks bright. And while environmentalists deride the company for rising carbon emissions, Wall Street analysts say the effluence smells an awful lot like money.

"The profits don't stink, that's for sure," said Roger Forrester, securities analyst at Bank of America. "The company was a complete mess before Walker entered the picture—bloated, unfocused, overextended, and uncompetitive. He brought in adult supervision."

What's really amazing, Robbie fumed, is that they attributed all this progress to that hillbilly dickhead. Did they not understand that Walker had a *boss*? Didn't they know he reported to a board of directors, of which Robbie was *chairman*, and that everything—*everything!*—ran through him? He wanted to call the magazine right now. *Hello, Fortune! This is fake news! I hired this fucking goober!* This, Robbie thought, is easily the worst story he'd ever read in his life. And by the way, that suit Walker was wearing really sucked.

In an interview in Hope's office in Crowe's historic Art Deco headquarters on

Broad Street in New York's Financial District, the unassuming CEO deflected praise with an aw-shucks shrug and dismissed speculation he could be lured from Crowe to another large industrial company seeking a turnaround. "I'm needed here," he said.

Guess again, asshole. After this strut around the magazine rack, you are as good as gone. How did Marty McGarry, the company's Chief Communications Officer, hired by Robbie's very own father, become nothing but a shill for this guy? Was this what they paid him for? Did he ever give a moment's thought to Robbie and his *essential* role in this turnaround?

Analysts say Robbie Crowe, who has declined interviews since becoming chairman, should do all he can to keep Hope alive. His family fortune is tied to stock in Crowe, whose iconic "Broad Street Blue" logo is on diversified energy holdings all over the world, including power plants, pipelines and refineries.

"Walker made $47 million last year, but he's worth three times that," Forrester said. "Should he bolt, I'd worry about Crowe reverting to bad habits, especially if Robbie decided to take the wheel."

Especially if Robbie took the wheel? What kind of gratuitous bullshit was *that*? If—and that's a very big "if"—*if* Robbie were to become CEO, he'd steer the company to a bold, brilliant future that included... well, he'd worry about that later.

Before ascending to the chairman's role, Robbie Crowe had an undistinguished career at the company, culminating in a disastrous turn as Executive Vice President for Strategy, where he pushed a huge gamble on renewable energy, losing more than $3 billion on Sungod Solar Systems and Windacious Energy. Hope, who arrived with a sweeping mandate from the board to increase profitability, made pulling the plug on Robbie Crowe's green gambits his first order of business.

"The board was smart to pair Robbie with someone who could check his worst impulses and minimize the damage he could do," said an institutional investor. "His most notable career achievement to date was being born."

Robbie could read no further. It was all so unfair. So biased. So mean-spirited. So *wrong*. He slapped the magazine shut and punched the intercom.

"*Winnie!*" he barked. "Get in here. *Now!*

2. GROUNDS FOR DISMISSAL

T he massive oak door to Robbie's office creaked open as plump Winnie Hummel, Robbie's matronly executive assistant, atmospheric stabilizer, den mother, and faithful gatekeeper of nine years, entered with her ever-ready steno pad and pen in hand. She plodded with a *swish-swish-swish* from her nylons to her usual mark on the oriental rug between the wingback chairs. There she faced the chairman, who slumped behind an intricately carved desk made of timbers salvaged from a long-ago shipwreck at the bottom of Long Island Sound, lined on three sides with tall stacks of dog-eared folders, reports and yellowed papers. Robbie's face was flushed an anguished crimson, his pin-striped collar showing a hint of perspiration in the humid air of his plant-filled office.

"Yes, Mr. Crowe," she said, breathing heavily from the short walk. She knew better than to sit down. That was well above her pay grade.

Robbie stared with watery eyes at the magazine on his desk. Winnie cleared her throat and Robbie looked up, unfocused, as if he were struggling to see her through his fog of rage and self-pity. Barely audible, he asked, "Did you see this story?"

"No, sir. I have not."

"It's un-*fucking*-believable," he said, his fury rising. "*Fortune* Magazine just stuck it up my ass. And Marty McGarry allowed this to happen. After all my family has done for him..." He shook his head. "It's beyond comprehension. Tell him I want to see him, right here, right now."

"He's in with Walker Hope at the moment, sir," Winnie said.

Robbie slapped an open palm on the magazine. *Whomp.* "Of course, he's in with Walker Hope. He's *always* in with Walker Hope. That's all he *cares* about, is Walker Hope. Do you understand that?"

"Yes, sir."

"You do?"

"I believe you've mentioned it from time to time."

"Well I've had enough. It's time he—and everyone else around here—started thinking about our *entire* company. There's a hell of a lot more to it than Walker Hope. Jesus. How do people think we survived for a hundred years? By luck? Accident? It was the leadership of my family. You read crap like this and you'd think, 'Well, damn. Walker Hope must be the only person there who doesn't have their head up their ass.'"

"I'll get the word to Marty right away." She turned toward the door.

"Hold on," he said.

She turned to see Robbie holding his cup of coffee from Café Che, his thumb covering the revolutionary image of Che Guevara in his trademark beret. "I hate to bring up a sore subject. But why in hell is my coffee so goddamn cold... again? This is *really* not the day for it..."

"I'm so sorry, Mr. Crowe. I sent Emma down to get it at nine-forty-five."

"Why so early?"

"That's when we expected you. Your driver said...."

"There was traffic, Winnie. It's New York *City. Hell-oo?*"

Winnie, through years of experience and practice, remained unruffled. "Would you like another coffee, Mr. Crowe?"

"Yes. But, this time, I want you to personally go get it and make sure it's right. Don't send some flunky."

"Yes, sir."

"I want a large Bolivian Jungle Roast, with exactly two ounces of soy milk. Not more. Not less. *Two ounces.*"

"Of course, Mr. Crowe. Everyone on our team knows how you like it."

He leaned back in his chair, exasperated. "Then why, why, *why* in God's name can't you deliver it, Winnie? If it's not the temperature, it's not enough milk. If it's not the amount of milk, it's the wrong kind of milk—almond, or skim, or some other bullshit. Honestly." He slapped his cheek and rested his elbow on the desk, staring at her with an expression of disbelief. "Do I have to do *everything* myself?"

"No, sir. Of course not."

"Well, I don't trust this Emma person. Where's she from, anyway? Australia or something?"

"She's British, actually, from a city south of London. Emma's a lovely girl who's going to school at night to get her degree in accounting. She's doing a wonderful job on our expenses."

"I can barely understand that damn accent. *Wot, wot, wot,*" he mimicked, then punched the desk with his well-manicured finger. "She didn't even deliver my calendar this morning. I have absolutely *no idea* what I'm supposed to do today."

"I'm sorry, Mr. Crowe. I told her not to bother with your calendar because there's nothing on it."

"Nothing... *at all*?"

"You said you wanted us to keep it clear, that we were booking far too many meetings for you, and that every appointment must be cleared with you in advance."

"*Fine*," he growled, looking away. "Maybe I did."

She looked at the notes on her pad. "You did say you might want to have lunch with your Uncle Chuck this week, but I never got the final word on that."

Robbie perked his head up. "See? This is exactly what I'm talking about. I need you to take *responsibility*, Winnie. You need to push me until you get an answer—"

"Mr. Crowe, I—"

He held up a hand. "No, no. Stop. You're not helping yourself. I really don't want to hear any excuses. I've had it up to here," he said, indicating a spot just north of his Adam's apple. "If you're not getting what you need from me, you need to stand up and *demand* an answer. Don't be satisfied until you get it. And that goes for your staff. Is that your team out there?"

"Yes, sir."

"*Own it.*"

"Yes sir."

"Do you understand what I'm saying?"

"You're quite clear."

"No, no. Listen to me. Do you *understand*?

"Well, I think so..." she said, her voice trailing off.

"I'm saying, get rid of this Emma English-what's-her-face. I don't want to see her, *ever*."

Winnie sighed. *Not again.* "What shall I tell her, Mr. Crowe?"

"I don't know. Take her down to the loading dock and say 'scram,' for all I care. We need the A-team in this corner. Nothing less. Not the B-team. Not the C-team. If she can't execute a simple cup of coffee, she has absolutely no business working in this office. Even the smallest tasks need to be executed flawlessly."

Winnie opened her mouth to protest, then decided against it. It was five minutes after ten and she was already exhausted. The only possible strategy was retreat. She'd return to her desk and look at a photo of her husband and grandchildren and remember that there were people in the world who were pleasant most of the time.

"And don't forget. I want to see Marty," Robbie said. "I don't care if he's with Hope, the Pope, or God himself. Tell him to get his ass in here *now*."

Robbie shook his head in despair as he watched her waddle out. The *ineptitude* of these people.

3. FOCUS ON EXECUTION

Walker Hope sat at his desk, straight as a smokestack, flipping through the *Fortune* story, occasionally biting his lip and shooting a squinty-eyed glance toward Marty McGarry, the company's Chief Communications Officer. Marty sat in a chair in front of Walker's desk, nervously waiting for a verdict while he checked his email, a mix of congratulatory notes and vendor pitches on how to leverage his good Fortune on social media. He considered the piece—timed to meet the proxy statement outlining Walker's lavish compensation—a slam dunk, perhaps the best he'd ever managed. Yet one never knew how Walker would view it. He had a knack for obsessing over obscure details.

Marty put down his phone and looked beyond his boss to Walker's newly installed black mahogany bookcase, studded with mementos and trophies. With its gleaming array of strategically placed spotlights, the bookcase was the central feature of Walker's latest office remodeling, his third in four years, and, at $2 million, the most expensive yet. It was a corporate altar suitable for worship, where visiting supplicants could admire a god of industry through his carefully curated collection of totems and artifacts from an increasingly celebrated life.

One shelf was devoted to Walker Hope, family man, with portraits of Walker, his wife Gloria, and their three well-scrubbed sons, as well as his beloved grandmother, Mamaw Hammy, who raised him. There were weathered black-and-white photos of ancestral Hopes in rural Kentucky settings, with hands on tractors, horses and plows, and a glass case displaying the heavy-duty work gloves his late father wore in his job at a steel mill on the Detroit River. A larger shelf was all about his business leadership, with awards from industry groups, tributes etched in Waterford crystal blocks, and photographs of Walker in black tie on a dais, holding an audience enthralled with his homilies on the virtues of hard work and humility. A third display showcased Walker Hope, statesman and possible future cabinet secretary, in grip-and-grin handshakes with Presidents, Prime Ministers and, here and there, a dictator or two. The credenza was reserved for thick binders of laminated press clippings and stand-up frames of magazine covers from his accomplished career. He had been the subject of many glowing stories over the years, but perhaps none more emphatic in its declarations about his singular greatness than this one. And, on a stand near the windows overlooking the harbor was the only artifact that survived every stage of the office's continual remodeling: a thoroughly beaten green wooden box, which held a special memory.

At last, Walker looked up. A gap-toothed Howdy Doody smile spread across his face. "Home run," Walker said, leaning back and rapping the cover with the back of his hand. "We can do business with this Sarah lady. She gets it."

Marty could exhale; his job was good for another week. "She can be a very tough customer. But you know, we worked very hard to help her understand all of our key messages."

Walker, puzzled, looked at Marty. Was he asking for a pat on the back? The story was about Walker's brilliant leadership and Robbie's incompetence. Couldn't have been *too* hard to sell. "Uh-huh," Walker said with a shrug.

Marty tacked back to speaking of Walker's wonderfulness, a topic of sure-fire engagement. "Photos came out very nicely," Marty said. "Spectacular shot on the cover."

"Yeah, yeah. See what you mean," Walker said, holding up the cover. "Handsome devil, ain't he?"

"Are you kidding me? That's got to pump up sales for the magazine."

Walker chuckled. "Get five copies for my family, will ya? Ship 'em to Gloria in Glen Arbor; she's keeping a box of mementos for each of the kids. And let's send a copy to everyone on the board. I want to make sure they all see this."

"Robbie, too?"

"Ah, hold on. You got a point there. This might put his diapers in a twist."

"He could see this as rubbing it in."

"Maybe. But what are the choices, Marty? I can save the company, or I can keep Robbie Crowe happy. Can't do both."

Walker picked up his trademark purple felt-tip pen and wrote on the cover in the perfect cursive style that earned him an A+ in third grade penmanship, then beamed as he walked around his desk and handed it to Marty.

To Marty McGarry,
We're firing up Crowe Power!
Walker B. Hope

Marty looked at the message and suppressed an urge to laugh. What the hell? An autograph? From his boss? With a *smiley face*? What kind of cornball nonsense was this?

Walker said jovially, "I'm *sure* there's a spot on your wall for *that*."

"Oh yeah," Marty said, summoning as much sincerity as he could. "If not, I'll make it."

Walker's held up an index finger as a warning. "Don't go puttin' it on eBay now."

"Are you kidding? I'll treasure it." *Treasure?* Did that word come out of his mouth? Marty made a mental note: dial back the obvious bullshit.

"But I gotta tell ya," Walker said. "There's one itty bitty part there I just don't understand."

"What's that?"

"The question mark."

"Where?"

"C'mon, Marty," he said, sharply. "Stay with me now. Right there on the cover. 'Best CEO in America,' question mark. Not a period. Not a statement. A *question*. I don't get that."

Marty had better tread carefully. "Well... I guess they're saying that it's a really strong *possibility* that you're the best CEO in the country. That's quite a compliment."

Walker managed to smile and sneer at the same time. "You think so? Really? It's okay to be just in the mix? Maybe, I dunno, pretty good? Is *that* the standard we should have around here?"

Marty slipped on his mental tap shoes and danced. "It's just their opinion, Walker. There's no objectivity with these sorts of things."

"Oh yes there is, Marty. It's called the *stock market*. That's our scoreboard. But they're not keeping score right."

"I'm sorry, Walker. I don't follow."

"She wrote that our stock was at fourteen dollars a share when I started. But really, it was eleven."

Marty considered his words carefully. "I don't mean to contradict you, Walker, but I'm quite sure it was fourteen. I checked the record myself."

"Then you checked the *wrong* record," he said, standing and pulling a binder from the credenza and flipping it open. "Here's the story from the Wall Street Journal on the day after the *announcement* was made." He laid the binder on his conference table and opened the tab "FEBRUARY 2014."

Crowe Power Names New CEO
Scion L. Robertson Crowe III Yields to Pressure
Market Embraces the News

"See down below there," Walker said. "Stock was *eleven-oh-nine* when I was announced as the new CEO a month before. You see that headline? '*Market Embraces the News?* Embraces, Marty. The market didn't shrug. It didn't yawn. It *embraced* the news. Dog-gone stock shot up twenty-seven percent just on word that I was coming," he said, shooting his hand into space. "Highest price in five years on that press release *alone*."

Wow, Marty thought. Walker must be thinking about his next contract. Making seven-hundred-and-eighty times the pay of an average worker apparently wasn't enough. "I see what you mean," Marty said. "But —"

"But *what?*" Walker snapped. "There's no 'but' here. You need to get this corrected."

Marty opened the magazine and took a deep breath. "Of course, I'll call if you insist, Walker. But I know Sarah will defend what she wrote as accurate.

Even without the run-up before you actually started, a fifty-one-billion-dollar swing is really, really impressive."

"Yes, it is," Walker said, his voice suddenly steely, his smile vanished, his famous geniality gone, his Forrest Gump twang fading, and his eyes taking on a decidedly feral look. "But it's even more impressive if it makes the point that investor confidence was restored *immediately*. Are you saying I should not get credit for that? I'm trying hard to understand your reasoning."

"I understand your point," Marty said, surrendering. "What she wrote is literally true, but it misses important context. Got it."

Walker stared at Marty as if he were considering whether he should remove his liver with a letter opener. "Stories like this are part of the historical *record*, Marty. As the leader in our communications, you, of all people, must get it right—*every dang time*. No exceptions. I shouldn't have to tell you."

"Understood," Marty said.

"Relentless attention to detail is how we turned this company around."

"I know that very well."

"There's no relaxin' now."

Jesus Christ. *Enough already.* "Yes sir."

"If we let these little things go, pretty soon we're lettin' big things go, too. We can't have that. And we *won't* have that. Not on my watch. I mean, if you don't care what happens to me or to this company... "

"I *get* it," Marty said, with more heat than he intended.

They sat in silence for a moment as both tempers cooled. Finally, Marty said, "I'll call her."

"I am *absolutely sure* you'll get this right. Of course, if you had made sure she had all the facts from the get-go, there wouldn't be a question mark at all. That's on you, Marty, and I have to say I'm disappointed."

The intercom buzzed on Walker's desk, saving Marty from further instruction. Walker, irritated, punched a button. "What is it, Flora?"

"Sorry to bother you, sir," said his executive assistant. "You've got your Leadership Team meeting at eleven and you've blocked out forty-five minutes for prep time at ten."

"Thank you."

"And Mr. Crowe's office called," she said. "He would like to see Mr. McGarry."

Walker let go of the intercom button and looked to Marty. "That guy still doesn't get it, does he?"

"What's that?" Marty said, standing up.

"You work for me—not him."

4. GREEN, WITH ENVY

With the autographed magazine tucked under his arm, Marty padded down the burled-maple-and-marble corridor separating Walker's corner office on the west side of the building from Robbie's larger office on the east, strolling past the spotlighted oil portraits of more than a hundred years of Crowe chief executives, all of whom bore the last name of Crowe. Somehow, Walker's portrait had not yet been hung, which is why the gallery was still known to denizens of the Crowe Power Company C-suite as the "Hall of Fam."

The company's official history, written by Marty for the centennial celebration four years earlier, touted the brilliant and caring stewardship of the Crowe family and the many contributions they made to the world's economic growth, improved standards of living, and charitable giving over the past hundred years. It saluted the company's role in illuminating remote rural areas of Africa with hydro-electric power, refining crude oil to create an essential ingredient in hundreds of useful products for everyday life, and building pipelines that delivered cleaner-burning natural gas to power plants. Portions of the company history left on the cutting room floor included Homer Crowe's violent suppression of a Depression-era coal miners' strike that resulted in eight deaths; his son Lester's spying activities on company workers; the fouling of various rivers and streams throughout the Eastern U.S.

with toxic PCBs; numerous violations of the Clean Air Act; a gruesome refinery explosion in Louisiana that killed 45 people; and a recent citation from an activist group naming Crowe Power the ninth worst polluter in the U.S.

All in all, Marty thought: not bad.

As he neared Robbie's office, his sense of dread colluded with a throbbing molar to instigate a massive headache. He slipped the phone from his pants pocket and called Carly, his administrative assistant. "Get me in to see Dr. Littmann, will you?" he said. "I can't take it."

"The job or the tooth?" she asked.

"Both. I've got a toothache, a headache, and I'm about to have a serious pain in the ass."

"Mr. Crowe?"

"I'm guessing he's on the warpath."

"We've all been told to stay away from his office. He fired one of the admins today because his coffee was cold."

"Great. This should be lots of fun."

"Speaking of which: Your wife called."

"Ex-wife."

"Sorry. Jill. She wants you to call her back."

"No, she doesn't. She just wants a check. And why not? I'd like one, too."

Marty hung up, pulled the ID badge from the reel on his belt, and waved it past the card reader next to the glass door. He looked up into a camera over the door and summoned a weak smile for Winnie. He heard a click and entered the outer reaches of the Chairman's 2,000 square-foot suite, a richly appointed reception area dominated by a three-dimensional Broad Street Blue and white logo of Crowe Power and a bronze bust of Homer Crowe benignly overlooking two plush sofas, a pair of chocolate-brown Paris club chairs, a glass coffee table, and a buffet counter featuring coffee, spring water, fruit and bagels. All the food would be thrown out by noon and replaced with fresh provisions that would also go to waste, making the Crowe Power dumpster a popular culinary choice for aficionados of suite-to-street cuisine.

Marty pulled open the glass door to Robbie's outer office and entered the administrative area, where Winnie, eying the magazine in his hand, greeted him with an arched eyebrow.

"You do not want to go in there with that," she said. "I'll hold it for you."

Marty handed it over, prompting Winnie to recoil at the autograph. "Oh *dear*," she said with a shudder, putting it face down on her desk.

"Is he ready for me?" Marty asked.

"Oh boy," she said. "Is he ever."

"Terrific," Marty said glumly.

"Well, don't worry just yet. He's got someone in there right now."

Behind Winnie, a shell-shocked Emma stood at her desk, sadly filling a cardboard box with her personal belongings while a stone-faced representative from Human Resources and a burly gum-smacking security guard stood watch, lest she try to steal her—what—desk? Marty turned his back to the sad scene and whispered to Winnie. "Didn't she just start?"

Winnie nodded. "Not a good fit," she mouthed.

"A fluid situation, I hear."

"Something like that."

The door to Robbie's office opened and out came Tom Michaels, the ultra-fit former Secret Service agent now running corporate security. He smiled grimly at Marty. "Good luck," he said.

Marty took a deep breath and headed toward the inner sanctum as a copy of *Fortune* came fluttering over the threshold, landing at his feet. Marty picked it up and walked in, pulling the door shut behind him. He assumed the wingback chair in front of Robbie's desk and sat on the edge, a respectfully submissive perch.

Robbie looked up, seething, his arms folded tightly across his chest, perspiration showing on his forehead and upper lip. It occurred to Marty that all the soothing greenery and expensive mood lighting in Robbie's office never seemed to help. "I'm sensing you didn't like the story," Marty said.

"Wow, Marty," Robbie said, raising his chin and clenching his teeth. "You must have ESP. How did you figure that out?"

"I got a message via air mail," Marty said, holding up the magazine and putting it carefully on the closest pile he could reach on Robbie's desk.

"So tell me, Mr. Public Relations Man: what did *you* think of the story?"

"Honestly? I thought the company looked pretty damn good."

"The *company*? No, no, no, no," Robbie said with a mirthless laugh. "*Walker* looked pretty damn good. Everything else about the company looked like total *crap*, especially me. You'd think I couldn't find the bathroom without him to hold my hand."

That was rich, Marty thought. Robbie had the bathroom ripped out of his father's old suite before Walker took occupancy to force him to use the executive washroom with the lowly VPs. Only Crowes were exalted enough for a private loo, which is why the guys on the building crew referred to Robbie—behind his back, of course—as His Royal Heinie.

"This story makes Walker out to be the second coming of Jack Welch, a reincarnation of Alfred P. Sloan and Steve Jobs. I look like I couldn't run a goddamn lemonade stand."

Interesting thought—Robbie running a lemonade stand. *Could he really do it? And turn a profit?* "Robbie, I know you're upset. But I thought you came off very well."

Robbie slapped his desktop. "No shit, Marty. How did you come to that conclusion?"

"Think about it. You're portrayed as a leader who does whatever it takes to make this company successful—even if it means sharing power with Walker. You could have had the CEO job, but you didn't take it. You're selfless. All you care about is the greater good of the business, which is doing spectacularly well because of your foresight and leadership."

Robbie mockingly flipped through the magazine. "Hmm. Let's see. Where does it say that I'm selfless? I must have missed that part."

Marty scooched forward, trying to peer over the piles. "You'll see it, if you read it closely."

"Looking... looking..."

"Okay. Maybe it doesn't say that explicitly. But it's clearly implied."

Robbie clapped his hands together. "You are a complete bullshit artist."

Well, yeah, Marty thought. *That's what I'm paid for.* He cocked his head like a dog trying to understand his angry human. "People admire what you've done here, Robbie. Everyone knows it takes a big man, secure in himself, comfortable in his own skin, to share the stage like you have. I hear people talk about it all the time. 'That Robbie. He's... he's... such a *good guy.*'"

"Really?" Robbie asked bitterly. "Then why in the hell couldn't you find someone to say that in the story?" He put both hands on his desk and pushed himself up. He walked slowly to the windowsill, where he was framed by his organic drapes, reputedly edible, and possibly in danger of being eaten imminently. Marty could feel the perspiration soaking the back of his collar. Why had he worn his suitcoat in here? Robbie maintained a rain-forest humidity in his office better suited for bananas.

"You know what really fries me?" Robbie said. "You'd think all we care about at this company is making money, that we're just a bunch of greedy bastards who boil oil and burn coal to line our pockets, the planet be damned. There's not one word in there about our green ventures, except that they supposedly failed. Do you have any idea how much crap I get about all the fossil fuels we use? It's everywhere I go. Restaurants. Clubs. Parties. And not just New York, but everywhere. Santa Barbara. Palm Beach. All over Europe. I can't go anywhere without somebody bending my ear about climate change—and blaming me for it. *Me*, when I'm the guy trying to do something about it. We had protesters down on Broad Street this morning. Angriest mob I've ever seen in my life. They were beating the *hood of my car*, Marty. Threatening my life! If I hadn't slid down in my seat so they couldn't see me, they would have dragged my ass out on the street and beaten me like a piñata."

"Really? I saw those people. I thought they were a tour group."

"Are you kidding me? They're terrorists. What I don't understand is why they don't go after Walker."

"Maybe because he gets in at 7. I don't think they're up yet."

Robbie sighed. "You know what? Hell with it. I'm done. I'm just going to hire my own PR firm to get my side out there. Nobody's standing up for me. There hasn't been one damn story in the past four years that said, 'thank God Robbie Crowe's keeping a watch over things, since he has a responsible view of the planet.' The path our company is on may be very profitable in the short term, and that's fine—*fine*—but it is not sustainable. We can't destroy the environment and expect the company to live. And I'm not hearing anything from Walker about what he's going to do about that. Oh no," he said, practically spitting. "Not loveable Walker, our hero—*the best CEO in America*."

Marty raised his index finger. "Question mark."

"Oh, please. That was clearly the idea. I've never seen such a slobbering suck-up piece in all my life. Especially for a guy who's a first cousin to Jethro Bodine."

So there it was—the real stick in his craw. Robbie couldn't stand the idea that Walker, an inherently inferior being, a mere hireling born to Kentucky bumpkins who migrated to blue-collar Detroit, was considered *better* than him.

"I can't throw Walker under the bus," Marty said. "That wouldn't reflect well on anybody, especially you. The world sees Walker as your guy, the one you and the board wisely turned to when you agreed, very graciously, as *everyone* knows, to focus your energies on leadership at the very highest level, which is exactly what you're doing."

"Walker's not my guy. He's Moe Klinger's guy. Which is why all he cares about is profits. *Money, money, money.* As if that's the most important thing in the world."

Marty bit his tongue. "Well, I know it comes in handy for some people."

"Look," Robbie said. "I'm not saying you should trash Walker. I mean, he's doing okay. But you've got to remember something. He might *think* he's more important than me, but he's *not*. He's a hired hand, like you, like that Emma chick, like everyone else around here. Maybe you haven't noticed, but there's a sign over the front door with my name on it. Not Walker's. I'm still going to be here long after he shuffles off to Michigan or Minnesota or wherever in that vast field of wheat out there. And I'm telling you, things will be very, very different around here when he's gone."

Marty was startled. "Walker's leaving?"

"Wake up, Marty. Everyone leaves at some point," he said. "*Everyone.*"

Robbie, tiring of his chew toy, stepped on a foot pedal under his desk, which activated a buzzer and blinking light on a phone line that went nowhere. He pretended to look at the digital readout on the console and furrowed his brow, as if he were getting a call. "I've got to take this," he said as he picked up the phone, effectively dismissing Marty.

"Yeah," Robbie said into the dead phone.

As soon as Marty crossed the threshold, Robbie hung up. First chance he got, he was going to fire that dunce.

5. NOWHERE TO RUN

So the sign over the front door said "Crowe" and the name atop the org chart said "Hope." No matter which way you read it, Marty figured, he was screwed. Walker, if necessary, would easily offer Marty as a human sacrifice to please the Crowe gods. And that would mean financial disaster.

At his desktop computer, Marty navigated to his private drive and clicked on the file entitled "Offer Letter" from October of 2010, when he had been recruited by Robbie's father, Lester, to run communications at Crowe Power. The letter detailed his salary, bonus, stock awards and other benefits. He pointed his mouse at "Find" and typed in "severance," which took him to the last paragraph on Page 5.

"In the event you are terminated without cause, you shall be entitled to one year's pay and a fractional share of your target bonus for the year, based on time served, and all Company shares awarded to you would be vested.

"However, should you resign your position or be terminated with cause, you will not receive severance pay and you would forfeit investiture in Company stock. All other benefits would cease immediately...."

It didn't take a lawyer to interpret this language: getting fired was a dangerous proposition and quitting was not an option without a soft landing elsewhere. Even with a healthy income, he was deeply overextended on his financial commitments. The monthly alimony payments to Jill, living in his old Westchester house with Jose, their 27-year-old Salvadoran gardener, drew nearly half his net pay. Tuition payments for Luke and Nicole, just beginning their college educations at Williams and Cornell, were cutting deeply into his savings. The nursing home for his mother in Philadelphia drained her accounts and were now leeching his. Even his smelly third-floor walk-up rental in Greenwich Village was running an appalling $6,000 a month. Without a job, his next living option might be a cardboard box and a subway grate.

Marty pushed back in his Aeron chair to regard his trophy wall, festooned with framed copies of the best stories produced on his watch at Crowe. There was the cover story profile of Robbie in *Forbes* when he was promoted to run Strategy in 2010: "The Next Generation of Power at Crowe is Green." Four years later, it was a cover story in *Barron's*, with a smiling Robbie and Walker, back-to-back: "Crowe's New Team at the Top—So Happy Together." The frame he was most proud of was empty, with nothing but a blank white sheet of paper. It represented the story never written: *Businessweek*'s planned cover hit piece in 2014 on "The Worst CEOs in America," which was going to feature Robbie's father Les. Marty successfully delayed the story for months until Les's death and Walker's appointment rendered the story moot and the piece was scrapped. In the prehistoric days of traditional media, Marty's press achievements would have helped him land another job. Now, with great publications withering away, there wasn't quite as much press for companies to worry about.

Marty dialed Jason Kleinman, a headhunter at Wylie & Crumm, who had placed Marty in two of his last three jobs.

"This is Jason. Can I help you?"

"I hope so."

"Marty? Hey, buddy. What's up?"

"I need to get out of here. Like now."

"Can't say I'm surprised," Jason said. "In fact, I was expecting your call."

"That's alarming. Why?"

"You've been in your job eight years. You're way beyond the average life expectancy for a post like yours. I mean, in dog years, you're basically dead. Then I saw the *Fortune* story and figured you might not last the morning. When a CEO gets more good publicity than the boss whose name is in the logo, lives are in danger. People die."

"Robbie's furious," Marty conceded. "He wants to kill Walker. But I think he'd like to practice on me first."

"I get it. He was upstaged by an underling. The man's pride took a hit, and we both know he's got an ego big as the Empire State Building. But if he were thinking clearly—granted, a big 'if'—he should let it go. The company was in pathetic shape when Walker joined. Robbie surely knows Walker Hope is making him rich."

"Robbie doesn't care about that. He's already rich. He's richer now, sure, as are all his cousins and kids and nieces and nephews. But this isn't about money."

"I get it. It's a cock fight."

"Yes, and here's the problem. It really doesn't matter who wins."

Jason sighed. "Well, I would strongly advise you not to quit, my friend."

"I know. I did the math. I can't leave until I find another gig."

"That's my point, Marty. There *are* no other gigs—not for you. I've got four CCO jobs to fill, but every one of them is looking for a diversity hire."

Marty sagged. "My grandmother once told me I'm something like one-thirty-second Cherokee."

"Look. Just because I go to Hakkasan for dinner on Christmas doesn't make me Chinese, alright? Unless you go transgender and I can call you 'she' or 'ze,' *fuhgeddaboudit*. A Martine, I can sell. A Marty? Not unless you spell it with an 'i' at the end."

"With the day I'm having, I can't rule out gender reassignment."

"Here's my advice, Tootsie. Put your head down and suck it up. Do the job they're paying you to do: making it look like everything's wonderful there, even when it's not. Keep working your magic. But just remember this: you can't stay in the middle between Robbie and Walker forever. At some point, you're going to have to pick a side."

Marty hung up, his toothache pounding his skull like an Anacin hammer, and looked out toward New York Harbor, cursing Ellis Island for having let Homer Crowe into the country a century ago. He clicked on LinkedIn and began browsing.

"Are you okay?" Carly said.

Marty turned to see his administrative assistant looking concerned. "No," he said.

"I got you in to see Dr. Littmann at 4," she said. "Maybe that will help."

"Could they just send over a general anesthetic? That's all I need."

"Mr. Crowe isn't happy?"

"Hates the story and hates me. Other than that, we're good," he said. "Can you get me Sarah Hudson on the phone? I need to ask for a correction."

"Will do."

"And do something with this, will you?" he said, handing her Walker's autographed copy of Fortune.

"Frame it?"

"Can't burn it," he said.

Carly looked around. "Where do you want to put it?"

"Honestly? Behind the door. But that won't do. Walker could show up here someday. He'd expect a display with votive candles underneath it."

6. HOWIE-DO-IT

O f all the petitioners to have standing in the Court of the King of Crowe, none was more improbable than Howie Doolin, who had previously flunked out of no fewer than four departments in company headquarters, yet retained a vague administrative job in the basement, where he spent much of his time studying porn and selling drugs to the building staff. Howie was a protected species because he was a genuine FORC—Friend of Robbie Crowe—a talent for which he had no peer, at least among men.

While Howie had proven himself an unreliable employee in IT, marketing, operations, and HR, he excelled at Robbie's black ops—the extracurricular activities that Tom Michaels and his security team of former Secret Service and FBI agents refused to touch. Howie had no such law enforcement training nor scruples; his mission was to defend Robbie against all demons by any means necessary. Throughout Robbie's rise to prominent leadership roles in the company, Howie exhibited remarkable skill at piercing the veil of anonymity of Robbie's social media critics and intimidating them to stop, spying on Crowe executives suspected of disloyalty, who found themselves suddenly dismissed, and delivering checks to witnesses of Robbie's more embarrassing behaviors to ensure they would never talk. Howie smelled opportunity in each successive crisis like a fruit bat sniffs out a ripening apple. His bias toward action, no matter how poorly it was thought out, earned him the sobriquet, Howie-Do-It.

And so it was that Robbie's second visitor of the day was the thick-necked, buzz-cut, tattooed, and dishonorably discharged Howard J. Doolin, wearing a track suit that looked like it was borrowed from the wardrobe of Paulie Walnuts, incongruously slumping into a seat in an elegant Chippendale wingback chair in front of Robbie's desk.

"What's this?" Robbie said. "Casual Monday?"

"Working out upstairs, man. Thought I'd better check in after seeing that piece-of-crap story."

Robbie gasped, still struggling to believe this latest indignity. "I couldn't believe it."

"Who is this chick, Sarah Hudson? Isn't that, like, the third story she's written about him?"

"Not that I care, but it was the *fourth*."

"She must be fucking him," Howie said with remarkable certainty.

Robbie leaned back, nodding. "That's what I'm thinking. What could she *see* in that dork?"

"Results, I guess. But, I mean, c'mon. That shit's *so* overrated."

"Give me a break. His so-called 'results' are strictly short-term," Robbie said. "Long-term? I have no idea where we're going. As usual, it's all going to be up to me to figure that out. I'm the only one around here who worries about the big picture. We don't need the best CEO in America. We need the best CEO *for the planet.*"

Howie-Do-It shook his head. "I totally get that. But nobody else does. It's just not fair."

Robbie skimmed the magazine, running his finger through the copy. "And tell me this: where do they get this crap about me being such a 'nice guy?' What's that supposed to mean? I can't be a prick if I have to be? I can't make tough decisions? C'mon. I can fire his ass. Let's see how they like that."

"People just don't know you. I've seen you be a real dickhead."

Robbie glared at him. "You made the point, alright?"

"C'mon, man. You know I'd take a bullet for you. You're tough when you need to be. That's the difference. You're not just a random, nasty-ass prick like Walker."

Robbie nodded. "That's right. You think Marty would ever tell a reporter that?"

"*No*," Howie said, practically spitting. "Marty's a total idiot."

"And they keep making Walker out to be some great leader. What the hell. I mean, look at what I had to deal with when I was running Strategy. Did any leader—*ever*—have a shittier bunch of followers than me?"

"Never," Howie said, looking grave. "You were dealt a really bad hand."

"They were all my *dad's* people," Robbie complained. "And you know who he put around him—his drinking buddies. What was I supposed to do? Fire them all my first day on the job? Well, you know the star of any show's only as good as his supporting cast. I had a bunch of washed-up losers. Somebody should say *that* in the press sometime. But no. It's *all* on me. Nobody around here gives a flying shit about me."

"Flying fuck."

"Whatever." Robbie leaned forward in his chair and spoke in a lowered voice. "Did you get that camera installed in Walker's office?"

Howie nodded and smiled. "Amazing what a hundred bucks and bag of weed can get you with our building crew."

"Where did they put it?"

"Behind his desk," Howie replied. "It's fantastic. You can see *everything* that goes on in there."

"So tell me," Robbie said eagerly, hunching over his desk. "What are you seeing? What's he doing? I gotta hear this."

Howie leaned forward, looking around conspiratorially before speaking. "It looks like he's working."

"I assume that. What else?"

"Nothing. From seven to seven, that's all he does."

"Oh, come on," Robbie pushed. "All he does is work? *Nobody* works that much."

"*He* does," Howie insisted. "It's kind of boring to watch, actually. I scroll through the video pretty fast."

"You think he's faking?" Robbie asked.

"Why would he do that? He doesn't think anyone's looking."

"I don't get it." Robbie shook his head. "What kind of work is he doing?"

"He reviews papers. Works on his computer. Holds meetings at his conference table. Talks to people overseas on his video conferencing screen. Stuff like that."

"So...*work*, work."

"Far as I can tell," Howie said with a shrug.

"Lot of good that does me."

They sat in glum silence a moment. "*Oh!*" Howie said. "There is something else he does."

"What?" Robbie asked.

"He practices his golf swing."

"No *shit*." Now, Robbie thought, we're getting somewhere.

"Yeah," Howie continued. "He keeps a club in his closet."

"He does that on *company time*?"

"Yep."

"Given the money we pay him, that's pretty outrageous, don't you think?" Robbie suggested. "How much does he do that?"

"Couple minutes a day."

"Oh."

"I think it's just to stretch his back because he's hunched over working all the time."

"Ah."

"Otherwise, like I said, he works," Howie said. "Works and works and works and works some more."

"Shit," Robbie said, leaning back. "You know when you think about it, that's the difference, right there. Of course, he works. He has the *time*. See?"

"I think I'm following you..."

"It's like this. He doesn't have all the distractions I do. Look at all these reports," Robbie said, waving a hand over the piles. "Can you believe it? I've got people running in and out of here all day, dumping their papers and their problems on me. Board issues, Crowe family issues, shareholder issues, outside boards. On and on it goes. Then I've got the calls from Lindsey and the kids and my friends. I mean, if I only had the time, I could clear off all this crap—"

"Of course. You'd be even *more* amazing."

"*Exactly!* All he has to focus on is the basics. Just run the business, which is *easy peasy* now. All he had to do was come in and grab the glory. And I'm stuck with everything else."

"It ain't right."

Robbie leaned back in his chair, looking up. For a moment, he pondered whether he had more ceiling tiles than Walker and made a mental note to ask the building department for a report on the square footage of every office on 24, just to be sure. "We should never have let anyone outside the family get their nose under the tent," he said. "Once they're in, they're like cockroaches. They never go away."

They sat in silence a moment, gravely pondering the injustice of it all. At last, Howie said, "You want me to take him out?"

Robbie frowned. "That's a little extreme, don't you think?"

"You tell me."

"Let's put it this way. I don't think 'murder' is one of our company's core values."

"You're probably right," Howie conceded.

They sat silently again. "I need something on him," Robbie said.

"Like what?"

"I don't know," Robbie sighed. "Some kind of leverage to get him out of here. Either I build a case with the board, which would be a tough sell, or we find something that could make him quit."

"I can get in there and dig around."

"That's a thought. It's all company property, right?"

"I think so."

Robbie nodded approving, pressing his fingertips. "Well. Why the hell not? I think we have every right to know what he's doing. He's a paid employee, just like everybody else."

"I like it."

"You know, I play by the rules every goddamn day," Robbie lamented. "What does that get me? *Nothing.*"

"Just because you do doesn't mean I have to," Howie offered.

"Well, however you handle this, I officially don't know, right?" Robbie said.

"Your hands are clean. As always."

"We never had this conversation."

"Anything I do is my own choice," Howie pledged. "They could torture me. Put me in stocks. Whip me. Beat me. Cat o' nine tails—"

Robbie held up a hand. "I get the picture."

"I'd never give you up. You know that, boss."

Robbie regarded Howie with dewy eyes: they really could torture him. He'd probably like it, too. Howie-Do-It. What a *gem*.

7. TAKING FLACK

Marty poured himself a coffee in the break room on the 24th floor and grabbed a table in the corner where no one could hear him. He dreaded calling Sarah Hudson for a correction, but he had no choice; Walker was sure to ask him about it. He looked up Sarah's contact on his mobile phone, took a deep breath, and hit the green phone icon. Up to this point, he'd built up a good pile of political capital with Sarah. This would likely draw down his chips.

"*Fortune*. This is Sarah."

"Hey, Sarah. It's Marty. I want to say thank you. That was a really terrific piece."

"I appreciate that."

"Great job on your part. I don't think anyone else has come close to capturing the essence of our success under Walker like you have."

"Thanks, Marty."

"You got almost every key fact in there."

Silence, then: "I sense a 'but.'"

"Well, yes, actually. I have just one."

"We all have just one, Marty. Tell me about yours."

Marty explained the additional value appreciation that should have been credited to Walker. By omitting that essential fact, he said, readers weren't getting the complete record of his magnificent achievement. If they understood *all* the market value that was created by Walker from the time he was announced as the incoming Crowe Power CEO, perhaps there wouldn't be a question mark on the cover. He would be, indisputably, the best CEO in America. His hiring alone is enough to lift a company from its misery and set it on a higher plane.

There was a long pause on Sarah's end, followed by a laugh. "Is it possible, Marty, that Walker actually *asked* you to call me about getting more credit?"

"Oh, no, no no. Not at *all*," Marty said with his best guffaw. "Are you kidding me?"

"You mean, plastering his mug on our cover wasn't enough?"

"I'm sure it was—"

"He's not that obsessed with his image, is he?"

"C'mon, Sarah. Of course not. You've come to know him as well as anybody. He's got his eyes on the big picture. You think he worries about little details like this?"

"To be honest with you, Marty, I bet he *obsesses* over details like this. Maybe I need to think about how that might factor into my next story. It makes an interesting little angle."

"Stop," Marty said. "Please don't pin this on Walker. He's the last person to worry about stuff like this. He's a very humble man, as you well know."

"Then why are you calling? I've got another story I'm working on and I'm right on deadline."

"I'm only calling because *I* care. I want to make sure the record is accurate. We're doing something historic here and, let's face it, you're the most credible source on our company."

"I'm credible because I don't put junk like that in my stories."

"So I guess a correction—just online—is out of the question?"

Another pause. "You know, Marty. I've always liked dealing with you because you've been relatively straightforward—I mean, for a PR guy—and you've minimized the corporate talking point bullshit. But I find this conversation extremely off-putting."

"I'm sorry, Sarah. Truly. I don't mean to upset you. Far from it. I respect you too much. I'm only thinking about you and your relationship with us. We regard you as the go-to person in the press. If we had a scoop of some kind, I think you'd be at the front of the line. I'd like to keep it that way."

"So, if I play ball, you'll be nice to me? Is that it? You think you can trade my, what, my integrity for a scoop to be named later? Well forget it. You should be grateful for the story you got—not because it's flattering, but because it's accurate and credible. And if you're going to come after me with some bullshit about exchanging favors, you can just buzz off. I don't play that game."

She hung up, leaving Marty for a moment to reflect: he hated this fucking job.

8. PITY PARTY

Robbie stared at the foot-high piles of reports, briefing papers, and presentations that made the perimeter of his desk look like a castle wall. Peering out over the parapets, his shoulders slumped. Some of this stuff, he thought, must be four years old. He craned his neck sideways to read the spine of an Annual Report—*2010!* How the hell did *that* get in there? Well, apparently nobody was going to lift a finger to help with this. And that was okay. This would be the week that he would finally do something about it himself, starting today, starting right now. *Now,* damn it. *Now!* Right... after he looked at the company's Twitter feed. *What were people saying about him?*

He grabbed his phone, swiveled his chair toward the credenza behind his desk, and pulled up his Twitter account. His chin dropped as he scrolled past one depressing comment after another extolling the leadership of Walker B. Hope and all he had accomplished. There were recommended buys for company stock, speculation about where Walker might go next, and shots at Robbie, whose leadership was discussed with derision and ridicule.

King Coal 1 hr
@CrowePower Walker Hope is a god.
Robbie Crowe should start each day
by kissing his ass.

Bullish 1 hr
@CrowePower Is that before or after
he beats off in the office? That must be

all he does.

Old Crowe 1 hr
@CrowePower Robbie: Charter member
of the #LuckySpermClub.

The thread went on and on, each commentator trying to outdo the other, casually ripping Robbie and praising Walker.

"Checking Twitter?" a woman's voice said behind him.

Robbie turned to see Maria Territo, the company's Associate General Counsel, standing in the doorway. His mistress for the past two years, she knew his habits too well.

"It's unbelievable," he said, his voice choking. "Everybody hates me."

She strode into his office, dressed in an elegant gray Chanel suit, her dark hair swept up in a chignon, and walked to the corner of his desk, where she touched the button for the door, which closed behind her.

She smiled sympathetically. "It looks like someone needs a hug."

Needs a hug? No, Robbie thought. He *deserved* a hug. If the people at the top of this company weren't so dead on their ass at defending him, he wouldn't be in this humiliating situation. He looked away, aggrieved, as she walked around the desk and stood over him, her breasts inches from his face.

"And that someone," she said, "*isn't you.*"

She reached back and swung the palm of her right hand—*whap!*—across his face.

"What the hell's the matter with you? What did you do that for?"

"'Cause I know what you're doing here"—pronounced *he-uh* in her deep-dish Lawn Guyland accent. "You read that story in Fortune and you started feeling sorry for yourself. *Wah-wah-wah.* You thought about how all those old Crowes out there in the Hall of Fam have been on the cover of *Fortune* and you never have. And then you looked at your Twitter feed and started feeling even worse. Well, you need to stop this crazy shit. Just *stop,* for God's sake. I can't take it anymore."

He straightened in his chair. "Did you see what they were saying on Twitter? I have every right to be pissed off."

She wagged a freshly polished index finger in his face. "No, you don't. You're a billionaire. You're at the top of the food chain. You've got six homes, teams of people catering to every whim, a private jet at your disposal. Your kids and their kids and their kids' kids are taken care of for the next five hundred years."

Robbie rubbed his jaw. "I'm really not a fan of tough love."

"Tough shit," she said, putting her hands on her hips. "That's probably why you're so pathetic. You never got enough of it."

"So I'm just supposed to take this lying down?"

"That's exactly what you *are* doing—lying down. You wallow in self-pity, nursing this unending grievance against the world. For whatever reason, you feed off this everyone-hates-me, I-got-it-so bad, poor-little-rich-boy crap. You know who had it bad? My mother," *muthuh*, "who was on her arthritic knees scrubbing floors for rich old biddies like your mother. And my father, who walked up a stairway in the World Trade Center on 9/11 with a 60-pound pack on his back and never came down. When the bell rang, he picked up his axe and strapped on his gear and went to battle. God forbid the bell rings for you. You'd curl up in a little ball."

"Stop. *Stop.* I get it. He's a hero."

"You're damn right."

"And I'm—"

"A fucking baby."

He sighed. "But..."

"But what?"

"You're a lawyer. Why can't we sue these people for saying this stuff?"

"Because you're a public figure."

"So anyone can say pretty much *anything*?"

"What would your claim be? 'They're saying nice things about my company president, who I hired, and I want people to stop?' That's just nuts. Why can't you just accept the fact that Walker has done you a solid and made your rich family a whole lot richer?"

Robbie shook his head. "You don't understand."

"You're right about that," she said, glaring at him. "I don't. Enlighten me."

Robbie turned his head from one side, then to the other, thinking. Should he say it? "He thinks he's me."

"Oh, brother." She shook her head. "And how do you figure that?"

"It's hard to describe."

"I'm sure it is. But you should try. 'Cause I don't get that at all."

"It's... the way he looks at me. The way he... the way he talks to me. His body language. Everything about him says he thinks we're equals. But we're not. He's a *fucking hillbilly*. All this Gomer Pyle, howdily–doodily bullshit. How am I supposed to take that?"

"Honestly, Robbie, you've got to get over yourself. I know you think you were somehow born under a special star that glowed only for you. But we're all just human beings here. You, Walker, me, everybody. I tell you what. Spend an afternoon at the Museum of Natural History sometime. You'll see a lot of dinosaurs with five digits on their hands and rib cages and eye sockets. We're all from the same family tree. The sooner you quit worrying about whether somebody might question, God forbid, whether you're some special species, the better your life—and my life—will be."

As she turned to leave, he called after her. "We getting together tomorrow?"

"I don't know," she said. "I'm not sure I'm on your level."

9. VICTORY LAP

Walker put aside 45 minutes of uninterruptible time at precisely 10 a.m. every Monday morning to study each line of the company Progress Report before his weekly Leadership Team meeting. Every week, Walker asked the top executives to prepare a scorecard, grading their progress towards corporate goals. He wanted to examine for himself whether every "A" truly deserved a top grade, to understand the fixable problems behind each "B," and to get a handle on any "C's," which indicated the possibility of failure. He reviewed each page, all the back-up slides in the appendix, scrutinized all details in the footnotes—a favored burial ground for bad news—and paid special attention to the asterisks. If there were a reason that any part of the company was forecasted to fall short of the business plan, Walker wanted to know who was accountable for it and what they were going to do about it. He let it be known that reports of low grades were not only tolerated but encouraged, for transparency was critical to running the business. But all C's had an expiration date of one week, as did the executives who posted them. The choice was, as Walker liked to say, binary: fix the problem, or someone else would.

At 56, Walker had reached a point in his life where he simply could not abide surprises—good surprises, bad surprises, birthday surprises—nothing that could distract him from his relentless focus on goals, which he reviewed at the beginning of every day. He had a plan for his career. A plan for the company. A plan for the wealth he intended to accumulate. A plan for each and every day.

His routines were all about meeting his various plans: Up at 5:30 a.m. and out at 5:35 for a three-mile run around the perimeter of Battery Park and Battery Park City, regardless of the weather; arrive at work by 7; consume a 15-minute lunch consisting of a sandwich and an apple at the stroke of noon; run a "bed-check" around the 24th floor at 6:45 p.m. to see who was still at their desk; and get out the door at precisely 7 p.m., usually with a take-home salad from the executive dining room. Throughout his workday, he made time for as many appointments as he could, often dividing his hours into 10- and 15-minute segments. Even his bathroom breaks were scheduled in advance, with peeing slated for two minutes before the top of the hour four times a day, beginning at 7:58 a.m. This discipline allowed no more than a half-cup of coffee in the morning, and very little water throughout the day, lest he need more bio breaks.

A little-known quirk in his daily regimen was that he worked only a half-day on Fridays, when he was picked up at noon in a black Escalade at the headquarters' back door on New Street and whisked off to Teterboro Airport in New Jersey, where he would board a company G5 for Naples, Florida, where his wife, Gloria, spent her winters, or Glen Arbor in northwestern Michigan, where she spent her summers in a house overlooking Big Glen Lake and the Sleeping Bear Dunes. After moving across the country every few years early in Walker's career, she put her foot down when Walker took the Crowe Power job in New York; she would move no more. She would sink in her roots more permanently, regardless of where he worked. He could join her on weekends, vacations and holidays. Walker made a condition of his employment at Crowe that he would have a company jet—the Crowe Bird II—at his personal disposal whenever he wanted for conjugal visits.

Regardless of whether he was flying northwest or south, Walker's jet always stopped at Detroit Metropolitan Airport for an afternoon layover, which he spent at the historic Book Cadillac Hotel in downtown Detroit, where he would have a swim at 2:30 p.m., a whirlpool at 2:45, and a massage in the penthouse apartment he owned at 3 o'clock, courtesy of Malaya Mendoza, an undocumented Filipino woman who was on his personal payroll. Once refreshed, he would re-board his jet at 4 p.m. for the flight home, arriving in time for cocktails with Gloria, dinner at 7:30 p.m. and bed by 11 p.m. The disclosure on the proxy statement about Walker's use of a company jet was noted by a line in eight-point agate type, saying that Crowe Power picked up the tab for roughly $450,000 a year as part of his compensation package. Beyond that, nobody at Crowe knew anything about his Friday travels. And why should they? It was nobody's business. And he knew how easily his stop in Detroit might be misinterpreted.

The intercom buzzed. "Mr. Hope, Mrs. Hope is on two," Flora said.

Walker punched a button on his phone. "Mornin', Glory."

"You should have said 'no' to that story."

"I thought you'd be proud of it."

"Big mistake."

"Why?" Walker stood up and paced.

"Too nice. Too flattering. You know Robbie's the most insecure human being on the face of the earth. He'll find it very threatening. He'll think you want his job, too."

"You know I couldn't care less about that. Let him babysit the board. Least interesting job in the building. Toughest part is pickin' out a catering menu with enough soft foods."

"Reading the story reminded me of your recruitment to go to Crowe. They did everything but send you flowers. You and Robbie were going to be a team. *Buddies.* Remember that? 'No daylight would separate you?' He was going to have you over for dinner. You'd meet for breakfast once a month. Sit with him in the box at Yankee Stadium. So you take this job. Now he wants you to shove it."

"Oh, come on now. I don't see that at all."

"Walker, I don't know him like you do, but I've been around him just enough to know. He hates that you *made* your money. His money was made for him, by his great-great-granddaddy and a whole lot of hired help. He has no idea how it all happened. In his heart of hearts, he has to realize he can't do what you do."

"He doesn't have to. All he has to do is sit back and enjoy the ride."

"Not if the driver's getting uppity. He's a Crowe. He was *born* better than you. I'm afraid this will bring hostilities out into the open."

"There's no way he'd take me on directly. He's a lot of things, but he's not stupid."

"Just be careful, Walker. Please. That man's a sneaky bastard."

Walker said goodbye and looked at his watch: 16 minutes until his Leadership Team meeting—enough time for a victory lap through the executive floor. Walker closed the Progress Report, wrote a few notes in the margins on the cover, and headed out the door, nodding to Flora on the way. He walked through the Hall of Fam and wondered how the Crowe family gene pool got so diluted that each successive generation was worse at running the business than the last. The fact that the company survived a hundred years was a small miracle. If Walker were to leave, would Robbie try to take his place? What were the odds that this family tree would sprout another Crowe who both shared Homer Crowe's genius for making money and was hungry enough to do it? Had they all lost the plot? Had they been too dependent for too long on outsiders to do everything but tie their shoes?

Jasmine Holmes, the Senior Vice-President for Human Resources, came walking briskly toward him with a broad smile on her face. "Walker, you really *are* the man," she said, spreading her arms to embrace him and jangling her gold jewelry, enveloping him in a cloud of Shalimar and smooching his cheek. "That story was just *wonderful*—and so true."

"Really?" he said, soliciting more gush. "You liked it?"

"Oh, my goodness," she said, fluttering her false eyelashes in a way that just might have spelled "LOVE" in Morse Code. "I ate it up with a big spoon. Tell me there's going to be a book about you."

Walker blushed. "Can't imagine anyone would buy that."

"I would," she snapped. "And if I were queen, I would make it required reading in every B-school in America."

Walker made two notes to himself. One, Jasmine already *was* the queen. Two, his shirt was going to smell like perfume the rest of the day.

He continued into the reception area, where an electronic sign carried the stock ticker that Walker installed the day he became CEO as a signal to all executives: we're here to serve shareholders—*all* of them, and by implication, not just those named Crowe. The ticker showed CRO up a dollar, which meant Walker had made, on paper, $1.8 million in the past 90 minutes. *Yeeha!* He slapped hands with the security guys behind the reception desk, as he always did when he walked by, and reflected that life couldn't get much better. He was making as much money in half a day as his daddy did in twenty years. He had his boss cowering in the corner suite. And with the company's outstanding performance, he was virtually untouchable. Imagine the money he'd make if he could double the share price! He could earn, what, a half-billion? He could buy an interest in a baseball team. Build a wing onto the business school at his alma mater. Create the Walker and Gloria B. Hope Foundation to cure... what? Rickets? Was that still a problem?

All that could wait. Today's concern was complacency on the Leadership Team. The people on this floor were getting a bit too comfortable with the fattening share price, paying more attention to the profit on their stock options than their business. He had seen leadership teams become complacent when things were going well, and it always led to trouble. It was time to shake things up, to put somebody in the hot seat.

Based on the report he just read, he had a pretty good idea who that somebody should be.

10. BLUE AS CAN BE

Winnie trudged into Robbie's lair just as he emerged from the bathroom in the back, a burbling toilet behind him. She held up a bound presentation as he took his seat behind his desk.

"Mr. Crowe, I have the weekly Progress Report for you."

"Fine," he said, stifling a yawn as he stretched his arms over his head. "Throw it on the pile."

Winnie studied the stacks of papers ringing his desk. Where should the Progress Report go? She decided on the heap closest to his right hand, minimizing the effort required for him to pick it up.

"Not that one!" Robbie yelped. He grabbed the report and placed it on the next pile over. "*Damn,* Winnie. What the hell are you thinking?"

"I'm sorry, Mr. Crowe. I wasn't sure."

"That's my *personal* stack. I'm going through all of that today. *These,*" he said, indicating the other 11 piles, "are my company papers and foundation papers and everything else."

"Oh. Did you move them?"

"No, I didn't *move them,*" he said, flopping around helplessly like a freshly boated salmon. "I've had it like this for almost a week. Honest to God, you need to pay attention."

She nodded. "The Leadership Team meeting starts in ten minutes, in case you wish to attend."

"I'm not going to that," he snapped. "*Complete* waste of time."

"Yes, sir."

"A slog in the weeds."

"Yes, sir."

"I can't bear to watch all that sucking up."

"I'm sure it's quite a show," Winnie clucked.

"And it's not like they ever listen to me anyway."

"That's obvious," she said.

"To hell with it," Robbie said, waving his hand dismissively. "Walker's the ringmaster of all those clowns. He can handle the circus. That's why we pay him the big... you know. Whatever we pay him."

"Yes, sir," she said, turning back toward her workstation.

Robbie reached over to grab the Progress Report and put it on his lap. He felt his eyes instantly glaze over. There was something about company reports that produced a Pavlovian response in Robbie. Why did he immediately want a nap? Why couldn't he focus? Was it all the numbers and charts? The agate type in the footnotes? Or was it the excruciating detail about revenues and taxes and free cash flow and all the financial stuff that made his head hurt. Let the other guys worry about this, he figured. Robbie's genius was the big picture, the really important matters, like the integration of the Crowe Power Company into the world at large. What great societal problems could he and the company solve? What essential issues demanded his leadership? What were the areas of opportunity that required his unique insights? There had to be *something*.

He sighed and picked up the report, forcing himself to focus on it. He would read this one for sure, cover to cover, and absorb every single morsel of information. *Yes, he would.* He took a deep breath and flipped to the Summary page, then to a tab called Forecast. Alarmed, he opened another tab, called Plan. With every page, he realized: something was *very, very wrong!*

He hit the button on his intercom.

"Winnie!"

He heard the wheels roll back on Winnie's vinyl chair mat. She appeared a moment later, panting. *What now?*

"Yes, sir," she said.

"Where did you get this?" he asked sharply, holding up the report.

"Flora emailed me a PDF from Mr. Hope's office. I just printed it out."

"On our printer?"

"Yes, sir. Is something the matter?" she said, coming around the desk.

"I'll say there is. It's the *wrong blue*."

"The wrong blue?"

"You hard of hearing? It's not our company color. Surely you can see that. It should be Broad Street Blue. This looks *way* too green."

"Hmm," Winnie said. "It looked fine on my computer. Maybe it's our printer?"

Robbie pulled his desk light closer and studied the cover. "I can't read a report like this when the color's not right."

"I'm sure it's distracting, sir."

"We need to do something about this." He looked at her, tapping the desk with a pencil, waiting for an answer.

"Well, I suppose I could get print-outs from other printers and compare. That might tell us if it's a problem with the printer or with the electronic file."

"I don't care how it gets fixed. I just want it *fixed*. We can't send out materials that don't even get our own company colors right. How pathetic is that? How are people supposed to believe anything else in there? My great-great-grandfather would be rolling over in his grave."

"Understood, sir. I'll take care of it right away."

Winnie skedaddled, and Robbie leaned back in his chair, interlocking his fingers, staring through the window at the Brooklyn Bridge below. Maybe this color problem was small beer. Maybe some people would think a detail like this did not deserve the attention of the company's chairman, paid $19 million last year. Maybe even Winnie thought he was overreacting. They would all be wrong. This level of attentiveness to the company's history and its iconography was part of his special gift, his contribution to the company's continuing endurance. Nobody else on this floor had been steeped in this company and its trappings since birth. Everyone else would come and go. He was here to stay, to defend the realm and preserve it for the next generations of Crowes.

It was damning, really, that the Leadership Team couldn't see the importance of issues like this, which reflected the company's very identity. Even during the six years when he was running Strategy and chaired his own leadership meeting in the rare weeks when he could make it, he could never get people on board with his vision—to honor the company's past and to make it even better in the future, to be a model corporate citizen of the planet and serve all their stakeholders. Every time he mentioned his revolutionary idea of becoming the first carbon-neutral diversified energy company in the world, they looked at him as if he were speaking Esperanto. They'd nod and mumble and glance about and then go on with their review of the business plan as if he had said nothing at all. *Someday, he would make them see.*

Winnie knocked on the door and entered with an armful of presentations.

"They're all coming out pretty much the same, Mr. Crowe," she said, plopping them onto his desk.

Robbie spread a dozen presentations inside the castle walls, pushing aside the Progress Report, an Annual Report, SEC filings, think tank white papers, and his most recent board briefing book, and scrutinized one print-out after another. *Hmmm.* There were subtle gradations of color, but it was hard to define the differences. Clearly, this was going to take careful examination. As he flipped through one of the presentations, it suddenly hit him that the shade of blue wasn't the only offense; blue was being used as a *secondary color!* It wasn't even used for headlines; it was for *sub-heads,* the second-tier words that weren't even important enough to get top billing. How could they treat the company color with such blatant disrespect?

Robbie looked up, mortified. "Somebody's going to have to fix this."

"Who do you have in mind?" Winnie said.

"Well it sure as hell isn't me. As if I don't have enough to do."

Winnie stared blankly at him.

"Let's start with our Great White Hope. Tell him to get off his duff and take care of this. And I mean *now.*"

There. Something accomplished. Something *significant.* Was it too early to knock off for the day?

11. C-FLAT MAJOR

All the executives on the Leadership Team assembled around the massive oval conference table rose as Walker entered the executive conference room, known as the Homer, after the founder. Each held a copy of *Fortune* magazine in front of their face so that it appeared to be a roomful of grinning Walkers.

"*Walker! Walker! Walker!*" they chanted.

Walker offered his best aw-shucks smile and shook his head—*this is too much, but please keep it goin'!* —as the applause and chanting continued. He walked to one of two empty chairs at the head of the table and allowed the commotion to go on for a good ten seconds before he finally raised his hands. "Alright. Thank you. Appreciate it. That's enough now. Please."

Walker took his seat next to Tim Padden, the Chief Operating Officer, who had served as his pliable, reliable gofer at three companies in a row. "Hell of a story," Tim said, gently patting Walker on the back. "You write that thing yourself?"

Walker bristled, and nodded toward Marty, who was seated at the far end of the table with the other administrative Veeps. "Marty tells me he had a big hand in it."

"Magnificent job, Marty," Tim said to a smattering of more applause.

"Yeah," Walker said. "He got most of it right, too."

Marty winced. *Most of it?* Was that necessary? "We've got a good story to tell right now," Marty said. "Makes that part of my job easy."

"Isn't that the truth?" Walker said, folding his hands together on the table. "Well, listen, gang. We can't get caught up in our own press clippings.

What success we've had, I attribute to all of you and the hard work we've done together. It's teamwork, collaboration, and discipline that's gotten us here. We need to continue that. But, as of today, what we've accomplished is all in the past. History. If we keep workin' together toward our strategy, and puttin' our focus on flawless execution, we can keep this thing going. And there's no tellin' how far we can go. Sky's the limit."

There were nods and smiles around the table. "Hear, hear," said Tim, never missing his cue to tickle Walker's balls.

Marty was impressed by the intensity of the subordinate suck-up, which was cresting near a 52-week high. He expected a butt-smooching exhibition from Tim, since, as Walker's perennial No. 2, that was part of his job. Yet there also seemed to be an uncharacteristically ardent pucker in the lips of Anna Pachulski, the normally stoic CFO; Wally Saxton, the Chief Engineering Officer; Jasmine Holmes, the politically savvy head of HR; and Cahn Ngyugen, the head of Government Affairs, who was looking in from Washington via a screen at one end of the room. Less enthused, if not thoroughly depressed, was Robbie's prepster brother-in-law, Digby, the General Counsel and Robbie's lone crony on the leadership team.

Attendants brought around plates of cookies and fruit and poured coffee as the executives opened their binders. One server put his hands on the back of the empty chair next to Walker. "Mr. Hope, shall I remove this chair?"

Walker looked around the room, then back at the server. "No, I don't think so."

Canh piped in. "You never know if Robbie might show up."

A roar of laughter rocked the room. Everyone enjoyed the joke at Robbie's expense except Walker, who knew better than to laugh at the boss, and Digby, who looked like he wanted to make a run for the window.

"Now, now," Walker said, noticing Digby's expression. "We don't make jokes at one another's expense. Especially our chairman. There's no one who cares more about the future of this company than Robbie Crowe. He deserves our respect and our loyalty."

With the solemn reproach, the bobbleheads nodded as if they had actually thought about it and agreed.

"Let's see where we stand against our plan," Walker said.

The methodical review showed that the company was doing extremely well. The forecast of revenues tracked well with the annual plan and shortfalls were more than made up for by greater-than-expected revenue from other parts of the business. Payrolls had shrunk from the previous year due to operational efficiencies and "synergies," a favored corporate euphemism for layoffs. The company's chief competitor, crosstown rival Staminum Energy, appeared to be in retreat, if not disarray, from management incompetence, and ready to sell off assets.

Their A–B–C scorecard showed more A's than Alabama, indicating progress across the board. The few B's were fixable, as billed. The only C came from the delayed conversion of the company's largest coal-fired plant in New Jersey to natural gas, which was proceeding more slowly than anticipated.

"Tim, can you tell us why we have a C?" Walker said, leaning back in his chair.

"It's pretty simple," Tim said. "All we need is about three-hundred feet of pipeline to tie into a gas supply, but enviros are tying us up in the courts. There's some sort of critter—a spotted salamander, I think—they say is endangered, with a habitat in the area."

"How long do you expect this to go on?"

"There's no end in sight," Tim said. "They seem very well financed. It's one lawsuit and appeal after another."

"Anna, how much is this delay costing us?"

"A lot," Anna said, opening a tab on her binder. "The delta between coal and natural gas is significant and it goes right to our bottom line. This year, a rough estimate after taxes is $300 million. That doesn't include our legal costs, which are mounting."

Walker shook his head, puzzled. "I don't understand this, Cahn. Wouldn't this pipeline actually be good for the environment?"

Cahn nodded. "Net-net, it is, of course," he said. "Carbon emissions would be half what we're pumping out of that plant now. But these people we're up against are scorched-earth in their tactics. They won't settle for anything that doesn't eliminate the use of fossil fuels, even gas. Their whole objective is to shut down our plant completely."

"Uh-huh. And replace it with what?"

"Wind. Solar. I don't know. Pixie dust."

Anna piped in. "Nothing that would be profitable for us."

Walker bore in deeper. "And how much sun do they get in that part of New Jersey?"

"It isn't Palm Springs," Cahn said.

"How much wind?"

"Not enough. The fact is, you would still need a steady supply of energy as a back-up, and that comes from carbon sources. They don't want to hear it, but it's the truth."

Walker turned his gaze to his left, where Digby sat uncomfortably. "Digby, it sounds like this problem lives in your shop."

Digby shifted in his chair. "We're on it."

Walker leaned forward, clasping his hands together, his expression hardened. "How long should we expect this grade to stay like it is?"

Digby winced. "I honestly can't tell you that right now."

"You're not suggesting we just wait for this C to change itself, are you?"

Digby could feel all the eyes in the room upon him. *Were some of them smiling?* He sat up a bit straighter and pushed his thick brown hair off his forehead. "No, of course not."

"Glad to hear that. Let's get a plan next week on what you're doin' to overcome this. We all want to see that C turned into a big ol' A."

"Got it."

Walker's tone softened. "And if there's anything I can do to help, you just let me know."

Digby nodded. "I will," he said.

This, Digby thought, was going to be a challenge. There were certain aspects of these costly pipeline delays that would never make this report.

12. CHAIRMAN OF THE POURED

"I've travelled with Presidents. Witnessed historic events. Uncovered assassination plots against heads of state. Chased down dangerous guys with guns. Now," Tom Michaels said as he placed a large paper cup of coffee from Café Che on Winnie's desk, "my career has come down to this."

Winnie grasped the paper cup. "It certainly feels warm," she said hopefully. "Hope he likes it. I can't afford to retire just yet." She carefully headed through the open doorway into Robbie's office, finding him at his computer with his back to the door, filling out his Fantasy Baseball roster for the week.

"Here you go, Mr. Crowe," Winnie said, putting the cup on his desk.

Robbie, startled, wheeled around. "*Damn,* Winnie. Don't barge in on me like that."

"I'm so sorry, Mr. Crowe. I knew you were waiting for your coffee."

Robbie put his hand around the cup and let go. He nearly smiled. "Well, it's certainly hot enough. I can tell you that." He picked it up and sipped. Then he looked at Winnie, wincing, as if he may have been poisoned. What a bitter disappointment—*not enough milk!* All around him there was nothing but plodding, pathetic nincompoopery.

"It's not the way you like it?" she asked.

Robbie, exhausted from his own rage and frustration with the people in this company, couldn't even bark at her anymore. Was it really their fault that they were all so damn *stupid*? After all, they came from—well, wherever.

"You know what?" Robbie said. "You and I are going over to Commie Coffee right now and we're going to get this right."

"I'm sorry, Mr. Crowe. I can't leave. I have to watch the phones."

"Forget that. Let what's-her-face do it."

"There is no what's-her-face. Emma was fired this morning, as you instructed. She's gone."

"Already? Well," he said, with a chuckle. "Glad we can still execute some tasks quickly around here. I tell you what. I'm going myself."

Winnie was alarmed. *Outside?* All *alone?* "Oh, no," she said. "Do you really want to do that? Why don't I send Tom with you, Mr. Crowe? Please."

"What the hell, Winnie," he scoffed. "You think I can't go to a coffee shop by myself? You know, they're not real commies over there. They just dress like them."

Winnie looked skeptical. In her nine years with him, there was precious little he could or would do for himself. And his helpless kids were even more challenged by the mundane details of daily life, calling her for restaurant and hotel reservations, train tickets, shopping, and passport updates. She was surprised they could dial their phones without assistance.

Robbie slipped on his suitcoat. "Seriously, Winnie. I'll take it from here."

He'd show her how it's done.

+++

Robbie, waiting at the Executive Express elevator, was surprised to see Digby loping down the hall, his usual stack of folders in his arm, his hair an unruly mop with a bit of a part on the left side, the very same style he wore to Harvard Law School twenty years before. His pale eyes drooped behind his wire-rimmed glasses.

"What's up, Digs? Time off for good behavior?" Robbie asked.

Digby shook his head. "That was dreadful. Worst meeting *ev-errr*."

"The Leadership Team?"

"Oh, my *gawd*. The Walker B. Hope Love Fest. It was like a cult in there. Absolutely appalling. Nothing but Kool-Aid drinkers. You would have barfed."

"*Tell me.*"

"They chanted his name. Actually stood up and roared over that ridiculous magazine piece. It was a freaking competition to see who could kiss his ass the most."

"Who won?"

"I'd say they all tied for first."

Robbie laughed. "I take it you weren't a contestant."

"I should say not. They were falling all over one another, as if he were the top dog in this company, rather than you. It was embarrassing. And..." He hesitated.

"What?"

"Somebody made a crack about you not showing up at the meeting."

Robbie's jaw dropped. "Walker?"

"Well, not him exactly. Somebody did. He might have laughed."

"He did, did he? What an asshole."

"And just for good measure: Walker decided to make *me* today's piñata, beating me up for sport."

"Of course. You're my guy. The last of the Mohicans."

"It's all about Walker now," Digby said. He nodded to the Hall of Fam. "You wouldn't know Crowes had anything to do with this company."

Robbie glowered. "I'm heading out for coffee. Come with me."

13. TAKING IT TO THE STREET

The mid-day heat rose off the cobblestones of Broad Street as Robbie and Digby walked quickly to the corner. Digby opened the door to Café Che for Robbie, and they took their place in a line of office workers, students, and tourists. Robbie scanned the menu on the wall before his eyes caught a tall, dark-haired barista with a name badge that read "Natalia." She was dressed in the shop's battle fatigues-and-black beret uniform. *Had she just smiled at him?* Or was that wishful thinking?

"Oh my god," Robbie said to Digby. "Do you see that chick behind the counter? She is so fucking gorgeous."

Suddenly, they were at the counter and she was looking at Robbie as if she could see right through him.

"Can I help you?" she asked.

"I... yes. Um—"

Was it Brazilian roast? It was a B-country of some kind. Burma? Botswana? No, no. *Shit.* It was in South America. Some place with a jungle. *What the hell.* All he could think of was Natalia's stunning beauty: caramel skin, black hair, and emerald eyes that seemed to glow.

"Digs, you go ahead," Robbie said.

Did he know her from somewhere? She looked so familiar. As Digby made his order and moved toward the register, Natalia turned again to Robbie.

"May I suggest something?" she said.

"Of course."

"How about a large Bolivian Jungle Roast with two ounces of soy milk?" she asked.

Robbie nearly exploded with glee. "That's *exactly* what I like," he laughed.

She smiled. "We all know that here. You are Robbie Crowe, right?"

"Well, yes. Last I looked," Robbie said, suddenly sheepish. "And how did you know that?"

"To be perfectly honest," she said, writing ROBBIE on a cup, "I've banged on your car a few times."

"You're... a *protester*?"

"Sure. We all are. We voted on what we could all do together to make a better world. You know, as a team-building exercise," she said. "We decided to protest against your company."

"For what?"

"Oh, you know. Destroying the planet. Stuff like that."

"But, I—"

She looked around him. "I'm sorry. I have to take the next customer."

Robbie staggered toward the register, dazzled by her coffee competence and extreme bodacity, and picked up his coffee, "Robbie" scrawled across the side by her lovely left hand. He carefully opened the lid to see it was the same color as Natalia's cheeks and wondered what the rest of her looked like. *Was there a tan line? Was it all one seamless color?*

"Can you believe it? She's a protester," Robbie said, joining Digby in a booth and looking around, suddenly feeling as if an imminent attack were possible. "They probably all hate me."

"You're an easy target," Digby said, stirring his coffee. "Convenient, too. They don't even have to cross the street."

"It's so unfair. Walker executes the plan; all I do is approve it. Why do *I* get the blame? I'm the guy who wants more solar and wind energy."

"You're right. It is not fair." No, Digby thought. It's also not fair that some people inherit a billion dollars, while others had their family fortunes frittered away by an alcoholic grandfather and a gambling father. What options were left, besides marrying the boss's sister?

"Here's the thing that really pisses me off," Robbie said. "Nobody seems to recognize that our company's greenhouse gas emissions were demonstrably *falling* when I was directing Strategy. Now look. They're not only rising, they're going through the roof."

"Literally," Digby said, stirring his coffee. "But to be fair, that's because our plants are all running at capacity now."

"Okay. Fine. But at the very least, we should be moving a hell of a lot faster on converting our plants from coal to natural gas. But when it comes to the environment, Walker always has an excuse. It drives me insane. I mean, how long has that New Jersey plant been delayed? And what's he done about it? *Nothing!* It's pathetic."

"Well," Digby said, sotto voce, "you do know why that's not happening."

"Of course. It's because Walker can't get off his dead ass."

Digby winced. "Not exactly."

"What then? Tell me."

Digby leaned forward. "It's because of these guys," he said, gesturing toward the coffee counter. "They're all members of that group, the Planetistas. They're suing us over our pipeline plan."

Robbie's eyes drifted back to the counter, where Natalia was scribbling another name on another cup. Why would she protest against him? If only she knew the purity of his motives. "I can't believe that."

"That's not the worst of it," Digby said. "We give them money."

"*What?*"

"We donated a hundred thousand dollars to them last year."

"We give them money to screw us over? How stupid is that?"

"Very."

Robbie practically exploded. "Who's the idiot who approved that?"

"Well, actually, you did."

"*What?*"

"Sorry."

"C'mon. I don't remember anything about that."

"We donated through the Crowe Foundation."

Robbie was dumbfounded. "Why didn't somebody tell me about this?"

"We did. It was in the report. It was in our meeting minutes. You signed off on all of it."

"Wait a second. I may have signed off. That doesn't mean I *agreed* with everything in there. I trust people to vet these things. Who recommended we give money to the Planetistas?"

"Annie Bolton."

"Oh, for God's sake. Why would anyone listen to her? She's an idiot."

"For one thing, people thought you were sleeping with her."

"*What?* That's ridiculous. I never did that," Robbie said, before sitting back. "Well. Maybe once."

"Ah."

"Possibly twice, at the most."

"Twice?"

"Okay, fine. A few times. What's the difference?"

"About $2 million. That's how much we paid to make it – and her – go away."

"All we did was screw around a bit in the back room off my office. It was nothing serious. And it's not like we ever went out in public or anything. Damn. How do people know about this stuff? The rumor mill around here is just vicious. People don't care at all about a person's reputation."

"You mean, like Annie's?"

"Like *mine,* you ninny."

Digby shrugged. "Well, now I've got a problem."

"What's that?"

"I need the Planetistas to back off. Walker is breathing down my neck. He wants this pipeline issue solved, like, yesterday. I've got a week to get it done or he's going to haul me up for a show trial at the next Leadership Team meeting."

Robbie exhaled hard, blowing his cheeks out. "What if we breathe down his neck instead? Put him back in his place."

"What are you thinking?"

"He's got his story out there. He's the best CEO in America, supposedly. What if we put out a different perspective?"

"Which is?"

"That he's not. That some people on the board aren't very happy with him."

"They're not?"

"I'm 'some people,' right?"

"No. You're 'some person.' Singular."

"There could be others. Possibly. You never know. Could we leak that somehow?"

Digby stirred his coffee, thinking. "An old friend of mine used to work at Forbes. Not sure where he is now. A dotcom, I think. Maybe I could reach out to him."

Robbie looked over at Natalia. How, he wondered, could he impress her? "Let's do it, Digs. Time to show that jerk whose name is on the building."

14. CLICK BAIT

Senior Writer James X. Bottomley could hear his editor's heavy boots shuffling down the corridor in his direction. At last he appeared in the doorway of the glass wall separating Buzzniss.com from the other startups on the floor of the Let's Work shared space in Brooklyn.

"Jim. Dude," Lex said. "Awesome story today about GE. Record traffic on our site. Our investors are going batshit, man. They love you."

"That's good to hear, I suppose," Jim said, clenching an unlit pipe in his teeth. His eyes rolled up from Lex's combat boots to his sweatpants, untucked plaid shirt, scruffy brown beard, bleary eyes and black knit cap. Why in God's name was this man wearing a knit cap inside the office on a 78-degree day? Lex held a black coffee mug that said "Let's Work" on one side, *"Chillin' & Billin'"* on the other.

"I thought you gave up coffee," Jim said.

"I did, basically. I'm down to, like, four cups a day. But they've got brewmosas on 19," he said, holding up his cup. "Beer and orange juice. Freaking awesome, especially for a hangover. Try one."

"It's a bit early for me," Jim said.

"Seriously, dude," he said with a soft belch. "This is like my third."

"Maybe later," Jim replied.

"There won't be a later. There's a whole line of Indian dudes from some tech company down there. They're quaffin', man."

"I'm sure I'll regret it, but I'll have to pass for now," Jim said. How in the hell had he gone from working under Randolph Erickson, one of the great business editors in publishing history, to this addle-brained doofus, an insult to journalism. "Perhaps you could enlighten me, Lex. Where did that headline come from? 'Time to Change the Dim bulbs at GE?'"

"Wasn't that great? Computer spit that out. Tested 10 different headlines when the story broke. That one got the most clicks, so that's what we went with."

Jim flushed red. The decision was made by a *computer*? "That story has my name on it. *I* didn't claim there were dim bulbs at GE. There was nothing in the story to support that."

"It wasn't necessary. The machine figured it out. Algorithms or something. The computers are smarter than all of us *combined.*"

They were certainly smarter than Lex. Jim sat up straight and pulled the pipe from his mouth. "I've got a real problem with this."

"Really? What's the big deal, man? It wasn't, like, the headline was a definitive statement." Lex cocked his head, puzzled. "You act like you're all upset or something. You should be happy. Impressions, click-through rates, stickiness—they're all totally amazing."

"I don't like it when somebody—or some *thing*—puts words in my mouth. Could you at least clear it with me before you make a call like that?"

"Dude. I had nothing to do with it. *You* had nothing to do with it. The *people* voted. Democracy in action. *Vox populi,* man."

"Vox poppycock! What about accuracy? Don't we have an obligation to tell the truth?"

"We're crowd-sourcing the truth."

Jim nearly choked. "We're *what*?"

"People must have thought it was, at least, a possibility that there are, like, some seriously stupid people over there, or they wouldn't have clicked on it. That tells you all you need to know."

"Sorry, Lex, but I don't equate click-bait with veracity."

Lex scrunched his face and scratched his stubble. Ver-*what?* "Look, Jim. I know you're old-school and you come from some far-away world in a distant analog galaxy—"

"Manhattan, actually."

"But it's a new day, man, and Buzzniss is the vanguard. I don't see why you don't just roll with it. Keep producing more great stories. That's why we pay you the big bucks."

Not quite, Jim thought; he was at half the salary he collected at Forbes, but with the promise of a fat payday if Buzzniss ever went public or were sold off. "Of course, I want this venture to succeed," Jim said. "I'm an investor, too. Half my comp's in stock here."

"Right. And sweat equity is cool. But we need to start closing a Series B round real soon. And that means we need all the clicks we can get. So if we spit out a headline that's good—but not perfect—is that so bad? I mean, if we don't get another $8 million by September, we're, like, el-fucked-o. And I'll be back in grad school."

Jim sneered. "Can your parents afford that?"

The jibe didn't register. "Just tell me," Lex said. "You think you might have a follow-up soon? We need more clicks."

Jim's phone buzzed in his pocket. He pulled it out, saw CROWE POWER on his screen, and sat up in his chair. "I'll let you know soon enough," he said to Lex, before answering his phone. "This is Jim."

"Hey Jim," the voice on the other end said. "It's Digby Pierrepont."

"I'll let you take that," Lex said before leaning over and blowing his beery-orange breath in Jim's face. "By the way, man. No payroll this week. Should be cool next Tuesday or so."

15. TAKING GAS

Emilia, the dental assistant, hovered over Marty like an angel, the spotlight illuminating her head in a halo. She peered down through her plastic goggles, a blue paper mask over her mouth and nose.

"Would you like some more gas, Mr. McGarry?"

Marty's jaw was numb from Novocain, but he was thoroughly enjoying the gas. A little boost couldn't hurt. He pointed up with his index finger, and she reached across him for the controls, smooshing her pillowy breast into his chest. He nodded affirmatively as the gas rushed through his nostrils and swirled around his brain. Suddenly, he was rising up from his chair, floating along the fluorescent lights on the ceiling, looking down at this poor limp man lying flat with a bib draped across his chest.

"Dr. Littmann will be with you in a moment," she said, rising from her stool.

Marty didn't particularly care when or even if he showed up. He was flying high over the World Trade Center when he heard footsteps in the sky. Where were they coming from?

"Mr. McGarry," Dr. Littmann said, breaking through the clouds. "Gas okay?"

Oh yeah. Marty gave a thumbs-up as Dr. Littmann kicked a rolling stool in his direction and sat down, as Emilia took her place across from him.

"Okay," he said, peering through magnifying glasses into Marty's mouth. "Let's see what we've got here."

A hand pulled on Marty's cheek and a drill whirred. "We received our copy of *Fortune* today and I saw the story on your company," Dr. Littmann said. "All I can say is 'wow.' Great piece. Your bosses must be pleased. I know I am. I've got a few shares in Crowe. You're up two bucks today."

Marty gurgled. "*Gah*," he said.

"I'm not happy with the returns from my mutual funds or, frankly, with my advisor. But I *really* like what I see at your company. I'm thinking of going big on Crowe."

Marty tried to speak, but his numb jaw, the suction tube over his lower lip, the gas inhaler over his nose, the finger pulling his cheek, the drill deep in his tooth, and Emilia's well-administered suction made the conversation one-sided.

"Everything I read about Walker Hope seems really good."

"*Argh*," was all Marty could offer.

"Although I have to say: it looks to me like he's got dentures. I think he would do better with implants. Tell him to come see me. I'll give him a 20 percent discount on the first visit," Littmann said, hitting something that made Marty flinch. "Sorry. You want some more gas?"

Marty's head felt like a large helium balloon—a huge improvement over his day so far. He signaled a thumbs-up and wondered if he could purchase a canister for his office. "*Anh-huh*." He was sailing over the Statue of Liberty, drifting toward the Verrazano-Narrows Bridge.

"You know, I recently inherited some money from my parents," the dentist said, leaning closer. "What if I put all of it into Crowe? My dad was a supplier to your company for years. He had a lot of respect for the Crowe family. He thought they were just very decent people. Really down-to-earth, which is interesting, considering how rich they are. That Robbie Crowe seems like a real mensch."

"*Ngha*," Marty gurgled.

"What a smart move for him to bring in Walker Hope. I mean, Robbie Crowe did whatever it took to make the company succeed. *That's* the kind of company you can believe in."

Marty was getting disturbing signals from Earth. In his mind, he responded with, "You understand that as an officer of the company, I can't offer stock advice." It came out sounding more like lyrics from the '50s song, "Witch Doctor." "*Ooh eee ooh ah ah.*"

"Yeah," Dr. Littmann said. "That's what I'm thinking, too. Alright. I'm putting a temporary crown in here and we'll bring you back in a day or two for the permanent one." Then to Emilia, "Alright. Let's rinse him out."

The nose mask came off and Marty's chair re-entered the atmosphere. He grabbed the plastic cup and rinsed his mouth, spitting bloody water into the swirling drain. Who knew this would be the most pleasant part of his day?

"The doctor said he'll want to see you when the new crown comes back from the lab," Emilia said.

Marty's head began to clear. "He knows I can't give him advice about investing in my company, right?"

"Oh, I wouldn't know about that," Emilia said. "You'll have to talk to him."

"Where is he?"

"He's with another patient now. Do you want to wait?"

Marty's phone buzzed in his pocket, signaling a text message.

JIM
See you for drinks at 6? Need to run
something by you.

Jim Bottomley. He was the last guy Marty wanted to see right now. He quickly typed in a response.

MARTY
Sorry. Can't. Have a commitment.

JIM
Cancel it. You'll want to hear what
we're publishing tonight.

The gas and Novocain fog lifted suddenly and completely, and Marty was on full alert. He turned to the assistant. "I can't wait. Tell the doctor what I said about investing, will you?"

16. COCKTAILS WITH A TWIST

"**W**ould you like to pay for that now, sir, or would you prefer to run a tab?" the bartender asked Jim Bottomley as he placed a glass of Oban scotch, neat, on the dark granite counter. The bartender's skeptical expression indicated he knew what Jim didn't care to admit: neither payment option was good.

"The gentleman I'm meeting is picking up the tab," Jim said, glancing toward the front door of Gotham Bar & Grill.

"Of course," the bartender said.

"I'm sure he'll be along any moment."

Jim scanned the Greenwich Village street through the tall windows of the restaurant hoping the next black car to stop out front would deposit Marty and rescue him from further embarrassment. There was a time when Jim wouldn't let Marty buy him so much as a bottle of water. That time was not now.

"Very well, sir," the bartender said. "I can hold open your tab with a credit card until he arrives."

Sir? Jim used to be *known* here when he worked around the corner at the *Forbes* offices on Fifth Avenue. They called him *Mister* Bottomley. Now he was George Bailey, unknown, about to get thrown out of Martini's. With the bartender's glare as penetrating as a barium scan, Jim fished inside the breast pocket of his tweed jacket and retrieved the lone card with available credit—Discover—and wondered how many of those they saw at this place. A credit card founded by *Sears*? Had the bartender even heard of Sears? Did he know it was like an upscale K-mart? The bartender regarded the card with amusement—was that a pitying smile?—and whisked off to the register, where he conferred with another bartender, leaving Jim to dwell on his financial prospects, which weren't improving, even with the scotch.

A muscular grip on Jim's shoulder was as welcome as a winning scratch-off lotto ticket. There, at last, was Marty.

"Jim Bottomley," Marty said, sliding onto the next stool. "Didn't you used to be somebody?"

"I'm still big," Jim said with a shrug. "It's the publications that got small."

"None quite as small as yours."

"Bartender seems to think so. I think he's calling for my credit score."

"That's ridiculous," Marty said, giving Jim an appraising glance. "You obviously can't run fast enough to skip out on your bill."

"I only have to run faster than you, Marty. And frankly, you don't look like you could make it past the hostess stand."

"Let's not test the theory, alright?"

Before Marty could order, the bartender scurried over with a chilled Hendricks martini. "Mr. McGarry," he said, sliding a bowl of mixed nuts across the bar top toward Marty and fluttering his eyes with the special love reserved for regulars. "A pleasure to see you." He slid the Discover card back to Jim. "Thank you, sir," he said sympathetically. "We won't be needing this any longer."

Jim looked up sheepishly. "Free from debtor's prison."

Marty smiled. "So how's life at the dot-com?"

"It's a long way from Fifth Avenue."

"Where's your office? Brooklyn?"

"Dumbo, which is apt, especially when you consider my editor."

"That's not so bad. Up and coming area, I hear. Your office is in a shared space, right?"

"One of those Let's Work outposts. The office walls are glass and you can scribble on them all you like. Crayons are appropriate for the children who work there. There's free coffee and beer in the reception areas. And sometimes, not often, they clean the bathrooms."

"Is it as glamorous as it sounds?"

"Come and see for yourself sometime. We can play video games in the lounge and throw back some margaritas. Tomorrow's Taco Tuesday. The line snakes down the hall, so stop by early—if you're still talking to me."

Marty sipped his drink and eyed Jim with suspicion. "That sounds ominous. Why wouldn't I be talking with you? You're an old friend."

"Let me ask you a question first. How did the *Fortune* story go over? I've got to believe Walker was ecstatic."

"Walker's never entirely satisfied. That's what drives him and his incredible success."

"I understand there are some people who disagree with its conclusion that he's the best CEO in America."

"Hard to imagine why. When you consider how far the stock has come since he was announced as CEO—" *take that, Walker!* "I think you'd be hard-pressed to find any executive in the S&P 500 who's performed better."

"Oh, I don't doubt that," Jim said. "Nobody questions whether he's an outstanding operator who's produced amazing results. But I understand there is some question about his vision for the future."

"From whom?"

"Your board."

Marty swallowed hard and his pulse raced. "I've never heard anything like that. And, frankly, I don't believe it for a second. Walker's run has been stellar—beyond dispute. Record profits, year after year. Stock at an all-time year high. We're at the top of every survey on the best places to work list. Best Places to Work for Women. Best Places to Work for LGBTQ—and the rest of the alphabet. You want me to go on?"

"Not particularly. I know it well."

"You think Walker didn't have something to do with that?"

"I'm sure he had everything to do with it."

"So where's this coming from?"

"All I can tell you is what I've heard. Apparently, there's some concern that Walker is using the same playbook at Crowe that he did at BFC and Goliath. He gets quick results by slashing costs, cutting investment in maintenance and capital projects and whacking the payroll. It bolsters the bottom line, for a while. But it comes back to bite the company in the ass. Look at what happened at those companies after he left. They all faltered."

"You can't pin that on Walker. He was long gone."

"I talked to people today who think he set up those companies for failure. And they're wondering if he's doing it again at Crowe."

"Did you consider the possibility that Walker is a scapegoat for people at those other companies who aren't doing their jobs?"

"I have. But here's what else they're saying. The board is wondering what happens in the future if coal's regulated out of existence—and not just in the U.S., but everywhere Crowe does business. They think Walker is a short-term thinker, that he's fine running operations that don't require any imagination, but he's done little to prepare for the future. And why should he? As hired help, a short timer by nature. It won't be long before he's retired, counting his money in Montana."

"Michigan."

"Fine—out there somewhere," he said, waving vaguely toward the West. "My sources tell me that Walker may think he's going to add 'Chairman' to his title, but that's never going to happen. He'll be lucky to hang on as CEO."

"Somebody's feeding you a line of crap, Jim. I'm surprised you fell for it."

"Don't get mad at me, Marty. It's not my opinion that counts. I don't get a vote. Maybe Walker has gotten a little lazy. Maybe his head's a little swollen with all those puff pieces you're getting him, so he's not listening anymore. He's too far above it all. People are starting to wonder whether Robbie should step in to help the company focus more on the long term—"

"Wait. *Robbie* should step in? You talked to him?"

"I'm not telling you who I talked to. But trust me: I have this from a source who should know."

Marty winced. "What am I supposed to do with that, Jim? Unless I know who said it, it's just grabbing smoke."

"You might want to start grabbing. I'm going with the story."

"Your editor allows you to run with anonymous sources?"

"My editor—the one that counts—is a computer. It proofs the story. Changes the spellings and syntax. Sometimes, it rearranges paragraphs. Then it spits out a dozen headlines and whatever clicks, sticks. And right now, I need—*we* need—clicks. That may be the grim reality, but it is my reality."

Marty folded his arms across his chest and raised his chin, regarding Jim with the affection he might show a cockroach. "And you probably don't mind sticking it to *Fortune*."

"They were my direct competitor for a lot of years. But I'm not after them, if that's what you mean. I just want a good story. And I've got one."

Marty shook his head. "It's sad to hear you say that, Jim. You were the gold standard in business journalism when you were at *Forbes*. I remember when we talked about you doing a book on Walker, and I thought that was a real possibility, especially with the relationship you were building with him. You do a hit-and-run job like this, and you realize you killed that idea."

Jim's face flushed. "If the board moves on Walker, I'll have an even better book, *Buzzniss* gets some real buzz, and my half-million shares in this dogshit dot-com start looking like they might actually be worth something."

"And if they don't—which they won't—you look like a schmuck."

"We'll still have our 15 minutes, if not an entire news cycle or two," Jim said, pulling out his notebook. "So tell me, do you have a comment or don't you?"

"On the record, you can say that as a matter of policy, we don't comment on speculation," Marty said. "Off the record, I'd say you're making a huge mistake."

Jim put his notebook away. "You know, what's really sad here, Marty, is that you're out of the loop in your own company. There are things going on above your head that you don't even know about. That puts you in a terribly awkward spot."

Marty summoned as much bravado as he could, croaking out a weak, "We'll see about that."

Jim stood and slung his bag over his shoulder. "Yes—at midnight tonight. Once we push the button, your boss turns from a prince to a pumpkin. He doesn't strike me as the kind of guy who's going to like that."

17. BED CHECK

Walker's routine of circling the 24th floor before leaving the office each evening had trained his Leadership Team to be at their battle stations between 6:45 and 7 p.m. Many of them departed for large chunks of the afternoon to get a workout, catch a child's soccer game or grab a glass of wine, but they all knew where they had to be when Walker flew around for inspection.

Per usual, Walker found Tim Padden at his desk, hands on his keyboard, staring intently into his computer screen, working over his beloved spreadsheets. Hearing Walker knock on his door frame, he offered the friendly smile that was always lacquered to his face whenever Walker appeared.

"Good day, chief?"

Walker nodded and sat down, propping a foot up on Tim's desk, which lifted the front legs of his chair off the ground and marked his alpha dog turf. "Not bad," he said. "Not bad at all."

Walker looked agitated, which always made Tim wary. He had worked with Walker for more than a decade and he could sense he was in for a corrective lesson of some sort. "What's on your mind?"

"Tell me something," Walker said, cocking his head. "You really think Marty deserves the credit for that story?"

So that's it, Tim thought, moving uncomfortably in his chair. He must be upset with Tim for suggesting some portion of the credit should be shared. "You mean, what I said during the meeting? I was just throwing the guy a bone," Tim said with a dismissive laugh. "Poor bastard gets beaten up every time there's a bad story in the papers. I thought he ought to get a little love when something goes right."

"Uh-huh. But you said, '*Hell of a job*, Marty.' As if, you know, he was responsible for it."

Tim took a deep breath and told himself to keep calm. "Well, I assumed he was. That's his job, to work with the reporter, manage the process, and shape the story as best he can, right? Didn't he arrange the interviews? Work up the briefing papers and the messaging?"

"Yes. But that's not the point."

"I'm not sure where you're going with this, Walker."

Walker sat up, his voice taking on an edge. "The point is this. The story of our success is irrefutable. The numbers don't lie. Marty's adequate, as far as that goes. But he's just the messenger boy, doin' the job we pay him to do. But *we* turned the company around."

"We?"

Walker shrugged. "All of us around here. We're the ones who deserve the credit for that story."

Tim reddened, and his smile evaporated. Ten years of smoothing Walker's prickly quills when he felt some ridiculous slight was getting to be more than he could take. "I get that. But you know, a *lot* of us didn't see our names in there."

Walker blanched. "You mean, like you?"

"For one, yes."

"Would you expect to?"

"No, frankly. I've pretty much gotten used to it."

"Really?" Walker said, irritated. "You have a grievance you'd like to share, Tim?"

Tim held up his hands, palms toward Walker. "Not at all. I've made my peace with where I am a long time ago. I thought we were just having a nice little conversation about the story."

Walker leaned forward, eyeing Tim with suspicion. "Are you saying you don't get enough credit?"

"I'm not. I just try to do the best job I can. I don't worry about the glory. That's not my department."

"You're sayin' it's mine?"

"Honest to *God*, Walker. You're putting me in a spot. I'm not complaining about anything."

"Good," Walker said, standing. "You know we can't be effective as a team if one of us tries to grab all the attention."

Tim suppressed a laugh. "Right," he said.

"There's no 'I' in 'team,'" Walker said, standing to leave.

"No sir," Tim said. "There surely isn't."

But, he mused, there is in "dick."

18. HOMEWARD BOUND

Marty slalomed through the crowds of NYU students on University Place shuffling along in a zombie trance, staring at their phones, oblivious to stoplights, turning taxis, and pedestrians maneuvering around them. He squeezed into a single-file shuffle under a scaffold, then stepped around a solemn young woman sitting cross-legged on the sidewalk with a dog at her side and a hand-written cardboard sign on her lap.

Homeless

PREGNANT

Need $$ for bus fare to Ohio

Well, Marty thought, at least he wasn't pregnant.

Marty found a bench in Washington Square Park as the evening chill settled in. He dialed Walker, whom he found at his apartment in Lower Manhattan, where he was eating a Cobb salad from the Executive Dining Room and watching a documentary on World War II.

"Walker, I need to give you a heads up on a very disturbing story."

As Marty walked him through the key points in Bottomley's piece, he could hear Walker breathing heavier and faster. After a pause, Walker said, "You can't let him write that, Marty."

"It's not a matter of giving permission, Walker. He's going with it, whether we like it or not."

"Well surely you can tell him it's not true."

"I can and I have. But the question is: is it?"

Another pause, this one longer.

"Walker?" Marty said. "You still there?"

"I'm here," he said solemnly.

"Thought I might have lost you."

"Not yet," he said, grimly. "I'm trying to make sense of this. You know, Robbie didn't say one darn thing about the *Fortune* story. You didn't send it to him, did you?"

"No. We agreed we shouldn't."

"Everywhere I went today, people were givin' me high fives and fist bumps. I even had people on the elevator askin' for selfies with me. But I didn't hear so much as a peep out of the corner. My wife said he'd be angry about it. Maybe she's right. Did he say anything when he called you down this morning?"

"Let me think," Marty said slowly, as if he were searching his memory. "He might have mentioned something in passing. I can't recall exactly."

"Well, let me tell you somethin', Marty, just between us chickens. I do not apologize for pullin' this company out of the ditch. Nor am I sorry for gettin' a little bit of press that says so. That helps us build our brand, capitalize on our positive momentum. And that's not about me, no, sir. That's about our *strategy*. Stories like this help attract recruits. Build morale among the troops. And I know our institutional investors are pleased about it. I had notes from a half-dozen of them today. Gosh. If Robbie doesn't like it, I do wish he'd come and talk to me first. Why would he go to the press?"

"We don't know for certain that he has."

"Stop pullin' my leg, Marty."

"Let me put it this way: I'm sure he didn't do it himself."

"I get that. My question is *why*?"

"Maybe he's afraid of you."

Walker practically spit. "That doesn't make a lick of sense, Marty. I work for *him*. He's the boss. Anything I do that's good for the company benefits *him*. Doesn't he see that?"

Marty briefly weighed the price of honesty before plunging ahead. "I've seen this movie before, Walker. He sees everything as a test of loyalty—not to the company, but to him, personally. And when he thinks someone on the team is trying to get an edge on him, he gets very nervous."

"Robbie has absolutely no reason to doubt my loyalty. I'm there for him—and his family. And I have been for four years, making them boatloads of money in the process, I might add."

"What can I say? God and Robbie work in mysterious ways."

"I want you to call Robbie and ask him about this story. See if he would like to issue a response. That'll tell me everything I need to know."

Marty looked at his watch. "He's hard to reach after 7."

"Oh heck, man. He's hard to reach after 3. Big story like this? He needs to hear about it. Right away."

19. SPIN CYCLE

As Robbie pedaled his bike around the southern loop of Central Park, his resentment of Walker grew with every turn of the wheels. If Walker had just had the sense to fix the company and leave within an appropriate time frame for a man of his station, then Robbie wouldn't be forced to attack him in the press and break into his office. No question about it, this was *all Walker's fault.*

Why was Walker still hanging around, anyway? For more money? More applause? Why couldn't he understand that he was an outsider at Crowe Power, and always would be. There was no future for him once he'd turned the company around. His job was finished. Walker's apparent assumption that he had acquired some special status—a level of equality with Robbie based on short-term accomplishments—was a preposterous conceit. It was one thing for Walker to cock around the 24th floor, slapping high fives with security staff and hugging everyone in sight. But for Walker to present himself so publicly as the face of the company in *Fortune* magazine, as though it were *his* name on the building, was beyond the pale. The Crowe brand, a great name in American business, had been minted by his great-great-grandfather and owned by the generations that followed—not some Joe-Bob-come-lately. Walker could never share Robbie's passion for protecting the family name, or his goal of making it mean something more than grubby old power plants and pipelines and refineries. Robbie had a *higher purpose...* of some sort.

Robbie steered his $40,000 Litespeed Blade to the right, staying clear of the faster cyclists and pelotons, passing joggers and walkers, and skirting around pedestrians scurrying to cross the busy road. As he rounded the bend and turned north, he caught sight of his grandmother's old apartment building on Fifth Avenue, where she spent her autumns and springs in a penthouse overlooking the park. She had lived long enough to see Robbie cruise up the corporate ladder and died assuming he would fulfill his birthright and eventually be CEO. What, he wondered, would she think now of this hick-from-the-sticks interloper taking custody of the family jewels?

Grandmother had been a keen observer of society, its castes and mores. When Robbie visited her for lunch on Saturdays during his childhood, she would peer at him through her vodka-induced haze, a cigarette dangling in her bony fingers, and remind him in her husky voice that 99 percent of the people down below were not of their peerage. She taught him that he had been born to a higher plane, destined to lead the miserable slobs beneath them to a better existence. His beneficence, his sense of *noblesse oblige*, was the tax one must pay for being superior. She reminded him that the special genius that created the family's great wealth was embedded in his DNA and could never be altered.

What would Grandmother think of Walker? No doubt, she would recoil at the idea that anyone other than a Crowe was entrusted with the keys to the family business. She would be particularly mortified that they were in the hands of a man as unrefined as Walker Hope, who didn't even have the grace to wear a proper suit to the office, or keep his elbows off the table when he ate, or pronounce his 'g's. One meeting with him and Grandmother would no doubt declare Walker "a rough cob." And she would be right. Which is why she would not only approve of Robbie dropping a bomb on Walker in the press, she would believe it was Robbie's *duty* to do so. It was time to restore the proper order of things.

As he wheeled up the east side of the park, Robbie mourned her absence. Grandmother had been one of the few people who knew him inside and out, a rare constant presence in his life. His father, Les, was largely a stranger, absent from the household through his constant work, travels, philandering, and golf at the finest courses in the world. His mother was busy with her boards and her friends and her homes and had assigned management of the children to a succession of nannies, one of whom, the beautiful and sweet-natured Brielle, Robbie had deeply loved. But Brielle was fired under mysterious circumstances—whispers said Mother had caught her sleeping with Father—and Robbie never saw her again. She never said goodbye, nor was she ever spoken of. She simply ceased to exist—*poof*—as far as the Crowe family was concerned. Meanwhile, his younger brother, Tap, and older sister, Bits, were shipped off to different boarding schools, his friends revolved in and out, depending upon where they were getting their educations, and his cousins were scattered about the globe, where they ran money-losing wineries, restaurants, and boutiques and supported charitable foundations, living off their trust funds and company dividends.

Who could he rely on now? Was there anyone who could remotely understand him, who appreciated the special circumstances under which he had been raised and the crushing expectations that were placed upon him at birth? Truth be told, Digby would never quite get it; his family fortune was relatively meager. Howie-Do-It was an ardent and devoted acolyte, but he was from another class entirely—and recreational drugs had taken their toll over the years. Maria Territo was an entertaining diversion and adventure into a wildly different culture, but her expiration date as his mistress was nearing, lest she develop expectations about a future together, which was obviously impossible. And Lindsey, his wife, whose grievance tumor seemed to be metastasizing, would never get what makes him tick—because he would never let her close enough to find out. Theirs was a marriage of social expectation, mutual convenience and, now, financial necessity, at least for Robbie. Were they to divorce, Lindsey's take would be devastating.

What, he wondered, about Natalia? Beautiful, exotic, coffee-slinging Natalia. What promise did she hold? She was a variety of forbidden fruit that excited him to his core. His amorous adventures over the years had taken him down many twisting paths, but never had he encountered someone so enticing yet so forthright in her rejection of him, which made her irresistible. What if he could seduce her? What if she could be persuaded of the righteousness of his intentions? Would she partner with him to make Crowe a more responsible company?

Robbie completed the last of his circuits and dismounted his bike at 66th Street and Fifth Avenue. As a warming spring sun set over Central Park, he fiddled with the music on his iPhone, turning up the volume on a song by Ten Years After. The lyrics were from a bygone era—some of them completely taboo under today's sensibilities—but Robbie reveled in their Utopian sentiment.

I'd love to change the world
But I don't know what to do

So *true!* He wished he had been of age in the '60s to protest the Vietnam War, or something important like that, or to be part of the environmental movement that swept the nation. As it was, he read Rachel Carson's *Silent Spring* long after its initial impact, at a time when America was more concerned about the destructive power of disco than DDT. It seemed that the timing of his life was unlucky, that he was either too late or too early to lead a great cause. But he could, perhaps, still use his position to create positive change for the world, starting in his own backyard. With Natalia at his side, together they could... *do something.*

Tomorrow, her recruitment would begin.

20. PLAUSIBLE DENIABILITY

As he walked home, Marty considered how he would approach his call to Robbie, ducking under the tree branches of Washington Square Park before heading south on LaGuardia Place to Bleecker. He jiggled the key into the lock of his apartment building door, just next to the wood-framed windows of The Bitter End, an iconic rock and roll club whose name captured where Marty was in his life. Inside the vestibule, two long flights of stairs loomed taller than the north face of K2. He grasped the handrail and trudged up the sagging steps, pausing at the landing to catch his breath and restore feeling to his legs. Marty made a mental note: *You're in pathetic shape.*

He squeezed past a couple of bicycles chained to the third-floor bannister, and stepped around the minefield of recycling bins, trash bags, and broken kitchen chairs to reach apartment 3R. There he was met with the faint odor of a gas leak and the vinegary smell of a kitchen where it seemed possible someone might have pickled cabbage every day for the past 30 years. Looking around at the shabby furnishings, it hit him how far his financial fortunes had plummeted since the divorce. From a spacious and comfortable 6,000 square-foot home in hilly, wooded, lovely Scarsdale to this condemnable dump.

He grabbed his legal pad and a pen off the coffee table and a bottle of Stella Artois from the fridge and headed outside to the apartment's most redeeming feature: a small outdoor deck with moderately fresh air. There, in the glow of the white Christmas lights the previous tenant had wrapped around nails in the brick wall, he plopped onto a wobbly Adirondack chair and called Robbie. He found him finishing up a bike ride in Central Park and filled him in on the outline of the story, pausing periodically for Robbie's reaction.

"Wow," Robbie said, at last. "Where do they get stuff like that?"

"Jim says he has a source very close to the board."

"Really? Gosh. I mean, you'd think I would hear about something like that, right?"

"One would certainly think so."

"Well, hold on there. *I* certainly never talked to him."

It was Robbie's standard rejoinder: plausible deniability. "I'm sure you didn't."

"Did you tell Walker?"

"Just now."

"Who does he think it is?"

"He can only hazard a guess."

"Well he better not think it's me, or it's your ass, Marty."

"I don't see how you can come to that conclusion when—"

"Stop, Marty. *Just stop!* Enough excuses. The fact that this story is running at all is entirely on you."

Arguing was futile, Marty knew. "Of course," he said. "What would you like me to do?"

"Maybe you should just deny it?" Robbie said in a tone that utterly lacked any conviction.

"I'd love to put that out there—squash this thing like a bug," Marty said, as he scribbled a possible holding statement out on his pad of paper. "What if we say there's absolutely no merit to the story and that Walker has the complete support of you and the board?"

"And attribute that to whom?"

"You."

"Mmm. I don't know," Robbie said. "That could be going too far. I mean, maybe there are some board members who really are upset with Walker and they just haven't mentioned it to me. Maybe they're frustrated that we're not set up for the future the way we need to be, and they're taking that frustration to the press. I'd hate to have a denial go out and then something happens."

"Like what?"

"I don't know. Something. Anything. I mean, we don't know who could have talked to this reporter. Could have been anybody."

Marty ticked down the board roster in his head. There wasn't one director who gave a crap about the pace of plant conversions, except in terms of financial returns, nor was anyone worried about a "lack of vision." If there was any doubt that Robbie was the source of the leak, Robbie's mealy-mouthed defense removed it.

"You know, Marty, what really pisses me off is that this company constantly leaks. You need to do something about that."

"Do you have any suggestions?"

"*Me?* No. How would I know? That's your department."

"Right. Not sure what I was thinking."

"Look. You and Digby should put your heads together. Figure out a policy. Get a note out to everyone at the company. Say this sort of thing will not be tolerated. Severe consequences. Blah, blah, blah."

Digby. Of course. "I'm sure Digby would have some good insights," Marty said.

"Absolutely," Robbie said. "He's one guy around here I can trust."

21. HOME IS WHERE THE ART IS

There was still a glimmer of daylight in the far western sky when Robbie neared his house. Endorphins always coursed through his body after a good ride, and his adrenaline flowed from anticipation of the story that would knock Walker off his self-constructed pedestal. He couldn't wait! He crossed Fifth Avenue and walked his bike down the sidewalk of East 67th Street toward the wrought-iron gate in front of his five-story Beaux Arts mansion. A uniformed servant, Frederick, came bustling down the stairs, his right hand extended toward the bike.

"I'll take that for you, sir," he said.

Robbie, his shirt still dripping with perspiration, handed Frederick the bike and his helmet and climbed the steps, tossing his cycling gloves into a basket in the foyer. He walked through the gallery, its walls decorated with impressionist masterworks from Monet, Renoir, and Degas, and headed toward the kitchen in the back, where he found Renee, the chef, making gluten-free bread.

"Are you hungry, Mr. Crowe?" she asked cheerfully.

"I could use a salad," he said, taking a bottle of spring water from a refrigerator. "Maybe with some chicken and hummus."

"Of course," she said, pleasantly. "I'll prepare it right away and bring it up."

"I hear the TV upstairs. I take it Lindsey's home."

"Yes, sir, she is."

"Did she eat?"

"No, sir. Mrs. Crowe said she wasn't hungry."

That was usually a bad sign, Robbie thought. He walked back through the gallery and up the grand staircase to the second floor, where he found Lindsey in the study, sitting on a sofa with her knees tucked under her, watching "Wheel of Fortune" with a glass of red wine in her hand. Robbie glanced at the word puzzle on the screen.

"Terms of endearment," he said.

She looked up at him with hooded eyes and practically hissed. "How many times do I have to tell you: *don't... fucking... spoil it.*"

"What?" Robbie said, sitting down on the edge of a club chair. "I figured you already had it. I mean, there were three letters left."

"I like to be sure before I say it," she said, indignantly.

At a glance, he knew this wasn't her first glass of wine—far from it. With her head wobbling slightly, she apprised him dully, her eyes fogged.

"Working late again?" she said.

"Do I look like I've been working?" he said, annoyed.

"No. Now that you mention it," she said, slurring her words slightly. "You've never broken a sweat at work."

"I usually don't wear this, either," Robbie said.

"Out for a ride?"

"Well, *duh,*" Robbie said. "You must be hammered."

"Oh, stop it. Why do you always say that? All I've had is a little *wine.*"

"Uh-huh. When you have a little wine all day long, it kind of adds up. Looks to me like you've got your Picasso face on."

"Kay and I were *shopping.*"

Of course. That's the way it usually started on days when she didn't have a board meeting for one of her civic institutions like the Met, Lincoln Center, or the New York Public Library. Her enormous spending habits gave her a free ride to all the high-end bars and restaurants on the Upper East Side, with tabs paid by the stores that she favored. First she might go to a favorite Madison Avenue boutique, which would pay for her brunch and champagne at Altesi whether she bought anything or not. Then it was off to Bergdorf for an afternoon tea, which meant more wine in the top-floor restaurant, BG. Kay's husband Jeff was the head of a private equity firm whom she rarely saw and, like Lindsey, Kay had her kids away at prep school in Connecticut. Before long, it was 5 o'clock and time for a serious cocktail or two in the warm glow of Bemelman's Bar in the Carlyle Hotel with a couple more of their cronies. Then, perhaps they'd grab a bite in a secluded corner of the café. Anything was better than going home to an empty house. Rather than rattle around all day in their mansions or penthouses with nothing but the help to keep them company, Lindsey and Kay bonded with other corporate widows in shared loneliness.

"You really should eat something," Robbie said, sipping his water.

"Kay and I split an appetizer at Cipriani."

"You need more than that, and," he said, nodding to the wine. "less of that."

"Really?" she said, carefully putting her glass down and straightening up. "Would that keep you home more?"

"Don't start," he said, standing.

"Start *what*? It's a simple question. When you decided to become chairman instead of CEO, you were supposed to have more time on your hands. I've never seen it. And just now, I read a magazine article that says Walker is basically in charge of *everything*. Rather than ask me what *I'm* doing all day, maybe I should ask *you*."

"Why would you believe some stupid reporter over me? That is so insulting. That entire story was obvious bullshit."

"I don't know what to believe," she said, standing, and following him around the sofa into the dining room, where Renee had placed his dinner. "The only thing I know is you're *never* here."

"Okay. I get it," he said, turning to her and crossing his arms over his chest. "How about I come home every day at 6 o'clock like some regular schlub. Would that make you happy?"

"Not with that kind of attitude. If you don't want to spend time with me, then maybe we need to think about whether this is even working anymore."

Robbie's life suddenly flashed before his eyes. Divorce was unthinkable. Lindsey would get half his fortune, including half of his Crowe Power stock, and with it, half his votes in the family bloc of shares. He would lose his clout with the board and his hold on the chairmanship. Goodbye office. Goodbye G5. Goodbye nineteen million dollars in compensation. And goodbye to the excuse that he was working every day, which was his license to do whatever he wanted without oversight. A more conciliatory approach was in order here, especially with the possibility of taking over as CEO, or at least being more involved.

He moved forward to hug her. "Let's not fight," he said.

"Don't hug me," she said. "You're gross."

He backed off. "Alright. Maybe I'm not around enough. How do I make it up to you?"

"Let's get away this weekend."

He blinked at her in horror but resisted the impulse to object. "Where?"

"The beach house."

"Seriously? It's only May."

"We have six houses and we hardly use any of them, except this one. You've said yourself spring is the best time of year to be out there. Before the crowds arrive. It will be just the two of us. And the weather's supposed to be beautiful this weekend."

Robbie was aghast. The two of them? *Alone?* What the hell would they do? Still, based on the urgency of her insistence, it was clear there was no option here. He'd have to suck it up.

"Fine," he said. "Whatever you like."

22. HOWIE DOES IT

As Howie-Do-It rode the elevator up from his basement cubicle to the 24th floor, he couldn't help feeling that he was on a mission from God—or least the closest thing there was to God on Broad Street. There was no greater privilege he could have in life than to serve Robbie, who treated him almost as an equal despite the vast difference in their social status. Impossible as it seemed, they were almost friends—the prince and the pauper. It was Robbie who paid for his two stints of rehab, neither of which quite took; Robbie who helped get him back on his feet after a personal bankruptcy from gambling debts; and Robbie who ensured that he kept a job at Crowe Power no matter how badly his supervisors wanted him fired.

What truly cemented Howie's allegiance was that Robbie was equally dependent on him, and even seemed to value his opinion. It was Howie whom Robbie would call in the middle of the night when he was distraught or depressed, Howie he would turn to when the straight-laced company security guys refused to bend the rules to avenge an insult or incursion, and Howie who provided comic relief for Robbie with his audacious tales of skullduggery and thuggery. Howie had no wife, no children, no enduring relationships, no education other than a semester at Borough of Manhattan Community College, and no career distinction. He was, basically, a nobody. Robbie had a storied name, vast wealth, an elite education, and a lifestyle that someone like Howie could only expect to see in the movies. Clearly, Robbie didn't need a job. But there he was, for several hours almost every day, doing what he could to advance the family's interests. It was an honor to serve him, and Howie derived an enormous sense of purpose for his life as well as a measure of reflected glory. Howie knew the price he would pay if he were ever caught while executing his duties on Robbie's behalf, which occasionally crossed the line into criminality; Robbie would disavow him, which would be even worse than getting fired.

Getting into Walker's office at 11 p.m. was easy, especially for a regular visitor to the 24th floor. All Howie had to do was nod confidently and wave to the lone security guard at the front desk, who seemed more concerned with concealing the video game he was playing under the counter and slurping his soda. Howie proceeded down the darkened hallway to Walker's corner, swiped the pass he pilfered from the IT department, and entered Walker's office. He punched the electronic controls to draw the shades before turning on the lights.

Howie settled into Walker's chair and opened the top drawer, meticulously organized into various compartments holding Walker's trademark purple marking pens, hand sanitizer, lip balm, paper clips, note pads, rubber bands, spare change, business cards, a Swiss Army knife, and other doodads. The left-hand drawer held hanging green files tied to various aspects of the business, such as the Leadership Team, the Board of Directors, and Walker's direct reports. Howie rifled through a file entitled "Succession," which contained folders on all the company's top executives, with performance evaluations marked by Walker's handwritten notations in purple. Howie photographed the notes on each executive, starting with Tim Padden, of whom Walker wrote "Topped out. A captain, not a general." Anna Pachulski, the CFO, was judged "One-dimensional. Poor people skills—fixable?" Lucy Rutherford, President of Australia and Africa, was deemed a "Strong candidate. Needs rotational assignment." And Digby was deemed simply "Not an option." Surely Robbie could use this information against Walker. How would these executives feel if they knew where they really stood with their boss—and that Lucy Rutherford was his apparent favorite? How would they like him then? On a scale from 1 to 10, this find might be a 7.

In the right-hand drawer were personal files and papers, marked "Naples" and "Glen Arbor," where Walker owned homes, along with files on Gloria and their kids. Howie looked through each one for material, but most of the papers were shopping receipts, travel itineraries and random snapshots. Nothing damaging. He pulled out a file labeled "Detroit" with several manila folders inside. One, entitled "Apartment," contained a real estate brochure advertising a two-story penthouse atop the Book Cadillac Hotel in downtown Detroit, along with papers showing that Walker had purchased the property for $1.2 million in 2016. Another folder, titled "Malaya," indicated she was a Filipino national who had applied unsuccessfully for permanent green card status and that she lived in the penthouse. It also appeared that Walker was paying Malaya's bills from an immigration lawyer in Washington. Was she his mistress? If so, this was too good to be true. He pulled all the papers from the files and laid them on the conference table, photographing each one with his phone.

This finding was at least a 9 – maybe a 10. Howie was so excited, his fingers trembled as he hurriedly returned the papers to the files and texted Robbie.

HOWIE
The mother load.

Robbie responded immediately.

ROBBIE
Lode, moron.

HOWIE
Dude. Whatever.

ROBBIE
Meet me at the house.

23. RECKONING

When Walker accepted the job at Crowe Power four years earlier, he decided for efficiency reasons to live close enough to the office to walk to work in 10 minutes or less. He selected a $4 million, three-bedroom apartment in the southern Battery Park City neighborhood of Manhattan with views of the Hudson River and New Jersey to the west, New York Harbor and Staten Island to the south, and the Financial District and Crowe Power headquarters to the east. When he wasn't traveling, he often sat for a few minutes by the windows each night before bed to review the day, think about tomorrow, contemplate his progress against his personal plan, and, lastly, say a prayer. Walker wasn't particularly religious, but he had to believe there were powers in the universe more potent than Robbie.

Tonight, he lingered in the dark longer than usual, deeply unsettled, processing the events of the rollercoaster day that began so promisingly. Why would Robbie refuse to let Marty deny the Buzzniss story? Could he really be on the way out? How was that possible, given his success and all he had done to enrich the Crowe family? He never expected to be Robbie's best friend, but he could not fathom how he could have earned his contempt. *This was not part of the plan.*

He looked down at the harbor, watching a tugboat push a dark barge past Ellis Island, where his grandfather, Liam Hope, arrived from Ireland in 1908, carrying all his worldly possessions in a green wooden box. After immigration processing and quarantine, Liam's American journey had continued on another boat to the Central Railroad of New Jersey train depot for transfer to Ashland, Kentucky, where he began work in the coal mines. At 21, Liam married 14-year old Earlene Hammons and raised three boys, all of whom followed him into the mines before the coal companies went bust during the Great Depression. One of those sons, Floyd, was unemployed for two years before he and his young wife, Iris, fit all their belongings, including Liam's green wooden box, into the trunk of his Plymouth and migrated north to Ecorse, Michigan, a blue-collar river town near Detroit, where he took a job in a steel mill ratcheting up wartime production.

Walker was the fourth of Floyd and Iris's seven children, which put him in the position of diplomat and negotiator among his siblings, all of whom shared the upstairs dormer in their white bungalow sided with asbestos shingles. Like its neighbors, the house had been stained brown by the soot from the mill. The kids played in a yard that was thirty feet wide, bordered by a cyclone fence that kept their two chickens on the lot, and went to sleep watching the flames from the blast furnace across the road cast a flickering orange glow on the ceiling. Floyd was a scarfer and wore a heavy fire-retardant suit to protect him as he burned the imperfections out of the molten steel slabs, and Iris worked in the cafeteria at Walker's school during the day and as a cashier at the corner drugstore at night. The money they made put a roof over their heads and paid tuition at Catholic schools, but its pursuit left them perpetually sallow, baggy-eyed, and exhausted. They rallied their energies toward one animating mission: to see their children lead a better life than they did, an objective that took a detour when the mill went bankrupt and Floyd was thrown out of work once more. The experience embittered him deeply. One late night, after a few too many rounds at the Jefferson Avenue bar where unemployed steelworkers gathered to nurse their grievances against the company and the system they regarded as grossly unjust, he staggered home, took Liam's green box into the backyard, and smashed it to pieces with a sledgehammer.

Walker, ten years old at the time, was awakened by the thunderous crash and looked out the window to see his father sitting on the ground, a dozen shards of splintered wood scattered around him, his shoulders heaving with sobs. Walker's heart dropped for the box as much as for his father. His grandmother had always told him the box only looked empty; inside, it carried the American dream. When Walker asked what that was, Mamaw insisted it was up to him to decide. He could be whatever he wanted to be—and he shouldn't let *anyone* tell him otherwise. As Walker watched his father struggle to his feet and stumble toward the house, he put his shoes on, crept downstairs and slipped into the backyard. It took a moment for his eyes to adjust to the light, but he ultimately found and gathered all the pieces of wood, put them in a bucket, and placed it in the rafters of the garage. Someday, he would put it back together again.

Two years later, Floyd died of emphysema, a grisly souvenir from the soot in the mill and his smoking, and his mother soon after suffered a fatal stroke. Mamaw, a widow, moved up from Kentucky to finish raising the kids who were still at home, and stayed in the house long after they had moved on and the neighborhood declined. Without her strength and guidance, where would he be?

Walker took one last look at the twinkling lights of the harbor, scanning the horizon before settling on an unusual sight in the east. Why, he wondered, were the lights on and the shades drawn in his office over on Broad Street? He picked up his binoculars and adjusted the focus, making out the singular shadow of a figure moving about. The cleaning crew generally finished by 9 p.m. and they never pulled the shades. Who was in there and why? Walker watched as the lights went out and the shades were raised, suggesting whoever had been there did not want to be seen.

He walked to the third bedroom, which he used as an office, and turned on the computer. The Buzzniss story was due at midnight, and he needed to know what it said about him—and where it stood against his plan.

24. CONSPIRACY THEORY

Howie and Robbie huddled in the study on the top floor of Robbie's home. One of the worst days of Robbie's life suddenly felt like it might be one of the best. Howie's report made him giddy.

"What did Walker's succession notes say about Digby?" Robbie asked, excitedly.

Howie, who had taken a black car uptown, held up the photo on his phone. "Quote: 'Not an option.'"

"You've *got* to make sure Digby sees that. In fact, show him everything. He'll be furious."

"You got it."

"And make sure Tim sees his review, too," Robbie ordered. " 'A captain, not a general.' That should rock his world. Tim will hate his guts."

"Consider it done," Howie said.

"I *love* this," Robbie said with a grin. "Now, tell me about this girlfriend."

Howie outlined his findings about Malaya Mendoza and the apartment Walker bought for her in Detroit. Robbie smacked his hands together with delight. "Can you imagine if that got out? An affair with an undocumented immigrant? The *New York Post* would have a field day."

"His family would be destroyed," Howie surmised.

"The threat of that alone would probably be enough to make him quit," Robbie said. "*God*. That would be so great."

"How do you want to proceed?"

Robbie paced behind his desk. "If we make this case, it has to be absolutely airtight."

"Right," Howie acknowledged.

"So. Is it?" Robbie asked.

"Kind of."

Robbie shook his head. "No, no, no. That's not enough."

"What more do we need?" Howie wondered.

"The evidence so far is circumstantial. Let's gather some more. Better yet, go to Detroit and catch him in the act. This *has* to be a clean shot, a kill. If all we do is wound him, he'll come back after us."

"Okay. So I get the goods. Then what?"

"We confront him," Robbie declared.

"We?"

"You."

Howie gulped. "*Me?*"

"Clearly, I can't do it," Robbie responded. "What are you, out of your *mind*? Chairmen don't do this sort of thing. I need to stay above the fray. 'Clean hands,' remember?"

Howie sighed. "Of course."

"You say something like, 'Robbie would really like to keep this quiet, because he's really concerned about how this would look for your family if it somehow got out.'"

"And if he doesn't quit, would that be enough to fire him?"

Robbie scratched his chin. "I think so—especially if we could establish that his extramarital affair was subsidized by the company."

"Subsidized? How?"

"It has to involve the company plane, right?" Robbie reasoned. "Surely, he doesn't drive to Detroit to see his little love bunny. He has to fly. And we pay for that. That's shareholder money. He's taking it right out of our pocket."

"Got it."

"Look into his itineraries, will you?"

"On it."

"And then go there. See for yourself. Get pictures if you can."

Howie held up his phone. "Shouldn't be hard."

Robbie clasped his hands together and laughed. "This is *fantastic*. I'm not sure I can get him fired based on performance. But this? The more I think about it, the more I think it would absolutely *ensure* he goes. What a hypocrite. Mr. Clean. Mr. Family Man. Always looking at me squinty-eyed, like I'm some sort of degenerate, just because I've had a little fling or two. Well look at him, getting a little love on the side with the wretched refuse. Time to kick his ass."

PART TWO

25. STROKE OF MIDNIGHT

As promised, Jim Bottomley's story appeared on the Buzzniss website at midnight, with simultaneous promotions on Twitter, Facebook, LinkedIn and Instagram that would run for the next 24 hours, at least.

Future of Crowe Power is Hope-Less
Board Pivots; Considers Change at the Top
Source cites Walker Hope's 'lack of vision;'
CEO may be out by June

By James X. Bottomley
Buzzniss Senior Editor
Superstar executive Walker B. Hope may produce an ever-rising stack of record profits and glittering press clippings to match, but that's apparently not enough for Crowe Power's restive board, Buzzniss has exclusively learned.

A source close to the company's board of directors tells Buzzniss they're concerned Hope's success in turning around Crowe has come at a steep price. By cutting the capital investment in environmentally-friendly projects favored by key members of the board, the company has risked running afoul of government regulators, green activists, and—in the long run—investors who are increasingly backing companies that take aggressive stances on climate change.

"The board isn't seeing a vision. Short-term gains are fine, but where does all this lead in the long run?" said the source, who spoke on the condition of anonymity because of the sensitive nature of the discussions. "At the very least, we need to be moving faster to convert our plants from coal to natural gas, which would mean a huge reduction in carbon emissions. We're not sure Walker gets that."

A darling of the business press, Walker Hope has been acclaimed as one of the best operating executives in the world for bringing Crowe, BFC Energy, and Goliath Industries back from the brink of bankruptcy, saving thousands of jobs. At the same time, the highly-accomplished Hope, whose amiable demeanor belies a steely ruthlessness, is considered an odd coupling with uber-wealthy Crowe chairman L. Robertson "Robbie" Crowe III, an Ivy League-educated descendant of company founder Homer Crowe.

Until now, many analysts considered Hope a likely candidate to break the Crowe family grip on the company chairmanship. Sources say that's unlikely now that he's

Jon Pepper

worn out his welcome. Deliberations have
begun on how Hope should be eased out.

"You have to give Walker oodles of credit.
He's done well," the source said. "But you
must give Robbie credit, too. He selflessly
agreed to share power when he realized the
company needed a different kind of CEO for a
short period of time. Now, that time has
passed, and we have to consider what's best
going forward."

Should the board move against Hope, the
candidates to replace him include Tim
Padden, the Chief Operating Officer; Anna
Pachulski, the Chief Financial Officer; and
General Counsel Digby Pierrepont, himself
an industrial scion and brother-in-law to
Robbie Crowe. Sources also indicated that, if
necessary, Robbie Crowe might be induced to
step into the breach, but he would be
reluctant to do so and would only add the CEO
duties to his role as chairman as a last resort
to protect his family's interests.

A company spokesperson reached
Monday evening said he would not comment
on board matters or the specifics of this
report, which he termed "speculation."

Marty's phone rang at 12:01. Walker didn't bother with hello. "*Vision?* We
need a *vision?* What about a profit? Holy freakin' *moly,* Marty. I've had four
years of meetings with our board. Not once has somebody asked me what my
dang vision was. The toughest question I ever heard was, 'What's for lunch?'
That's the only time I've ever been stumped."

"No doubt about it, Walker—it's a hit job."

"And we know exactly who hit us. Who says things like 'oodles of credit?'
I'll tell you who. Digby, that... *dodo.* And he's the guy who can't get the permits

100

for the plant conversions that I'm now getting blamed for. The *nerve* of this guy."

"Understood. But you do know Digby is just a proxy."

"Of course. He's Robbie's attack poodle," Walker sighed. "You know what the board asks me? What's my strategy, and how am I going to execute it. That's it. Did we hit our targets or not? And if we didn't, what was I going to do about it? All this green stuff this story says the board cares about? If it helps us make money, or builds a bit of good PR that doesn't cost too much, okay. Otherwise, I haven't heard one question about it. If Robbie's got his knickers wadded up over Sungod or Windacious, why doesn't he bring it up at the meeting? Or talk to me? I'm right down the hall. Maybe he should come to our meetings once in a while. He's always invited."

"That's not his style," Marty said, as his phone vibrated and dinged with calls and texts. Reporters were already chasing the story, which would no doubt make headlines overnight and become a hot topic on CNBC, Fox Business Network and Bloomberg TV all day.

"I need you to help me on something," Walker said. "Nose around with the reporters you talk to. Is there anyone else on the board I need to be concerned with, other than Robbie?"

"I can do that, if you like. But the bigger question may be this: does it matter?"

"What do you mean?"

"If Robbie wants to move against you, does he need any allies? Or can he go it alone?"

There was a long pause. "I never thought I'd have to worry about that. I assumed that if we made outstanding progress, that's all that mattered."

"Interesting concept," Marty said. "But in this company, I'm not sure that has anything to do with it. In fact, it can work against you."

26. MORNING HAS BROKEN

Marty rose to find that the market rendered a devastating verdict on the story overnight, with shares in Crowe Power plummeting eight percent in pre-market trading as analysts and commentators pummeled the company board for even thinking of dispatching their most effective leader in a generation.

Marty had taken calls until 2 a.m. as reporters chased the Buzzniss scoop. Sleep came fitfully, with percussion from a band at The Bitter End pounding through the floor. Marty tossed and turned, dreaming of talking points, struggling to find the right words for a credible rebuttal that didn't paint the company into a corner. Several times, he awakened in the dark to scribble out a dreamy brainstorm on a scrap of paper, but all his ideas looked terrible in the morning and his handwriting was worse. Reporters and producers began calling again at 6 a.m. as the morning shift began working follow-up stories and requests for Robbie and Walker to appear on the cable shows. Marty reiterated on the record that no one would be available and that the company did not comment on speculation. On background, he reminded them all that Walker had done a widely-admired job at bringing Crowe Power back from the brink, and that if anyone on the board had other ideas, they had not expressed them to him. He insisted, wishfully, that the story was a one-day wonder that would be instantly forgotten. And, he emphasized to each reporter that Crowe stock was $11 a share when Walker was announced as CEO, and that it had closed the day before at $95. He didn't mention it, and didn't need to, but the overnight loss of $5 billion in market capitalization was all on the chairman.

On the cable TV business shows, sell-side analysts lauded Walker and questioned how the company could do better with another CEO. The consensus was that Robbie was a truly wonderful guy—family-oriented, charitable, quick with a smile at black-tie events all over the city—but that the CEO job was well beyond his capabilities. By virtue of his name, he skipped the normal weigh stations on his express-lane trip to the top, making meaningless pit stops along the way to take jobs between experienced leaders above and functional operatives below. That left Robbie with no duties other than taking credit when things went well and second-guessing those responsible when they didn't. A former Crowe Power executive opined in Business Insider that Robbie's insulation from responsibility bequeathed him no favors, since he never had the chance to learn from failure. He was not only no Homer Crowe, he was no Lester Crowe, Charles Crowe or Les Crowe. The board should bypass Robbie again in picking the next CEO, the exec said, but the list of possible replacements from the inside was underwhelming and recruiting an accomplished executive from another company might be impossible. Who would want to follow in Walker's outsized footsteps? Better to follow a disaster, like Walker did.

Marty was in his bathrobe at the kitchen counter digging into a bowl of Cocoa Puffs when his phone rang again.

"As if the story isn't bad enough," Walker said. "Somebody's been in my office."

"How do you know?"

Walker explained what he saw from his apartment the night before, and what he encountered in his office a moment earlier. "My files have been disturbed. Whoever went through them was pretty careless in putting them back."

"That's Howie-Do-It," Marty said.

"That's not how *I* do it," Walker said, prickling.

"I mean Howie-Do-It, the guy. Robbie's henchman. He bugs offices. He beats people up. He does whatever it takes to keep Robbie happy. Breaking into your office must be a new part of his job description. Did he take anything?"

"Not that I can tell."

"Well, all I can say is look around you and smile, Walker. Odds are good you're on candid camera."

27. CODE BLUE

Walker returned from his 7:58 a.m. bathroom break to find that Flora had placed a copy of the week's Progress Report on his desk. Still standing, he picked it up to read a handwritten note from the chairman clipped to the top.

Wrong blue!
Unacceptable!!!
LRCII

What the heck? There were 70 pages of narrative, charts, and data points about the health of Robbie's company in this report, a comprehensive evaluation of its progress as a business, and a detailed analysis of all areas that needed improvement. All Robbie could focus on was the *color?* Walker looked at his watch. Robbie wouldn't be in for another hour or two. He buzzed Flora, who appeared at his door in an instant.

"Looks like we have a Code Blue here," he said, holding up the report. "Get Wally Saxton to convene a task force for me. I want an answer for our chairman by the end of the day."

"On it," she said, turning to leave.

"And see if you can get time on Robbie's calendar for me. I want to see him as soon as possible."

Walker flopped into a seat behind his desk as Flora departed. It never failed that communications from Robbie sucked the life out of him. He rested his elbows on his cushioned armrests, pressed his fingertips together, breathed deeply, and contemplated his situation. Was he leaving the company? He could use a read on things from his most reliable supporter.

The intercom buzzed. "Mr. Crowe isn't available today, Mr. Hope," Flora said. "Winnie says his calendar for the next week is jammed."

"I've seen his calendar. It has more white space than the South Pole."

"She says he's preparing for next week's board meeting."

"See if he's taking walk-ins. And get Moe Klinger on the phone for me." A moment later, line one was blinking.

"Mr. Hope? This is Emma from Mr. Klinger's office."

"Emma? Didn't you work in Robbie Crowe's office?"

"I did indeed, Mr. Hope. I departed just yesterday."

"Glad you found something so quickly."

"Thank you, sir. It was rather fortunate that I met Mr. Klinger. May I put him on?"

"Please."

Walker heard a phlegmy roar as Moe cleared his throat. "You got me before I could call you," he said.

"You saw the story."

"Everyone saw the story," Moe replied. "That's why I haven't been able to get off the phone. My clients are wondering what the hell's going on over there. And they're turning on me for not getting them out of the stock by now. They say I should have known Robbie would fuck it up. And I've got to concede: they have a point."

"Have you spoken to Robbie?" Walker asked.

"I haven't been able to get through."

"Join the club," Walker said sadly.

"He hasn't talked to you? You have to be kidding me."

"Crickets."

"Well, this little story cost me about $50 million today before I started dumping shares."

"Oh, no. Please, don't do that, Moe. I need you to hang in there with me."

"I've seen this movie before, Walker. It doesn't end well for investors. I'm not sure I've got the stomach for another offensive on Crowe Power. Not when Captain Robbie seems determined to scuttle his ship. Are you going to try to see him, at least?"

"They say his calendar is full."

"Right. Maybe he's blocked off time to catalogue his baseball cards. From what Emma tells me, he does jack shit all day long. She said, 'I couldn't be certain whether he was staring out the window envisioning the next hundred years or just staring out the window.' It's just too bad he didn't jump."

"I may have to, before I'm pushed. You free for lunch off-campus?"

"Unlike Robbie, it looks like I actually have several things scheduled," Moe said. "But I'll move them. In the meantime, don't do anything rash."

28. OH, WHAT A HORRIBLE MORNING

R obbie opened the door of his home and stepped through the threshold to discover what appeared to be a lovely spring day. A bright sun sprayed a leaf-dappled sunlight onto the sidewalks of East 67th Street. Robins, cardinals, and sparrows engaged in a raucous competition of mating songs and territorial fights. The rose-like fragrance of the first blossoming cherry trees wafted in from Central Park. And people liberated from walking their dogs with their heads down against bitter winds wore smiles and exchanged head-nod greetings as they passed one another. For them, the weather was about to get even better. The forecaster on 1010 WINS said temperatures for the day could reach a record high of 84 degrees.

For Robbie, it was a sign of the apocalypse. As he ambled down the steps toward the idling Cadillac Escalade, he could hardly breathe. All he could feel was an overwhelming sense of guilt over a warming climate that threatened to sauté all these people on their sidewalks like so many fillets of trout. And he knew deep in his bones that he must share the blame for these temperatures, and so must Homer Crowe and his successors, all the way down the family line. Unwitting or not, they were contractors in the devil's bargain to improve standards of living by exploiting the planet's resources and pumping massive amounts of carbon dioxide into the atmosphere, where it would remain forever, entombing the world.

Boris spotted the boss descending the stairs, jumped out of the driver's seat of the Escalade, and ran stiffly around to the right rear door, opening it for Robbie to step up and in. Then he hobbled back to the driver's side, hopped in, fastened his seat belt, and adjusted the rear-view mirror to frame the boss's glowering mug.

"Temperature okay back there, Mr. Crowe?"

Robbie glumly shook his head. "No," he grumbled. "It's awful. You're running a meat locker in here, Boris. I hate this fucking AC. Turn it off and get the windows *down*."

"Whatever you say, boss."

Robbie plopped his briefcase on the back seat and pulled out his iPhone to find 22 new text messages and 84 new emails in his company mailbox. A second phone, tucked deep into a pocket in his briefcase, had a single text.

MARIA

Someone's Taking Care of Buzzniss.

C U later.

Robbie didn't respond. There would be nothing on the record, digital or otherwise, that could be used against him by Lindsey or, potentially, her lawyers. God forbid he should end up like his Uncle Robert, whose three divorces left him and his children with significantly reduced shares in the company—ceding enormous power to relatives like his Uncle Chuck, who had stubbornly remained married to Aunt Sylvia for 57 years. Robbie was careful to never let his extramarital activities go too long or too deep, lest they place the foundation of his power at risk.

Robbie's affair with Maria had lasted two years, the longest of any relationship in his long string of paramours. Maria, more than any of them, was the opposite of Lindsey—earthy rather than polite, witty in her conversation rather than cautiously dull, cutting edge in her fashions rather than a prudent year behind, a tightly-wound overachiever always looking to go higher, farther, faster, including during sex. Most enticing, she was socially taboo for a man of his lineage, which made her especially desirable. While Lindsey was the dutiful daughter of wealthy parents in Chicago and attended school abroad, Maria was deep-dish New York. Italian on one side and Polish on the other, she was the rebellious daughter of a fire department captain in Brooklyn. She left home at 17 to attend SUNY Stony Brook on academic scholarship for her undergraduate degree and borrowed $200,000 in student loans to attend Fordham Law School, where she made Law Review. After graduation, she received a dozen job offers and accepted a role at the white shoe firm of Rothstein Lucas & Pratt, which managed the Crowe family business. That led to a flirtation with Robbie, an offer from Digby to become Crowe Power's Associate General Counsel, and an invitation from Robbie to join him for an afternoon in a suite at the Peninsula Hotel. Their encounters soon became the only weekly appointments that weren't subject to cancellation, at least until this point.

Robbie scheduled their rendezvous for Tuesday afternoons, when he blocked his calendar for water polo at the New York Athletic Club, an event that certainly would have come as a surprise to the people who actually played water polo there. For two years, Robbie hadn't even seen the pool and wasn't precisely sure where it was. He always went straight upstairs to a suite on the 21st floor, where he and Maria had their weekly romp overlooking Central Park. Now, as Natalia began to occupy his thoughts, he began to think there might not be room in there for Maria.

Boris's phone rang and he tapped a button on his steering wheel, which put the call on the car's speakers. "Boris, it's Tom Michaels. We've got a situation down here at HQ."

"Yeah. Tom. Whattaya got?"

"Protesters out in front of the building on Broad Street. You'll need to bring the boss in on New Street."

"Okay, Tom. You got it."

Boris hung up and steered toward the FDR, then looked in the rear-view mirror. "I don't know if you heard that, Mr. Crowe, but we got protesters again today. I'll take you around the back way."

Robbie kept his eyes on his phone. "Whatever," he said absently.

He saw another text, this time from Digby.

DIGBY
Stock down five dollars at open—and falling.

Robbie rang him up. "Good Lord, Digs. That's worse than I thought."

"Overreaction, if you ask me," Digby replied. "All the follow-up stories say losing Walker would be catastrophic for the company. I'm hoping there's a correction as the day goes on and people realize the sky isn't falling."

"You know what?" Robbie said. "I'm fine with this. I don't mind taking a short-term hit. Let the people who don't believe in us get out. To hell with 'em."

"I've also had a couple of board members asking what's going on."

"What are you telling them?" Robbie wondered.

"Exactly what we agreed: we have no idea where the story's coming from, but there have been rumblings along these lines for some time."

"Perfect."

"Otherwise, all hell is breaking loose. People are running around the 24th floor with their hair on fire."

Robbie laughed. "Excellent!"

"Are you coming in?"

"Heading in now."

"You have a welcoming committee on Broad Street," Digby warned.

"Protesters? So I heard. We're going in the back way. I don't need that shit."

"You'll miss your girlfriend."

"Natalia?" Robbie asked, excitedly.

"She's right out front, chanting with the rest of them," Digby said. "They're yelling, 'Hey, hey, ho, ho. Something-something's got to go.' I couldn't make out the something. It might have been you."

"Me? *I've* got to go? What the hell. I'm on their side. If I could, I'd be out there protesting *with* them."

"They don't know that."

"You need to make sure they see the Buzzniss story."

"It's digital, Robbie. What should I do? Throw them my laptop?"

Robbie pondered his options. He put the phone down and called up to his driver. "Boris, let's go in the front."

Boris looked at Robbie in the rear-view mirror. "There's a mob out there, Mr. Crowe."

"I know," Robbie said, defiantly, "and I don't care."

"Mr. Crowe, it could be dangerous."

Robbie flushed red. "Just fucking *do it*, will you? Does everything have to be a goddamned *negotiation*?"

Boris put his head down. "Yes, sir."

"I can't take it," Robbie muttered into the phone. "This guy's an idiot."

Digby heard the conversation. "You're coming in the front door? Are you insane?"

"I understand these people, Digs—certainly more than I understand Walker and his stupid Leadership Team. All I need to do is talk to them, reason with them, tell them where I'm coming from."

"They *know* where you're coming from. A mansion on the Upper East Side."

"That's not what I'm talking about."

"Well, I think it's very brave of you. The natives appear to be rather hostile."

"I'm not the least bit afraid," he scoffed. "But... meet me down there just in case, will you?"

"Right-o."

"And, uh... bring Tom Michaels and some of his guys. I might need back-up."

29. MAN OF THE PEOPLE

Digby, Tom Michaels, and three of his most intimidating Crowe Power security agents awaited Robbie's car on the west side of Broad Street, surveying the dozen drowsy protesters, several of whom were wearing battle fatigues from Café Che and the badge of the radical Planetistas. As New York protests go, it was tame if not lame, and nobody was giving it much attention. The usual smokers and vapers hanging out on the sidewalks close to building entrances were looking at their phones and blowing plumes in the air. Commuters walking the last blocks to work from the subway or the ferry were more interested in finding a decent bagel and dodging the various sidewalk obstacles put in place by NYPD to block suspicious vehicles. Kiosk operators kept their eyes on the hands of people who browsed their stands. And Tom scanned the brigades of beat cops, Anti-Terrorism police, and Rapid Response teams patrolling the neighborhood, who he knew would only get excited if someone shouted *Allahu Akbar*. Otherwise, *fuhgeddaboudit*.

As Robbie's Escalade turned the corner from Water Street toward headquarters, Robbie took a deep breath and considered his reception.

"Boris. Drop me off here," he said.

Boris was puzzled. "Sorry, sir?"

"I can't show up in a massive fucking gas guzzler. What's *wrong* with you?"

Boris pulled over at the corner of Beaver and Broad, put the vehicle in park, and ran around to let out Robbie, who gathered his phone, newspapers, bottle of water, and briefcase and stepped out onto the cobblestone street. From there he walked the last block alone, a brave, solitary figure ready for any and all takers. Was this, he wondered, how General MacArthur felt as he waded ashore in the Philippines? Gary Cooper walking down Main Street in *High Noon*? That Chinese man staring down the tanks in Tiananmen Square? Surely, this was bravery in action, an illustration of *character*, the kind that springs from righteousness.

As the protesters recognized Robbie, they were roused from their lethargy. *There he was! A genuine planet criminal! A capitalist piglet!* A man in green fatigues with a scruffy beard and cap, à la Fidel Castro, shouted through a megaphone to the group, which began a new chant.

> What do we want?
> *Clean energy!*
> When do we want it?
> *Now!*
> What do we want?

With Digby, Tom Michaels, and his well-armed team keeping close watch, Robbie courageously strode over to the group and raised his hands over his head to a smattering of boos, glancing over the crowd for Natalia. He located her in the back, peering into a compact mirror and adjusting her beret.

"Hold on. Hold on," Robbie said. "I want to tell you something."

A protester yelled, "We don't want to hear it."

Another shouted, "You got nothin' to say to us, greedy pig."

"Well, I'm going to say it anyway," Robbie said. "And this is the truth: *I understand.*"

That brought snorts, laughter and a few shouts of "bullshit."

"You don't fucking *get it*, man!" a protester shouted.

"The fact is, I do," Robbie said. "Seriously. You want clean energy? Well guess what? So do I."

The bearded guy with the megaphone walked over to Robbie as the protesters gathered around. "You got some serious *cojones*, man. I'll give you that."

Robbie glanced at Natalia to see if she heard that. He had *cojones! Great big balls! Castro himself said so!*

"You may find this hard to believe, but I really am on your side," Robbie said. "In fact, I couldn't agree more. We—and by that, I mean corporate America, not just Crowe Power—we need to do more to combat climate change. And we need to move much, much faster than we're moving now. This is about our children and our grandchildren and our grandchildren's children and the generations after them."

Castro strode to face Robbie, *hombre a hombre.* "Well, if you're such a believer, why don't you do something about it?" he said. "You're the big man over there."

"I'm working hard on this—very hard. You could ask our Leadership Team. They're tired of hearing me push them all the time to do better. But I promise you: I'm going to push *even harder*. I'm going to do everything I can to make people listen. We're going to get this right. You know, my great-great-grandfather was one of the original conservationists. I'm sure he'd want to see us doing more. Just like I want to see us doing more. And we will. We have to think about more than profitability. This is about the future of our planet."

There were a few nods of heads in the crowd, but not from Natalia, whose arms were folded across her chest, her skeptical expression easy to read. *Prove it.*

Somehow, some way, he had to win her over.

30. RAVE REVIEW

"Good lord," Digby said, trailing Robbie into his office like a tail-wagging puppy. "Such heresy, a block from the New York Stock Exchange. I thought a building might fall on top of you." Digby took his usual perch on a chair in front of the desk as Robbie hung up his suitcoat in the closet around the corner.

"You thought it was good?" Robbie called, excitement in his voice.

"I thought it was terrific. Inspiring, actually," Digby said. "I was proud of you."

"Really?"

"Absolutely. That's not the way Marty would recommend. In fact, he'd be mortified if he knew you were out there. What if there were reporters?"

"I wish there were," Robbie said, walking back to the desk and sat down, smoothing his hair. "It needed to be said, and nobody else around here was going to say it. I mean, I've got to find a way to get through to them."

"All of them? Or just Natalia?"

"We win them over one at a time, Digby. But I wouldn't mind starting with her."

"That looks like a tough sell. I don't think she's buying."

"It's not like I haven't done this before."

It suddenly dawned on Digby what Robbie was doing. "You want to hire her, don't you?"

Robbie laughed. "You know me too well."

Digby rolled his eyes. "I've seen this maneuver once or twice."

Robbie laughed. "Or three or four or five times."

"So tell me," Digby said. "What did you think of the Buzzniss story?"

"You tell me," Robbie said, leaning back.

"Personally, I thought it was fabulous."

"Yeah," Robbie said flatly. "I guess it came out okay."

Digby sensed Robbie's discomfort. "What didn't you like?"

"Nothing, really. It's just that—I don't know how to say this—I was really surprised to see you on the list as a possible successor to Walker. Where did they get that idea?"

Digby blushed. "Well... that would be from me, I suppose."

"You and I talked about Tim and Anna. I didn't mention you in there."

Digby's face blanched from pink to white. "You don't think I'm qualified?"

"I'm not saying that. It's just that I hadn't thought of it at all. I mean, usually CEOs come from a finance or operations background. You have neither."

"That's true," he said, leaning in. "But let me tell you what I do have."

"What's that?"

"Your back."

"And I appreciate that." Robbie said. "But I can't have my brother-in-law in there. How would that look?"

"It worked for the Kennedys."

"We're not the Kennedys."

"You're doing a passable imitation."

"Don't tell me how."

Digby leaned in. "Look, Robbie. Nobody else here is going to care about the Crowe family interests like I do. I'm the only executive outside this office who understands those interests, who knows that Crowes are the only people who are in this for the long haul. I may not be blood, but I'm a reasonable facsimile. I'm all in on this family and this company. In that order."

"I hear you."

For the first time ever, Robbie looked at Digby differently. Was it possible that he, aside from being part of the family, was exactly like everybody else? That he wanted something from Robbie? That he had been carrying his bags all these years hoping for a big payoff? Family or not, Digby was suddenly diminished—just another guy waiting for a handout.

Digby sensed Robbie's withdrawal. He pressed ahead. "Of course," Digby said, "I'm also the only one who also knows where all the skeletons are buried, some of them in the basement of this building. That's helpful, too, no?"

Then why did it sound more like a threat? Maybe this was a trap and Robbie had just stepped in it. He tried to think of what he might have on Digby and drew a blank. For all the years that they had known each other, from Eton to Harvard to marrying his sister and immediately joining Crowe Power, Digby had never shown Robbie any real dark side. Was that on purpose? What if he secretly hated him?

He looked across at Digby, whose mop top, wire-rimmed glasses, and bow tie suddenly looked less like a law professor's and more like a menacing prosecutor's.

"Look, I think it very well could happen for you at the right time," Robbie said, turning his back to Digby and flipping on the desktop computer on his credenza. "But that time isn't now, Digs. I need an ops guy in that spot, somebody who can execute my vision,"

"That means the only candidate is Tim."

Robbie looked over his shoulder. "I could live with that."

"Seriously?"

"I hear he secretly hates Walker."

"And that makes him qualified?"

"No, but it helps," Robbie said.

"How do you even know that?"

Robbie turned back around and smiled. "A little bird told me."

"A little bug? Planted by Howie-Do-It?"

"You don't want to know."

"No, I don't. What about the succession plan the board asked Walker to draw up?"

"I'm not leaving this up to Walker. Are you nuts?"

"You don't even want his opinion?"

"Look, Digs," he said, swiveling back around. "I already know his opinion and, frankly, I don't care. This will be a board decision. Period. And, let's face it, that means it's *my* call on when he goes and who takes his place. In this case," he said, pounding a knuckle into the desk, "the buck really does stop here. And if Walker objects, or tries getting tough with me, *too fucking bad.* I'd hate to get nasty with the guy, but I will if I have to. And he won't know what hit him."

The intercom buzzed. "Mr. Crowe, Mr. Hope would like to see you," Winnie said.

Robbie looked at Digby. "Can you believe this?" he muttered, before hitting the button to talk to Winnie. "Tell him I'm busy."

"He's on his way down."

Robbie's voice rose, panicked. "Oh, *shit.* He can't come in."

"I'll try to stop him—" Winnie said.

Robbie bolted out of his chair. "I've got to go."

Digby stood up. "Where?"

"I don't know," Robbie said, starting for the door.

"You can't go out there," Digby said. "He's on his way in."

"Right." Robbie pivoted around and jogged toward his private sanctuary in the back. "Tell him I'm... I don't know. Gone." He pushed on a bookshelf in the far corner and the doors to his lair swung open. He stepped inside, closing the shelf behind him.

As Digby gathered his papers to go, the office door opened and Walker stood in the frame.

"Chairman around, Digby?" Walker asked.

Digby shrugged. "He was here a minute ago."

"Well I'd like to see him. Maybe he went to the little boy's room back there?"

"He dashed out somewhere. Couldn't tell you where."

"Couldn't or can't?"

"Won't."

"Uh-huh. And he left you here in his office? Alone? C'mon," he said, laughing. "You guys can do better than that."

Digby summoned a shaky indignation. "What are you saying, Walker?"

"Let me say it loud enough for both you and him to hear, 'cause frankly, I suspect he can," Walker said. He called loudly in the direction of the back room, channeling his inner Arnold Schwarzenegger. "Tell him *I'll be back.*"

Walker left as Digby's phone dinged with a message from Robbie.

ROBBIE
Well?

Digby typed a response.

DIGBY
Gone.

The bookcase swung open, and Robbie reappeared. "The *nerve* of that guy," he said. "I should kick his ass for barging in like that."

"You might still be able to catch him."

Robbie snorted. "What? You think I can't?"

"I'm sure you'd thrash him from top to bottomus."

"I get the allusion, asshole. Cowardly Lion? Go to hell."

31. FLUSH WITH SUCCESS

Within a minute of pressing the button to transfer $11,000 from his bank account to that of his ex-wife, Marty heard the piano riff ringer of his mobile phone. He didn't have to look at the screen to know it was Jill.

"You're short, Marty," she said.

"I don't think so," he said, turning his chair toward his office window. "I looked it up. And you know what? At five-eleven, I'm actually *taller* than average for the U.S. And in Sri Lanka, I'm a freaking giant. I could play center on the national basketball team."

"Don't get cute. You're a thousand dollars under on your payment."

Marty sighed. "I know it's a little light. I'm waiting on my bonus."

"I'm not. Pay me."

"Can you cut me a little slack? I'm getting killed here. Between the rent and the groceries and these payments, I can't even go out for a beer unless it's on the company credit card. I buy six-packs at Duane Reade and ration them."

Jill shifted into a baby-talk voice. "Can you hold on, Marty? I need to get a Kleenex for all these tears."

"Get yourself more than one. I may be losing my job."

"Not surprising. You have a flair for self-immolation."

"I'm not the one lighting the match, alright?"

"Listen up, Marty. That's not my problem. *My* problem is I'm paying for everything else in this family you left behind."

Marty reddened. "*I* left behind? You kicked me out to take up with—literal description here—the fucking gardener. How was I supposed to know manure wasn't the only thing he was spreading around there."

"Oh Marty. *Puh-leeze.* We're not going to litigate this again. But I will take you to court if you don't pay me. Like now. So just do it, and I don't have to call you anymore."

She hung up. Marty, furious, hit the call back button on his phone.

"How about this?" he said. "You call the court and I'll call Immigration and sic ICE on your boyfriend. Then, if you want to continue living with Jose, you'll have to do it in El Salvador. You might like it. They have gang warfare down there, sure, but Jose can garden all year round and, hey, so can you. I'll send your money in pesos or colons or whatever they call the currency. Sound like a plan?"

Silence. "You wouldn't dare."

"Here's the beautiful thing about my pathetic situation, Jill: I've got nothing to lose."

Marty hung up, took a deep breath to compose himself. His analysis was, unfortunately, correct. He had little to lose with Jill or at Crowe Power. Playing it safe had gotten him nowhere but behind on his payments. And if Robbie succeeded in removing Walker, his job was as good as over. The times called for a futile and stupid gesture, like trying to save Walker's job. And if that didn't work, the least he could do was torment Robbie a little bit on his way out.

+++

Marty found sanctuary in the last stall on the left in the Executive Men's Room, a dark and quiet place where he could read his tablet in peace. He scanned the lead stories in the *Financial Times*, oblivious to the opening and closing of the door to the hallway, the shuffling of feet, running faucets, flushing urinals, and muffled conversation until he heard Digby's voice.

"Morning, Tim," Digby said.

"Some story today," Tim said, stepping up to the urinal next to him.

"How about that," Digby said.

"Kind of shocker, actually," Tim said. "Anybody in here?"

Marty raised his feet off the floor in case Tim or Digby peered under the stalls.

"We know Walker isn't," Digby said.

"Right," Tim laughed. "It's not quite 10:58."

"Or 2:58 or 5:58. Between us girls, I avoid his pee schedule," Digby said. "I don't need a performance review in the bathroom."

"I hear you," Tim said. "So tell me. Do you think there's any truth to that story? Kind of surprising given the run we've had."

"Nothing surprises me around here," Digby said, jiggling his johnson and folding it back into his boxer shorts. "People have been coming and going for a long time."

Digby pivoted toward the sinks. Tim finished his business and joined him, addressing Digby as they washed their hands. "You have any sense how this might play out?"

"No," Digby said. "But I do know this much. Once Robbie makes up his mind, things start moving fast. I would advise that if you have any interest in moving up, you should raise your hand soon, in case a vacancy opens. Robbie thinks very highly of you."

"Really?"

"He told me himself he sees some unique qualifications in you."

"Well, that's very nice of you to say—"

"I'd dispense with the modesty," Digby said, pulling down a hand towel. "There's no time for it. If you don't move, Anna could try jumping in ahead of you. That wouldn't be good for anybody."

Canh Nguyen entered the men's room with a "Good morning," and the conversation ceased. Digby dried his hands and headed toward the door, pausing and speaking softly as Canh went into the first stall. "Think about it. But don't think too long."

Marty waited until the restroom cleared before he left the stall, processing what he heard. Tim, the perennial second banana, could steal the spotlight at Crowe Power? Marty was quite sure Robbie would regret it. And, sooner rather than later, so would Tim.

32. CHUCK ROAST

C harles Francis Crowe II emerged from the executive elevator on the 24th floor and walked down the hallway, craning a peek into the various executive offices, each guarded by an executive assistant dutifully working at a desktop computer. *Who were these people anyway? Damned if he could keep track anymore...*

Tanned from his winter in Palm Beach and crowned with a mane of immaculate white hair, Chuck was, as always, an elegant portrait of old-money wealth. Impeccably dressed and groomed, he wore a tailored light gray suit, crisp white shirt, pale green Hermes tie, and brown Salvatore Ferragamo cap-toe shoes, and carried a Burberry raincoat over his arm, just in case. As he entered the reception area, two security guards snapped to their feet behind the desk.

"Good morning, Mr. Crowe."

"At ease, guys," Chuck said with a smile. "Really."

They resumed their usual seats and Chuck walked past to a large office off the beaten path where his aged secretary, Greta, sat at her desk idly flipping through *People* magazine. Chuck showed up at headquarters a dozen times a year for board meetings, haircuts, and luncheons, but as the patriarch of the Crowe family, retained an elaborate office and a small staff. Greta swooned at the sight of her boss.

"Good morning, Mr. Crowe," she said, rising. "So nice to see you. May I get you anything? Coffee? A bottled water, perhaps?"

"No, thank you, Greta. Thought I'd drop this off before I head upstairs."

"I'll handle that for you," she said, taking his coat. "They're expecting you in the Founders Room."

He nodded and headed toward the spiral stairway that would take him to the 25th floor, where the Board Room, gym, Executive Dining Room, and other corporate facilities were located. The Founders Room was a private dining room reserved for Robbie, Chuck, and other members of the founding family to host luncheons away from the common folk in the Executive Dining Room down the hall. Both rooms were joined at the center by a shared kitchen, but the Founders Room had its own dedicated chef, its own private washrooms with towels monogrammed for the Crowe family rather than Crowe Power, and its own wine list tied to the family's exclusive cellar, stocked with wines from family vineyards in Italy and California as well as the cellars that were bought at a steep discount from companies that went bust during the financial crisis. Referred to as the "Crowes Nest" by the help, the room was Old World elegant with Chippendale chairs, Sterling silver service, Wedgwood china and finger bowls, and staffed by two white-gloved waiters in tuxedos.

Chuck found his seat along the side of a small dining table and was met by Horace, the ancient waiter, with a Waterford tumbler of Johnnie Walker Blue. Chuck sipped his drink and reflected on the consequential meetings that had taken place here over the years. There were good times, like the celebratory dinner when he was named, at age 29, a Vice-President and joined the company's Board of Directors. And there were difficult times, like the meeting four years ago following Les Crowe's death, when Chuck told Robbie that the conga line of Crowes in the company's top job had come to an end and the party was over. Given Robbie's piddling record and the company's dire condition, there was too much pressure on the board to allow him to succeed his father as CEO. He would have to settle for chairman, where he could preside over the board and the family's interests, and another person would run the business. Rather than protest, Robbie seemed almost relieved. As chairman, he could dabble in the business as much as liked, but he'd never have to work again.

Chuck felt a friendly pat on his back.

"Uncle Chuck," Robbie said. "Please don't get up."

"Don't worry," Chuck said, turning to shake Robbie's hand. "I can't."

"You look terrific," Robbie said, sitting down.

"All you see is the paint job," he growled. "Thank God you can't get under the hood." Horace placed a glass of green slime in front of Robbie. "I hope that swamp water you're drinking has medicinal properties."

"Anti-oxidants," Robbie said, taking a sip.

"I have lots of things to worry about at my age," Chuck said, picking up a menu. "Rust isn't one of them."

They ordered Dover sole with sauce meunière and caught up on family issues, gossiped about various retired executives, and discussed the merits of their servants, before Chuck blotted his lip with the linen napkin and set it on the table. Through it all, Robbie was assiduously polite and deferential, carefully cultivating Chuck's favor. His uncle still held 15 percent of the family's shares and, importantly, maintained enormous credibility and influence with Robbie's cousins, nieces, and nephews.

"I read the story this morning from that dot-com publication—Bizzy, Buzzy, whatever the hell it is," Chuck said, lighting a cigarette. "And I'm really curious. Who are these folks on the board who are upset with Walker? I go to all the meetings and I chair the Finance Committee. And I talk to Carlton Lucas at least once a week. I haven't heard one damn word about this. In fact, all I hear is praise for the job he's doing. He put a plan in place four years ago that everyone on the board approved. And he's executing it flawlessly. For my money—and I have a fair amount invested in this joint—he's the best CEO we've had since Homer Crowe. Did they just make up this story?"

Robbie wriggled uncomfortably in his chair. "Hard to say, Uncle Chuck. But I'm not terribly surprised that something like this came out. No doubt, Walker has done a superb job. The key word there is 'done,' past tense. After four years, I would expect board members to wonder: how are we set up for the future? The world is changing fast. Are we changing fast enough to keep up?"

Chuck leaned over the table. "Those are fair questions. But they ought to be raised in the Board Room, not in the press. I hope to God this isn't your doing."

Robbie snapped his head back, indignant. "Why on earth would I do that?"

"That's what I'd like to know."

Robbie considered his words carefully; at crunch time, he would need his uncle's backing with the family and the board. "Uncle Chuck, you of all people should know that all I want is to see this company succeed—and I mean on all measures, not just financial. We must win in the market *and* in our communities as a good corporate citizen. That's our family name on the shingle. We need to do the right thing in all aspects of the business, including how we treat the environment."

"That sounds an awful lot like the story I read this morning."

Robbie, rolled his eyes, exasperated. "I can say unequivocally: I did not talk to them."

Chuck regarded him skeptically. "Are you thinking *you* want to run the company?"

"Heavens no. But I would if I had to."

Chuck guffawed. "What the hell's *that* supposed to mean? Nobody's got a gun to your head. Although I might if you make a move like that."

"I'm only saying I would in an emergency, say, if Walker left and we didn't have anyone else right away. I could step in for a short period of time."

Chuck vigorously shook his head and stubbed out his cigarette. "Let's be candid here, Robbie. There were reasons it didn't happen last time. Your strategy was one of the reasons we nearly went bankrupt. I do *not* want to go through that experience again."

"I remember it all very well. But those were different times, and the company is in a different place now."

"That's right. It's in the best shape it's ever been—at least in my lifetime."

"How's this?" Robbie said, pushing his hair off his forehead. "Let's take that off the table."

"Take what, precisely?"

"I will not move to become CEO."

"Good, because I wouldn't support it," Chuck said, lighting another smoke. "I know it makes you uncomfortable that we make our money in an unfashionable way. It's not exactly environmentally friendly. But the fact is, somebody's got to do it. Otherwise, the lights don't stay on. The planes don't fly. The cars don't drive. So it may as well be us."

"Fine. But even if you're not worried about the environment, we all should be worried about the business. And it's just a matter of time before we're regulated out of existence. People *hate* our industry. I hate our industry. We've got to develop alternative forms of energy before it's too late."

"I'm all for high-mindedness," Chuck said. "But have any of your ideas on wind or solar ever panned out? I mean, seriously, Robbie. We might as well generate power by throwing dollar bills into a furnace. That's essentially what we did."

"You can't look at this as a short-term proposition," Robbie insisted. "I'm looking twenty, thirty years out."

"I'm not," Chuck said. "I'm 82 years old. I don't buy green pineapples."

"Then think about your legacy, about saving the planet. Look at the weather today. People are practically *frying* out there."

"Golly," Chuck said, blowing a thin stream of smoke. "I thought it was just a nice day."

"Not to me. It's alarming," Robbie said. "We have a responsibility here. I know we don't like to think about it, but we're contributing to climate change."

"Right. By almost everything we do, including breathing. Would you like me to stop?"

Robbie sighed. "I'm saying we must do something to fix it."

"Fine. Do something. But don't run this company onto the rocks while you're doing it. Have you checked in with the rest of the family lately? Might be good for you to ask them how they feel about Walker and the direction we're going."

"I get it. They're reasonably happy."

"Happy? No. They're fucking delirious," Chuck said. "The dividend is five times what it was. They don't have to dip into the principal of their trust funds anymore. Christ. When you and your dad were running the show, some of them were seriously having to think about getting jobs. How do you think our voting bloc would have held up then?"

"No question, this has been a good run—"

Chuck stood, abruptly. "You're damn right it's been a good run, Robbie. Which is why I want to offer you a bit of advice: don't fuck it up."

33. A NEW PLAN

Walker and Moe Klinger found sanctuary from the Financial District's lunchtime crowds on the outdoor balcony of Cipriani Wall Street, where they held court at a secluded corner table behind a potted palm tree and a massive Corinthian column. On the street below, tour guides carrying colorful pennants guided groups from Shanghai and Tokyo and Paris through the cobblestone corridors of American financial power.

"I want you to be honest with me," Walker said, poking aimlessly at a plate of taglioni. "Do I have trouble with the board?"

Moe broke open a crust of bread. "You mean, aside from Robbie? Nah. I've never heard a peep."

Walker exhaled.

"From what Harvey and Jayne tell me, they're all supportive," Moe continued. "And they should be. You've made their shares worth something. But I wouldn't say they're deeply invested in you personally. Aside from my guys, most of them have been Crowe family lapdogs for so long, the only trick they know is to roll over and play dead. Which, from what I can tell, they do rather convincingly."

"So if Robbie moves against me, do the rest of them follow?"

"Like sheep to a shearing. Crowe boards have buried more executive bodies along Broad Street than I can count. It's one reason I went after them four years ago, and why I'm thinking of getting out now. They have a knack for chasing out the best talent."

"It's astonishing to me," Walker said. "Why don't these directors have more backbone? These are accomplished people."

"Right," Moe said, "but they were accomplished back in 1890. They're all past their due dates. Carlton Lucas was a stud lawyer back in the day, but I'm told now he can't stay awake past the reading of the minutes. Tommy MacDonald was one of the best CEOs in America, ever, but his wealth is tied up in Armaco Steel, a company supplier. And Virginia Einholz? Problem with her isn't that she was bought when she was governor of Delaware; it's that she stayed bought. There's no energy in this group anymore. Harvey tells me that once the lights go out in the Board Room, it's lights out for half the board. You can barely hear the presentation over all the snoring."

"So, if Robbie asks, they'll vote the party line."

"That's my guess." Moe waved his fork. "I've seen this sort of thing at other family-run corporations—at least, the bad ones. Somewhere along the way, they lose the plot. They think they're special because they're born rich and they have a famous name. They name their kids Homer the Second, or Charles the Third, or Frankie the Fourth—like they're American royals or something—when they should have named them with fractions, Fred the One-Eighth or Mary the Three-Sixteenths, which would be a hell of a lot more accurate. Fact is, there wasn't a second or third or fourth Homer Crowe. There was only the original, and he was a frigging genius. No other Crowe since has come close, especially when you get down to the fifth or sixth generation. Not that there aren't some very decent people in there. I have a lot of time for Robbie's Uncle Chuck; that guy's smart as hell, but nobody knows how to run a complex corporation like this. They can't even run their own households."

Walker was too deflated to eat. "Where does that leave me?"

"I think you're in the torture phase now. Robbie will make you as uncomfortable as he possibly can in the hope that you'll quit. That would spare him an uncomfortable conversation."

"So if I quit," Walker said, "that makes it easy for him."

"Don't give him the satisfaction," Moe advised. "And don't box yourself out of another gig. You quit and you can't run another company for at least a year. Robbie will enforce the non-compete. But get yourself fired, that goes out the window. You can go anywhere you like, as long as you don't let them slap on some golden handcuffs."

"What really bugs me is this: I built this company, as it stands today."

"Yeah. So what?"

"It's not finished. There's more work to be done."

"Who gives a shit?"

"I do," Walker said.

Moe laid down his utensils on the plate and sat back in his wicker chair. "Let me ask you something, Walker. Are you a missionary or a mercenary?"

"I don't know. I've never thought of it like that."

"Well, I have. And Crowe Power already *has* a missionary. His name is Robbie Crowe. He's all about legacies and the family's reputation and making the world a place of sunshine and lollipops. He wants to be a man about town, proud of his name, celebrated at cocktail parties and civic board meetings. He's a greedy bastard like the rest of us, of course, but his name matters more than anything else. If you fall into that same trap, where all you're worried about is your standing with the swells, you're screwed."

"You're saying I'm a mercenary."

"You're goddamn right you are," Moe insisted. "You're a hired gun. You were brought in to clean up Dodge. Which you did. The minute you start caring about what happens after you throw down your badge, you may as well put your head in the noose. That's why you need to think about moving on sooner rather than later."

Walker slumped in his chair, like he'd been socked in the gut. "I've never been fired in my life. I really don't want to start now. I mean, I do have my own reputation to protect."

"Yes, you do. But with all due respect, Walker, you're thinking short-term. In the grand scheme of things, this is just a battle, not a war. You —*we*—can win this thing, as long as we don't fight by their rules."

"How so?"

"I have a couple of thoughts."

"That's good," Walker said. "Because I think I need a new plan."

34. UPTOWN RENDEZVOUS

Tim Padden had always been a man with a finely tuned sense for survival, and it had served him well. From his graduate school days at Purdue, where he earned his master's in mechanical engineering, through his climbs up various corporate ladders, Tim demonstrated a knack for recognizing danger and opportunity and acting accordingly. From the moment he met Walker ten years ago and dazzled him with the clear labels and multiple tabs in his color-coded weekly report, Tim knew that from there on, he would navigate his way through the shoals of corporate America with Walker's butt serving as his North Star. There was a man who knew where he was going, and he was getting there fast.

Now, for the first time in his career, Tim sensed an opening. With Walker possibly on the ropes at Crowe Power, Tim had a chance to vault ahead. And why not? He was ready. He had studied Walker like the Bible at three companies and knew his every move. Even more enticing was the opportunity to at last escape his giant shadow. Tim's dependence on Walker for every promotion and every raise, his deference to Walker for every bit of credit for each company's success, and the diffidence that allowed Walker to constantly elbow him out of the way had taken their toll. The anonymous document he received in an inter-office envelope showing Walker had written him off as a "captain, not a general" was the last straw. Tim had enough. He'd show him—and everyone else.

He left the office at 3 p.m. and told his assistant to advise anyone looking for him that he had a doctor's appointment and expected to be back at the office around 5:30. To cover his tracks, he booked an Uber rather than a company car up to the Metropolitan Club at Fifth Avenue and 60th Street. There he took an elevator to the top floor, where he headed to the bar looking south over Midtown. Since Robbie was notoriously late, Tim was pleasantly surprised to find him arriving right on time. Perhaps he was as eager for this meeting as Tim.

Tim rose and shook Robbie's hand. "I hope this wasn't inconvenient for you, Robbie."

"Not at all. I have an appointment at the Athletic Club at five, so this works out perfectly."

A server brought a double espresso for Robbie and a decaf coffee with skim milk for Tim. Tim waited until the waiter departed before speaking. "I appreciate you meeting with me."

"Glad to do so," Robbie said. "We haven't spent a lot of time together, but I'd like to get to know you better."

"Likewise. That's one reason I called you."

"There's another reason?"

"I wanted to ask your help on something. But I want to give you context first."

"Shoot."

"First of all, I want you to know that coming to work at Crowe has been the best move of my career. It's been a real honor and a privilege to work for you and your family, which has done so much for the world."

Robbie almost blushed. "I don't hear that very often."

"Well, it's true. To be perfectly honest, you're the reason I came to this company."

"Really?"

"Yes. I've always thought your willingness to work every day—even when you obviously didn't have to—was inspiring. That's the kind of commitment that employees need to see, with leaders who do their job for the right reasons. Not for power. Not for glory. Not for money. But to make the company an instrument for creating a better world." Tim had done his homework. The last line was lifted from Robbie's Letter to Stakeholders in the last Corporate Sustainability Report.

"That's very thoughtful, Tim. I didn't know you felt that way."

"The question I'm sure you wrestle with is how you continue to make sustainable progress. It's not easy when you have the shareholders breathing down your neck. You need a partner as committed as you are to help drive it."

Robbie twisted a lemon peel over his espresso. "Are you saying Walker's not that guy?"

"That's not for me to say."

"That's surprising. I always figured you were Walker's guy."

"Of course, you would, and in some ways, I am. Walker brought me on, and I owe a lot to him. We've worked together for ten years, and I think we accomplished a great deal as a team. Especially through the management process that I originated."

"*You* originated? I thought that was Walker."

"I can certainly understand why you'd think so. He's received all the credit for it."

"But it was your system?"

"I hate to say it, because it sounds disloyal, but it's the truth. I came up with the format for the spreadsheets, the letter grades, the way we report our milestones, the at-a-glance forecast relative to the plan, the whole thing. I make sure our team prepares those documents properly each week."

"And Walker?"

"He reviews them."

"You're *shitting* me. That's it?"

"Well, he does a few other things, like setting the overall priorities. You know, sorting out where we should focus our time and our resources."

"Oh, sure," Robbie said. "The easy stuff."

"And he also makes sure the strategy is aligned with the board's expectations."

"Management 101. *Anyone* could do that."

"And, of course, he holds people accountable—rewarding performance and getting rid of those who can't do their jobs."

"Isn't that an HR function?"

"At some level, sure. And I should also mention, just in fairness, that, at the end of the day, he takes responsibility for the performance of all aspects of the company."

Robbie scoffed. "Well, yeah. That's the job we pay him for. But what I'm hearing is you basically do everything else."

Tim nodded. "Basically, yes."

"Wow," Robbie said, sitting back in his chair. "I can't say I'm shocked. When it comes to worrying about who gets the credit, Walker leads the league."

"Yes, and in some ways, that may have been helpful for running a company this big. It takes pressure off the rest of the management team when things aren't going right to have someone else stand as the lightning rod. But it seems now the company's in a different position than it was four years ago, and that brings me to my other point. I'm in a situation that's really no longer viable for me."

"How so?"

"I read the story today about how there might be a change coming. If Walker is out, then I'm on my own. I've been with him in three companies already. I'm not doing it a fourth time."

"Especially if he doesn't have a job."

"Even if he does. I'm done. It's time to go our separate ways. I need to take the next step in my career. Which is why I'd like to know if I could count on you as a reference. As much as I love this company, and respect you and your family, I know I have to think about life after Walker Hope."

"Hold on there, Tim," Robbie said. "Maybe we can find a way to align your goals with mine. Let's kick this around a bit, shall we?"

35. LAST TANGO IN NEW YORK

Robbie's thoughts were racing faster than he could assimilate them when he arrived at his suite at the New York Athletic Club, but a glass of Puligny-Montrachet slowed him down. So, too, did a half-hour of venting to Maria about Walker, Marty, the management team, Uncle Chuck, Winnie, and anyone else who came to mind. Once he exhausted his rage, it didn't take long to get down to business. Nor did it take long to finish it. These late afternoon trysts were increasingly quick affairs. If the thrill wasn't quite gone, it seemed headed for the exits.

Maria stood at the mirror in a monogrammed robe, brushing her hair and glancing at the reflection of Robbie, reclined on the bed, checking his phone, a top sheet draped over the lower-body parts that frequently governed his brain. The day had warmed up as predicted, and Maria opened the door to the veranda overlooking Central Park, hoping a spring breeze might thaw the frosty air inside.

"What are you looking at?" Maria asked.

"Oh. Nothing. Usual crap," he said. "Memos. Reports. It's ridiculous how much stuff I have to read."

None of which concerned him now. He was searching the internet for information on Natalia, hoping to discover snippets of career information on LinkedIn, a bikini shot on Facebook or Instagram. He found nothing, and his patience was thinning. Had she changed her name at some point?

"You'll have to read a lot more if Walker's gone," Maria said.

Robbie looked up with a start. "What's that supposed to mean?"

"Meaning: you won't be able to slack off."

"Whose side are you on?"

She sat on the edge of the bed. "Yours."

"Then why do you say stuff like that? You should be encouraging me."

"You want uncritical support? Seriously, Robbie. Call your nanny. *Somebody* needs to give you the straight scoop."

"I don't know why that has to be you and why it has to be now."

"Because I *know* you and I think you're about to make a big mistake."

"Oh really."

"Yes, really. Getting rid of Walker doesn't solve your problem."

"Which is?"

"You want to be the star of the show."

He put the phone down. "Oh please. You're saying this is about *me*?"

"Of course. It's *all* about you. And look. I get it," she said, massaging the back of his hand. "Walker's a preening prima donna. This company's not big enough for the both of you. Fine. But if you think Tim's the answer, you're smoking crack. You like him because he's a corporate drone. He'll be glad to flutter around the hive and cede all the honey to you. But for that to work, he'd have to run the company as successfully as Walker has and I don't think he can. You need a leader in that job. Tim's not it. You know they call him 'The Mechanical Man,' right? He's got the personality of a mall cop. People wouldn't follow him out of the building in a fire."

"I don't need charisma. I need operations experience, somebody who rolls up their sleeves and gets their hands dirty. He'll do that. He's basically been running the company for years. He just hasn't gotten the credit for it."

"He told you that, huh?"

"You don't have to believe it," he said, indignantly. "I do."

"Oh, please. Whatever success Tim has had is because he gets strong direction."

"Fine. I'll give him all the direction he needs."

Maria shook her head. "No, you won't."

Robbie sat up, angry. "Why the hell not?"

"Because you don't know what you want this company to be."

"Of course I do. I have a vision, you know."

"So I heard. What is it?"

"Stop this. You know what it is. And if you don't, that's an even bigger problem."

"Humor me."

"Oh, come on. It's about... you, know, being a more responsible corporate citizen. Making a better world for all. Investing more in renewable energy. Stuff like that."

"Seriously? Sounds like boilerplate gibberish from the CSR Report. What does that actually mean? What would you do differently?"

"That's something we just have to figure out."

"Right. And when—with all these *burdens* that are weighing you down—do you think you're going to get around to that?"

"As soon as Walker's gone."

"You and Tim will figure it out."

Robbie smiled, defiant. "The Dream Team."

Maria stood up. "I have to get dressed."

"Where you going?"

"Back to the office."

"It's six o'clock. What are you, nuts?"

"I have to work for a living," she said, pulling her thong up beneath her robe. "If Tim gets that job, you will, too."

36. MANHATTAN PROJECT

Walker convened the Crowe Power Company's newly appointed Code Blue Emergency Task Force at 6 p.m. Around the table was a panel comprised of electrical engineers, mechanical engineers, the building manager, a graphic artist, and Flora, who was there to take notes.

"Alright," Walker said, taking his seat at the head of the oval table. "Can you help me understand the problem here?"

"Yes, sir," said Wally Saxton, the company's Chief Engineer. "As you might imagine, I'm more of an expert on the electrical systems for large refineries, pipelines and power plants, but we've been able to conduct a full review that should provide the answer our chairman is looking for."

"Thank you," Walker said.

"As a bit of background for you, Walker, I'd like to read from our company's brand manual from our Marketing department."

"Go right ahead."

"Broad Street Blue was specially designed for our company by founder Homer Crowe in 1920 to reflect the vibrant energy that is at the core of all we do," Saxton read. "We bear this color proudly in our logo, our signage, and on the uniforms in our plants because it reflects our culture of working together and caring for one another."

Walker nodded. "Golly. I don't think I fully appreciated how much thought went into this."

"I know Mr. Crowe takes it quite seriously," Saxton said. "This isn't the first time he's asked questions about our color deployment."

"That's why we're here," Walker said.

Graphic artist Melissa Kennis, nervous to be participating in a meeting of such obvious importance at the very top of the house, stuttered a bit and her voice quaked as she explained that Broad Street Blue in print was a mixture of three colors: 100 percent cyan, 58.8 percent magenta and 32.9 percent black. On a computer, the mix was a little different: 27.9 percent green and 67.1 percent blue.

"Would you like to know the hue, saturation, and lightness, sir?" she asked, quavering. "I can also give you the wavelength in nanometers."

"No. I think I'm good," Walker said. "It's dark blue, right?"

"Basically, yes," Saxton piped in.

"Got it," Walker said. "Please continue."

"We checked the digital files," Saxton said, "and we found that while there are miniscule variations that are undetectable to all but the most trained eye, they were all using the right RGB formulations of color. So we proceeded to a CMYK forensic evaluation of all the printers on the 24th floor."

"And?"

"We can say that they are remarkably consistent. Whether they're HP or Toshiba didn't seem to make much difference. They all came out pretty similarly."

"So there was nothing wrong with the digital files or the print-outs?"

"That's correct, sir."

"So is our chairman seein' things?"

Saxton shook his head. "Not exactly, Mr. Hope. It appears that when he issued the decree that we were to get rid of all incandescent lightbulbs because of their impact on our carbon footprint, he changed the lighting on his desk lamp. The LED bulb he selected casts a warm light, adding a yellowish hue that makes the blue in his print-outs look slightly greenish."

Walker scoffed. "You've got to be kiddin' me."

"No sir," Saxton said, pulling a light bulb from his brief case and holding it aloft. "Replace his current bulb with this one, and everything should be fine."

"Uh-huh. And tell me this: how much of your day was taken up with this?"

"It's been pretty much the entire day for everyone."

"Well," Walker said, standing, "all I can say is thank you. Sorry to waste your valuable time on such an exercise."

The task force members stood. "No problem at all, sir," Saxton said. "Any time."

"Please. Let's hope not."

37. TRANSCENDENTAL NEGOTIATION

After the morning rush hour traffic subsided, Robbie and Digby set off on their mission, walking slowly down the middle of Front Street in the South Street Seaport and struggling to avoid spraining ankles on the uneven cobblestones.

"I don't see any addresses," Digby said, looking from one side of the street to the other.

"She said it was above the coffee shop on the left," Robbie said.

"That figures."

"I think that's it—Koffee Klatch."

They approached a dented metal door with a chicken-wire window and hit the buzzer next to the mailboxes. They heard a click and pulled hard to open the door to a dark vestibule lit with a single light bulb. They began trudging their way up the cast-iron stairway, made longer by the high ceilings on each floor. Given their levels of fitness and eagerness, the first three flights were a breeze, but the fourth was a study in slow motion and the last flight a surprising ordeal. By the time they hit the fifth-floor landing, they were both gassed, with their hands on their knees, trying to catch their breath.

"I guess... this means..." Digby said, panting, "you're... heart-healthy enough for sex."

Robbie stood up and threw his head back. "Who lives in a building without an elevator?"

"Hippy-dippy commies, like your girlfriend," Digby said with a shrug. When Robbie shot him a look, Digby said, "Hey, it's sustainable."

"Not for me. This works out, I'll get her a place at the Plaza."

Digby nodded toward a door at the end of the hall. "That's her apartment, 5B. I'm going to head downstairs. See you in the coffee shop."

Robbie, alarmed, grabbed his arm. "Wait. What do I do?"

"What do you mean? You knock on the damn door."

"You do it."

"I walked you over and helped you find it," he said, pulling his arm away. "My job's finished. You're on your own, big boy."

Digby headed back down the stairs and Robbie approached the door. He smoothed his hair over and knocked tentatively. From the other side of the door, he could smell jasmine incense and hear sitar music, but no stirring. He knocked again, harder.

Natalia called to him softly. "Door's open."

Robbie opened the door and stepped in front of a folding screen separating the entrance from the living room. He stepped around the screen and a stand of potted plants to find Natalia sitting with her back to him on a yoga mat on the floor. She was naked, looking through the window, her face toward the sun. Candles burned next to her and a cat stared at Robbie suspiciously. The sitar music was louder here than it was in the hall and the morning sun lent Natalia's remarkable body an unearthly golden glow.

Robbie stopped in his tracks, his jaw fallen, mesmerized.

"Oooooooooooommmmm," Natalia chanted, her hands before her as if in prayer. "Namaste."

She bowed down until her head nearly hit the floor. She sat back up, then stood, turning to look at Robbie, her eyes radiating tranquility. He was stunned by her perfect figure, as well as the profusion of tattoos on her left arm and midriff. Was that a tattoo on her breast? What the *hell*? Who puts tats on tits? It's not like they need adornment. They're *tits*, for crying out loud.

Natalia reached for a silk robe on the back of a chair and slipped it on, casually tying the sash around her waist.

"Those are some *amazing* tattoos you have there," Robbie said, nodding toward her arm.

"Yeah," she shrugged. "Different sayings from philosophers."

"What's does that mean?" he said, pointing. "The one with the Chinese characters."

"Oh, that," she said flatly. "This was *supposed* to be a saying from Confucius. Instead it's something from a menu in Chinatown."

Robbie suppressed a laugh. "What does it say?"

"Moo shu pork," she said, disappointed. "I mean, it's not even vegetarian."

"That sucks. Are you vegetarian?"

"Vegan, actually."

"No kidding," Robbie said. "Me, too."

"You are?" she said. "That's surprising."

"Well, let's put it this way. I am for certain side dishes."

"I'm not sure that counts."

"I like to think every bit helps."

There was an awkward pause, before she indicated a cushion on the floor, between easels and a drawing board, and they both sat down. "Sooooo," she said, looking puzzled. Her posture was completely erect, as was a portion of Robbie's. "Why are you here?"

"I had this crazy idea that maybe you'd like to work with me at Crowe Power."

"That is crazy," she said. "Why on earth would I want to do that?"

"Look. As I told your group: I'm on your side," Robbie insisted. "I want to change things. I mean, what if you channeled your passion for the environment into helping me at Crowe Power? I've got an opening in my office for an assistant. No, better than that—an *aide-de-camp*," he said. "We'd work side-by-side, every day."

"I don't want to work every day. That's why I like Café Che."

"Fine," Robbie said. "Part-time then—a few days a week."

"I don't want to work for corporate America. I've already done that. Didn't much care for it."

"I don't like it either," he said. "In fact, I *hate* corporate America. That's why I want more people like you, people who want to change the company, just like I do. And the fact is, you can't change it from the outside. You have to be inside to make a difference."

Natalia rubbed her temple, thinking. "Do you know that I was a sell-side analyst for Poundstone?"

"No," he said. "I didn't know."

"I made a lot of 'sell' recommendations on your company stock."

"Why?"

"Because I didn't like the direction it was heading."

"*Exactly*," Robbie said. "And that's my point. I don't either."

"I mean, the direction under you and your father."

"Oh."

"I thought your instincts were noble," she allowed. "But your strategy was terrible. I mean, seriously. Windacious? That was a dog-ass company."

"Then help me make better decisions," he pleaded. "Help me make this a sustainable enterprise."

"Isn't part of that making money?" she asked.

"Of course. I just want to make money the *right* way."

"You mean, planet before profits? Is that what you're saying?"

"Yes," he declared. "Sort of. Absolutely."

"Sorry," she said, trying to follow. "Which one?"

"Planet before profits, of *course*," Robbie said. "I'm committed to that."

"How much?"

"*Totally* committed."

"No. How much *money*?"

"How much would you make?" he asked. "I don't know. What are you making now at the coffee shop?"

"Minimum wage, plus tips."

He glanced toward the outline of her breasts under the silk robe. "So that's what? Fifty thousand?"

She burst out laughing. "Why, yes. We get *enormous* tips."

"How about if I double that? A hundred thousand?"

Astonished, she decided to play it out. "You're getting warm," she said.

"A hundred and ten?"

"Make it twenty."

"If that's what it takes," he said, "that's what you'll get. I want you."

"Yes," she said, standing. "Apparently you do."

38. THE EPIPHANY

The fact that a return trip to the dentist was his most eagerly anticipated event of the week forced Marty to take stock of his life as he stood at the elevator in the lobby of Dr. Littmann's building. He concluded quickly that he wasn't having much fun. Between his sorry financial plight, battles with his ex-wife, his pathetic apartment, and the monkey-in-the-middle between Robbie and Walker, he had sunk about as low as he could go. So it was more than a little disappointing to learn upon reaching the dentist's office and climbing into the chair that he would not be administered gas for his follow-up procedure.

"No gas?" he asked the hygienist.

"Sorry, Mr. McGarry," Emilia said. "Dr. Littmann say no."

"How can that be? Are you out of it or something?"

"I don't know why. You have to ask Dr. Littmann. I just—" *yust*, "do what he tells me."

As Emilia lowered the back of the chair, Marty looked up into the bright lights and heard the shuffle of the dentist walking into the room. Littmann plopped down on a rolling swivel stool and pulled himself up to the chair.

"Open," he said curtly.

Marty dutifully opened his mouth and Littmann poked a rubber-gloved finger around the temporary crown. He used a lever to pop it off, peered inside the cavity with a mirror, then poked inside with a curved sickle scaler, hitting a nerve that prompted Marty to jump.

"I guess that hurt," Littmann said drily.

"Sure as hell did."

"You know what else hurts? Losing a hundred thousand dollars in three days. That was some stock tip you gave me."

"Dr. Littmann, I'm sorry, but I did *not* give you a stock tip."

Littmann continued his probing around the tooth, jabbing the nerve again and prompting a yelp from Marty. "I said I was going to invest a million bucks," Littmann said. "You could have stopped me."

"I *can't* give stock advice. It's against the law."

"I figured maybe the drugs I gave you clouded your brain. So I'm keeping you off them in case you want to give me some more bullshit advice," Littmann said, reaching for another tool. "We've got to clean this tooth out a bit more before I put on the crown."

Marty heard the drill whirring and held up a hand. "Can I at least get some Novocain before you do that?"

Littmann rolled back on his stool. "I suppose," he said, retrieving a needle.

"Doctor, do you want me to swab the gum first?" Emilia asked helpfully.

"Nah," Littmann said. "It'll be alright."

Littmann stuck his thumb behind Marty's front lower teeth, then brought the needle down and, with a jerk on his jaw, stuck Marty in the gum, causing him to arch his back and suck in his breath. *What the hell?* Was Littmann watching *Marathon Man* last night?

"Couple more," Littmann said.

Marty was seeing stars. Without the gas, there was no delightful floating over Manhattan this time—just the throbbing of his jaw, the coffee-and-corned-beef-hash breath of Dr. Littmann, a bright yellow light in his eyes, and the Spanish conversation of the receptionists in the lobby echoing down the hall. Now, even the dentist wasn't relief.

Then, as he heard Littmann step on the pedal for the drill, a switch in Marty's brain turned on and he had a sudden moment of perfect clarity. He would stop playing the role of helpless victim—for Littmann, Walker, Robbie, Jill, or anyone else. He would stand up for himself and let the chips fall. What harm could there be in that? Things certainly couldn't get much worse.

As Littmann brought the drill toward Marty's mouth, Marty held up his hand. "*Stop!*" he demanded.

Littmann pulled back the drill. "What is it?"

Marty sat up and looked Littmann in the eye. "Give me some fucking gas. *Now*."

After a shocked moment, Littmann nodded to Emilia, who slid a nose mask onto Marty's face and opened the valve for the nitrous oxide. Marty laid back and breathed deeply as he heard it flow.

"Pump it up," he said, with a thumbs-up.

Marty was magically transported away from it all, rising above the dreary dentist office, floating southeast over Coney Island, then along the shore to Fire Island and into the Hamptons, looking over one magnificent estate after another, before focusing on a massive shingle-style house nestled in the dunes near East Hampton. From 30,000 feet, he could clearly see Robbie Crowe's compound, delineated by ten-foot boxwood hedges on three sides and a broad white-sand beach on the other, a manicured lawn and gardens with fountains, the glimmering swimming pool and immaculate tennis court, the gray-shingled guest house, the long veranda on the main house overlooking the ocean, and a horizon dotted with pristine white sails on a Broad Street Blue ocean. He swooped down to street level to see the glistening black Range Rovers and Mercedes SUVs cruising slowly down the road, the preposterously fit and good-looking joggers, and the quaint roadside stands offering fresh fruit, homemade pies, and cut flowers.

As Dr. Littmann drilled deep, Marty had a flash of inspiration. If he couldn't set fire to Robbie's wondrous idyll, he could at least disturb its feng shui. And he had a hunch how to do it.

39. WINDMILLS OF HIS MIND

Walker convened the monthly Strategy Committee meeting in the Lester, the small executive conference room on the 24th floor named for one of Homer Crowe's three children: Lester Robertson Crowe. Lester was Robbie's great-grandfather, who grew up to become president of the company, leading it through two decades of consistently underwhelming performance, for which he was rewarded handsomely since he was, after all, a Crowe.

Now, after consecutive years of record revenues and profits, Walker recognized that the company was reaching the limits of organic growth. For Crowe to take another great leap forward, it would need to consider an acquisition, which is why he asked for recommendations from HM&S, the Midtown investment bank. Walker sat at the head of the table next to the usual empty chair reserved for the chairman. Tim was perched on his right, Anna to his left, and Marty sat at the far end of the table in the shadows, where he played the card game Spider on his iPad.

"The good news is that your stock had been appreciating enough to give you significant buying power," said Leonard Halliday, the HM&S banker. "The bad news is that reports of a possible change in executive leadership sent your company stock plummeting in an unfortunate spiral, diminishing your flexibility. Nevertheless," he said, hitting his clicker and bringing up a slide on a screen in the front of the room, "you still have enough market muscle to explore three options.

"The first is to consider firms that expand your global footprint in your current sectors. Second is to acquire a company that offers synergy with what you already have. And third is looking at distressed companies in the renewable energy field that have the potential for new life under the right circumstances."

Walker took notes as Leonard walked them through the pros and cons for various companies in each area. "I'd like to drill down on the second option," Walker said. "What do you think of Staminum Corporation?"

"Staminum. Right. A long-time rival to Crowe," Leonard said as he brought up a global map showing icons representing Staminum's refineries, pipelines and power plants around the world. "They're an interesting match for you, since you have the same lines of business. Our view is that they have very good assets and a management team that doesn't know how to operate them. In fact, they look an awful lot like Crowe Power did four years ago."

"Could we get 'em?"

"That would be a stretch. They're a lot bigger than you are, so it would take cash as well as stock. Not sure you'd want the debt and the pressure that would put on your finances, especially if there's a downturn. I don't know if you recall this, but Staminum was rumored to be considering a takeover of Crowe before you arrived."

"So I heard," Walker said.

"I don't think you have to worry about that anymore. They appear to be a rudderless ship."

From the shadows in the back of the room, Marty raised his hand. "This may seem a bit out of the blue, but I have a question about option No. 3 and renewable energy: have you looked at BlowCo?"

Leonard laughed. "Not very hard."

Walker glared at Marty. "Why are you asking, *Martin*?"

"Couple reasons," Marty said, blushing. "For one thing, our chairman continues to call for us to get into renewable energy."

Walker cleared his throat and sat up. What the hell was Marty thinking? Was he on drugs? He wasn't there to offer suggestions. He was there to shut up and take notes and nod when Walker said something smart, or, actually, anything at all.

Leonard said, "BlowCo is certainly *not* a game changer. It's much too small. They might be worth a look if you wanted to place a small bet in the green space. But they don't seem to be getting anywhere with their Atlantica project, which their company is built around. If that doesn't go, we don't see a Plan B."

"What's Atlantica?" Walker asked.

"A wind farm BlowCo wants to build offshore in the Hamptons," Leonard said. "So far it hasn't generated any electricity—just resistance. Homeowners out there have it tied up in court, maybe forever. We hear the company needs a cash infusion to keep going."

Suddenly, Walker understood. He looked at Marty and smiled. Then he turned to Leonard. "How much do they need?"

Leonard flipped through a notebook. "They're trying to close a Series C tranche of $20 million. I'd have to question whether they'll get any of it."

"Well," Walker said. "Twenty million seems like a small price to pay to help save our planet. Our chairman is so passionate about this issue, I'm sure he'd have to agree."

"Hard not to, right? Marty said.

"I've seen complaints in the press recently that we lack vision on such matters," Walker said. "If we back a wind farm out there in the Hamptons, perhaps that would change their point of view."

Said Marty, "Yes—from just about every room in the house."

40. ACCOUNTS PAYABLE

The intercom buzzed, distracting Robbie from checking the baseball box scores on ESPN.com. "Mr. Crowe, I know you're busy, but Digby's here to see you."

What the hell does he want now? "Fine," Robbie sighed. "Send him in." He closed the window on his screen and wheeled around in his chair as Digby entered, carrying an accordion file under his arm.

"Whattaya got?" Robbie said, slumping wearily. *The weight of the world...*

Digby took his usual place in a wingback chair and pulled out a yellow legal pad. "I've worked up some numbers," Digby said, holding up the pad. "If you want to move on Maria, it's going to cost you."

"How do you figure?"

"I'm looking at our other settlements. They're not cheap."

"Let me see," Robbie said, reaching out his hand to grab the legal pad. "Annie Bolton, two million. Okay. Fine. Knew that," he said, running his finger down a page. "What does this mean: 'Janet Quigley, three.' That can't be three million?"

"That's what we paid her to go away."

"*C'mon.* I can't believe it was that much. She wasn't even that great."

"She was one of our top marketing people."

"That's not what I'm talking about."

"Oh, please. We haven't based our settlements on how good they were at jiggling your nuts. You wanted her gone. She's gone."

Robbie looked further down the page. "Priscilla Neumann—four-point-five *million*? Are you kidding me?"

"The numbers went up as you moved up in the company. She was in a high-level finance job at the time you wanted her out. When you consider the compensation she left on the table, that's what it came out to."

"Who the hell signed off on that?"

"You did."

"Okay. Fine. Where do we get the money for this stuff?"

"It's out of your discretionary budget—totally off the books."

Robbie laughed. "My indiscretionary budget."

"More accurate," Digby said.

"What about Laura Edinger? I don't see a number."

"We got her a transfer to Latin America."

"Ah. Right. Forgot where she went."

"So that's kind of what I'm thinking with Maria. I work closely with her and I know her pretty well."

"I know her, too, jerk."

Digby ignored it. "I'm saying I don't think she'd take a payoff. And even if she did, I don't think you'd have the budget. A settlement could be eight figures."

Robbie sat up, alarmed. "What do you think she'd do? She wouldn't sue, would she?"

"She's a lawyer, Robbie. And a damn good one. Probably my best."

"We can't have a suit. No way. Can you imagine the media? Especially now, with all this #MeToo crap?"

"That's why we need an offer she can't refuse."

"Which is?"

"She told me in her last performance review that she'd eventually like to move out of Legal. She'd really like to get some operations experience. And, you know, she's got family in Italy."

"...And we have an opening for a VP of Operations in Rome."

"Bingo. That's exactly what I was thinking. Nice, big promotion. Huge raise. A great location."

"What about her husband? He's got a big job here."

"That's another reason why I think she might like this. He's apparently got a girlfriend. I think she'd like to tell him to go to hell."

Robbie nodded his head. "Would she go for this?"

"If she thinks she's not being manipulated in some way, yes. You'd have to sweet talk her a bit."

"*Me? I'm* not doing that. *You're* her boss."

"C'mon. This is your deal."

"C'mon nothing. This is company procedure."

"Which I know you strictly follow."

"When it suits me," Robbie said huffily, "yes."

Digby slouched in his chair. "Well, alright. I can do it, of course. But you know her first stop after I talk to her is going to be your office."

"What do I care? Just give me some notice. I'll get the hell out of here."

"I'll do what I can."

"Damn," Robbie said, clasping his hands behind his head and smiling. "This could be *perfect*. Walker wouldn't have to approve?"

"Not at this level. All we need is the President of Europe, Middle East, and Africa and our head of HR to sign off. I've already run the traps. They're in, especially when I told them you backed it. They can tell which way the wind is blowing."

"Oh my god," Robbie said. "This is *great*."

"I wouldn't mention how delighted you are when she comes to see you."

"Of course not. I'm sorry as hell to see her go. When can you make this happen?"

"When do you need it?"

"As fast as possible. Natalia starts tomorrow."

"From barrister to barista? That's quite a jump."

"I don't need commentary, Digby. I just need you to do your fucking job."

"Well, here's some commentary you *do* need to hear. And as your counsel, I must tell you this: you can't afford any more of these. There's no budget for them. And there's no tolerance for it anymore. Someone goes public on one of these and you could hit the loser trifecta: marriage, job, and money."

Robbie stepped on the button beneath his desk that flashed a red light on his phone. "I have to take this," he said, picking up the phone.

Digby didn't move. "Go ahead. I can wait."

"No," Robbie said, clenching his jaw. "You can't."

Digby stood. "Okay," he said. "But you should realize: everyone knows your bat phone is phony."

41. CORRIDORS OF POWER

As Walker emerged from the executive elevator, he thought for an instant that his eyes were deceiving him. Was that *Robbie* coming out of the stairwell? Walker was about to call out when Robbie caught sight of him and took a sharp right turn on the 24th floor in the opposite direction of his office, walking rapidly.

"*Robbie!*" Walker called, quickening his pace.

Robbie ignored him, sped up, and turned the corner. By the time Walker reached the corner, Robbie was nowhere in sight. Walker walked as fast as he could and turned again, only to find another empty hallway. He switched back, breaking into a jog through the Hall of Fam toward Robbie's office. As he rounded the last corner, he thought he caught a glimpse of the chairman peeking around the corner, then quickly pulling back.

The guy's like a groundhog, Walker thought. He held his breath and walked as quietly as possible across the plush carpet toward the opening where Robbie's shadow last emerged. There, ten feet away, he leaned back in wait, both palms against the wall. Had he blinked, he might have missed Robbie's leap toward his office door.

Walker was on him in an instant as Robbie fumbled with the ID reader on his belt.

"Mr. Chairman."

Robbie turned, flushed red and angry. "What? *What?*"

"Do you have a minute?"

"Actually, I don't. *Huge* hurry."

"I think we need to talk."

"Get with Winnie. She can get you on my calendar." He opened the door, but Walker pushed it shut and glared at Robbie.

"Apparently, she can't."

"What am I supposed to do about that?"

"How do I actually get to see you?"

"Just stop in. You're right down the hall."

"I've tried that. It doesn't work."

"Look," Robbie said, exasperated. "I'm sorry if you feel neglected, but I can't see just everyone who wants to pop by whenever they snap their fingers. I'm jammed. I've got to get ready for the Board next week."

"As do I. All the more reason for us to get together."

Robbie leaned against the glass door as Walker stepped closer, clearly violating Robbie's personal space.

"Okay," Robbie conceded. "*Fine.* See me in the morning. Is that good enough for you?"

"What time?"

"I don't know."

"I'd like to plan accordingly."

"Fine. Does 10 o'clock meet your approval?"

"Looking forward to it," Walker said with a triumphant grin. "See you then, big fella."

To Robbie's worsening annoyance, Walker made a small fist and tapped him on the shoulder, as if they were *buddies*. The fucking nerve of this guy.

42. ROBBIE LOBBIES

Uncle Chuck was surely right about one thing: for Robbie to remove Walker, he would have to go through Carlton Lucas, last surviving principal of the storied Park Avenue law firm Rothstein Lucas & Pratt, longtime chairman of the Crowe Power Board of Directors' Executive Committee, and, not coincidentally, the richly compensated lawyer for the Crowe Family Trust and vice-chairman of the $3 billion Crowe Foundation. Every other outside director, save Moe's two proxies, Jayne Willson and Harvey Mandelbaum, would fall in line behind Carlton and whatever the family wanted them to do. Through the lavish grants they received in company stock, the full-time jobs and internships provided to generations of their offspring, the campaign donations that purchased their political principles, or their continuing dependence on the Crowe Power Purchasing Department, the company's Board of Directors was a spaghetti bowl of intertwined interests that retail shareholders would never see, much less untangle.

Carlton, a dependable rubber stamp of the family agenda under Robbie's father, had in his old age suffered inexplicable bursts of passion for good governance, much to the astonishment of his colleagues. He had privately opposed Robbie's ascension to Chairman & CEO four years earlier, citing the need for an experienced turnaround specialist to run the company, and helped broker the deal that split the job in two. Now, at 89, he was still the board's most formidable outside director and its best debater, with an argumentative style honed before the nation's highest courts.

If Robbie couldn't win over Carlton, he at least needed to neutralize him. The first step was showing respect by trekking uptown to meet Carlton at the Union League Club in Murray Hill. There, he found Carlton seated in a large black leather chair in a corner reading *Barron's*. Elegantly attired in a pin-striped charcoal gray suit, white shirt, blue tie, and pocket square, Carlton's shrinking frame looked rather small in the massive chair. Still, he mustered every bit of strength he had to push himself up to shake hands with Robbie.

"Wonderful to see you, Carlton," Robbie said, taking a seat on the adjacent sofa and glancing around at the oil paintings of Lincoln, Teddy Roosevelt and other Republican presidents. "Haven't been here for some time."

"I like to be reminded there were leaders I actually admired," Carlton said ruefully, as he resumed his seat.

"Should I take that as a commentary?" Robbie said with a laugh.

"You can interpret that any way you want. I don't talk about politics anymore," he said with a dismissive wave of his hand. "Too upsetting."

"How do you feel about business?"

"Even worse," he said, casting an icy glare at Robbie. "What the hell's going on down there on Broad Street? That story going around about Walker leaving is a disaster."

Robbie sucked in his breath and plowed ahead. "Two things, I think," he said. "One is that we have a leak somewhere, obviously. That really—excuse my French—pisses me off. Believe me, I'm doing all I can to find the source."

Carlton looked doubtful. "I understand companies leak from time to time, sometimes for good reason. Floating a trial balloon, perhaps. Testing out interest in a product or service. But, goddamn it, Robbie, boards should *never* leak. It's bad governance and it looks terrible for all concerned—including you and me."

Robbie shook his head, feigning exasperation. "I couldn't agree more," he said. "That's why I have Digby leading an investigation into where this leak came from. When we find out, I promise you, I will deal with the perpetrator in no uncertain terms."

Carlton nodded. "Good. We need to send out a message that this—" he punched a finger into his armrest, "will not be tolerated."

"We're absolutely on the same page."

"Fine. So what's the second issue?"

Robbie looked around to see if anyone could eavesdrop, then turned back to Carlton. "Bad as the leak was, I'm getting a sense there's actually some truth to it."

"You don't say," Chuck said, crossing his legs and eyeing Robbie suspiciously. "I've never heard a word of criticism of Walker from the other directors, including your Uncle Chuck. And everything I've seen says he's been an outstanding leader whom we're extremely lucky to have. The company's performance over the past four years is the best stretch we've had since I joined the board 40 years ago."

"I don't disagree. Walker's done a wonderful job to this point. And don't get me wrong—I *love* the guy. But I've heard rumblings that there's some real concern about where we go from here."

"The path we're on isn't good enough? I don't understand. What is it they don't like about record profits? It wasn't so long ago we were suffering record losses."

"Of course, we're doing well profit-wise," Robbie conceded. "But you and I know that companies are expected to do more these days."

"By *whom*?" Carlton demanded.

"Stakeholders."

"Hogwash. Who gives a shit about them?"

"We do," Robbie insisted. "Or at least, we should. Communities, NGOs, social investors all have a say in our license to operate. We've had protesters camped out at our entrance for the past two weeks. I thought they were going to string me up the other day. What happens if they decide to blockade one of our plants? Or contest our permits from the EPA? That could certainly impact our bottom line. And those record profits vanish."

Carlton peered at Robbie. "So, for argument's sake, let's assume for a moment that Walker isn't the one to lead us through this thicket of tormentors. Who would take his place?"

"I think we have a very capable replacement in Tim Padden, the COO."

Carlton guffawed. "Timid Tim? You're not serious. He's never said a word in our meetings."

"That's because Walker won't let him," Robbie claimed. "But I'm telling you—and you know I sit in on a lot of management meetings—he's been instrumental in Walker's success. Do you know he does all the forms?"

"What forms?"

"You know. The stuff we see in our board meetings. Spreadsheets. Letter grades. All the things that track our progress as a company. He just hasn't gotten the credit."

"He pushes the fucking *paper*? That's your idea of a great CEO? Are you looking for a leader of people or an outbox?"

"Carlton, please. I take exception to that. This isn't about *me*, for God's sake. This is about the company."

Carlton pressed his fingers together and glared at Robbie. "Let's be clear about something here, Robbie. You have a very important role at Crowe, watching out for your family's interests and your family name. I respect that. I support you in that position, just as I supported your father before you. That said, I'm very skeptical about this. What would you expect Tim to do differently?"

"I would want him to address environmental and social issues as aggressively as he does financial performance."

"Have you ever told *Walker* you'd like him to do that?"

"Not directly, no."

"Well, then," Carlton said. "How do you communicate your ideas to him?"

"Oh, gosh. A million ways," Robbie contended. "I've given speeches. I wrote—okay, I signed—an op-ed in the *New York Times* a couple of years ago. When I ran Strategy, I was on TV a bunch of times talking about how we need to build a better world. It doesn't seem to matter what I do, I never see my thoughts reflected in our plan."

"Here's a radical thought," Carlton said. "Why don't you *talk* directly to your CEO? Explain where you're not on the same page."

"He knows my wishes," Robbie said. "He doesn't want to change our priorities, or they would be done. And, I've got to tell you, I find our performance embarrassing. There's got to be more to Crowe Power than setting fossil fuels on fire. There are long-term implications for our planet that are already playing out. I don't want to go down in history as a guy who had a chance to do something about climate change and did nothing. I'm concerned about my family's reputation."

"As am I. And, frankly, I don't believe it would be enhanced by sweeping out the best chief executive this company's had since Homer Crowe."

"Will you withhold a final judgment on that until the board meeting next week?"

Carlton leaned forward and looked Robbie in the eye. "You need to understand something here, Robbie. I've got a fiduciary responsibility to the shareholders—all of them, not just your family. We send Walker packing and we're subject to shareholder lawsuits. I can't afford that and neither can you. So my recommendation is that you try a whole lot harder to reach an accommodation with Walker."

"As a matter of fact, I was finally able to get on his calendar. I've got a meeting with him in the morning."

"Good," Carlton said. "I urge you to put your arm around him and tell him how much we appreciate all that he's doing for the company. I just hope to God it's not too late."

43. THE PLANETISTA

Natalia was happy to shed her dull barista fatigues for something more fashionable, using the prospect of a significantly fatter paycheck to go on a shopping spree for sustainable clothing at Reformation in Soho. If Robbie truly wanted a non-traditional corporate environment, she'd show the way. And so she strode into the Office of the Chairman in a Bohemian style quite unlike any that had ever been seen there before: A slim-fitting crushed velvet stretchy skirt and silk satin blouse unbuttoned far enough to display a range of assets, including an array of long necklaces. Her long sleeves hung halfway over her hands, and she looked even taller in lace-up sock booties. She topped it off with a floppy hat and aviator sunglasses. It was enough to make the gray-suited Winnie blink hard as she hoisted herself up on her chunky pumps to offer a welcome.

"You must be Natalia," she said cheerily.

"Hi," Natalia said, extending a hand.

"I'm Winnie, Mr. Crowe's executive assistant."

"Spectacular view," she said, looking around at the panorama of Lower Manhattan and the Brooklyn Bridge.

"We like it," Winnie said proudly. "Not that there's any time around here to look out the window. Oh no."

"I like the chill vibe, keeping it kind of dark."

"Perhaps," Winnie said, "that has something to with your sunglasses?"

"Ah," Natalia said with a chuckle as she took them off and folded them into her purse. "Forgot I had them on."

Winnie walked Natalia over to the desk once occupied by Emma. "You can put your things here, which is where you'll be working. I've got your log-in information for the computer on this sheet. Our office hours are 8:30 to 6. I'd like you here by 8 to cover the phones."

Natalia placed her purse on the chair, tossed her hat on the desk, and ran her fingers through her hair. "I don't do phones."

"I'm sorry?"

"I don't know what Mr. Crowe told you, but I'm not here as an admin."

"You're working in here," Winnie said. "I just assumed..."

"Well, you shouldn't assume, really. And, just so we get things straight from the start, I'm not coming in at 8. I have yoga in the morning. I'll see you around 10 or so."

"Oh dear," Winnie said. "I was really counting on you to give us some coverage. Since Emma left, it's just been me."

"I feel for you. Seriously. I know what a drag that can be. But that's not what I signed up for."

"Well, golly. That just doesn't work for me."

"Right," Natalia said, flatly. "And *I* don't work for you, either."

"I wish someone had told me."

"I guess you're referring to him?" Natalia said, nodding to the office, where the door creaked open and Robbie stood in the threshold.

"Natalia. Hey!" Robbie said. "C'mon in."

Natalia breezed past Winnie's befuddled stare and followed Robbie into his multi-million-dollar enviro-cave, letting the door close behind her. He walked past his desk toward a sofa along the far wall. "Please," Robbie said. "Have a seat."

Natalia sat at one end of the sofa, her back to the armrest. Robbie sat at the other end, facing her. "Love all the plants," she said.

"Everything in here is sustainable," he said, grandly. "The lighting is LED. The wood in my desk comes from salvaged timbers. All the upholstery is made from recyclable materials. The dyes in the fabric are completely natural. They tell me you could even eat the drapes."

"Hopefully, you won't have to."

"No," he said with a laugh. "They usually bring me lunch. But the important thing is that all this sets a tone. I want everyone in the company to think about the little things we can do to create a healthier planet. I mean, if we all do our part, things can change for the better."

"That's interesting. I saw a piece in the Styles section of the *Times* that says you have six homes, a private jet, a fleet of SUVs, and this office that's, what, about 2,000 square feet? That would give you a pretty significant carbon footprint—one of the biggest in the world."

"I saw that piece. What a malicious pile of crap."

"It's not true?"

"I'm not saying that. I'm saying I have terrible PR. That article should have *never* been published. We've got a guy running Communications who doesn't seem to have *any* idea how to defend me. He's absolutely dead on his ass. I can't wait to get rid of him."

"So the article was wrong..."

Robbie blinked hard. "Factually, I suppose there was some accuracy to it. But... but—" *But what?* "You can't lose sight of the larger picture. What we do as a *company* is much more significant. *That's* where we can make real change. You see that, right?"

Natalia nodded. "I suppose. So, tell me: what do you have in mind for me?"

Robbie looked at her, unconsciously licking his lower lip, and staring, his head listing to the side. She was so exotically beautiful, from no world he'd ever known. She shifted slightly on the sofa and her necklaces dangled between her concealed breasts. God, he would love to be a necklace right now. Natalia waited for him to say something, but he seemed lost. Finally, she lowered her head to look into his eyes. "You still with me?"

Robbie's head jerked back. "Sorry. I was just thinking. I want to take Crowe Power where no other power company has gone before. And I want you to help me create the future. Imagine. We could be the first carbon-neutral power company in the world."

She smiled. "*That,*" she said, "is very exciting to me."

"Even enough to give up Café Che?"

"Tough call," she said, with a smile. "But yeah. I love it."

Robbie could feel a stirring in his balls. He had better stand up or Little Robbie might pitch another tent pole in his pants. "So glad," he said. "Let me show you around."

Natalia followed Robbie as he walked her around the office, pointing out his many books on sustainability and the environment, his awards from various interest groups, a few framed articles, and photos of his famous family.

"My great-great-grandfather Homer Crowe was the original recycler. Nothing went to waste at his power plants. Everything was recycled."

"He was an environmentalist?"

"Truth be told, he was just cheap. But regardless of his motivation, he did the right thing. And that's what I want to do—the right thing."

"What about your own family? Your wife and kids? Surprised you don't have any photos of them."

Robbie blushed. "I do, actually. Somewhere. I think Winnie sent them out to be reframed."

"Ah."

He walked her into the pantry at the back of the office, where an Organic Exotika coffeemaker sat on the counter. "I'd offer you some coffee but, frankly, I don't know how to operate this damn thing."

"You're kidding right?"

"No," he said. "I've never had to. Winnie always makes it for me."

She smiled. "What would you like?" she asked, flipping through the coffee pods in a basket next to the coffeemaker. "How about a Gorilla Decaf? It says it's 'strong, yet mellow.' Like you, right?"

"Oh yeah."

She made two cups and they continued their journey around the office. "I've got to show you my secret hideaway," he said, walking toward the opposite end of the office.

He stood in front of a bookcase and pulled on a book, which caused the shelving unit to slide off to the side, opening a portal to a small suite containing a bathroom and a dressing room.

"Check this out," he said, punching a button that brought a Murphy bed down from the wall, and another button that activated Sonos speakers, bringing up classic jazz from Chet Baker.

"That's pretty cool," she said.

"People have said it's like something out of James Bond."

"Or maybe Austin Powers."

Natalia walked slowly around the room, appraising a painting by de Kooning, a cupboard for tuxedos, casual wear and shoes, and the bathroom, which had a surprisingly large shower, suggesting recreational use.

"Nicely done," she said, turning to find Robbie standing uncomfortably close.

"Feel free to use it if you need to some time," he said.

"I can't imagine. Although I suspect you could."

"I'm just thinking, if you needed, you know, a little break or something."

"*That's* not happening." She turned to leave.

"Of course," he said, sending the Murphy bed back into the wall and following her out of the bedroom, "I wasn't suggesting anything by that."

"I'm not saying you were," Natalia said, taking a seat on the windowsill. "But it's probably good that we both get our orientation today. I, like you, want to do 'the right thing.' If our goal is sustainability—that is, I last more than a week—we need to focus on work."

"I couldn't agree more."

"That means we don't hang out in there, alright?"

Robbie gulped. "Of course not. I wouldn't expect to. I'm sorry if you got that impression."

"No. I'm sure," she said. "You don't know anything about me, do you?"

"I know you make a great cup of coffee," he said, with forced cheer.

"I told you before that I'd been a sell-side analyst for Poundstone. I quit because I hated recommending companies I couldn't believe in."

"Then why did you recommend them?"

"Because they were Poundstone clients. So even when all the data suggested a company might suck, we were pushed to issue 'conviction buy' recommendations. It was complete bullshit. I decided I'd rather sling lattes and work with people I like than sit in an office all day touting bad actors. I'm here because you suggested there was a chance to do things differently in corporate America. I've seen a lot of companies say they want to be green. The question is how?"

Robbie exhaled. "That's the challenge I keep throwing out to these guys. You know, I give a speech about what I see for the future, and what do they do with it? *Nothing.* And they know what I want. They just refuse to do it."

"Then what's the solution?"

"What do you mean?"

"If what you're doing isn't working, what are you going to do differently? You can't just throw up your hands and say it's someone else's fault. You're the chairman. Make a move." She nodded toward the outer office. "I mean, with your management team, out there. Not with me, in there."

"That's exactly what I intend to. And that's why I hired you. Will you help me?"

"I'm here, aren't I?"

"Yes."

"I'm in."

44. MEETING OF MINDS

Robbie paced his office, trying to settle his racing heart before Walker's arrival. He hated meetings like this, but there was no evading it any longer. He grabbed a satin pillow off his sofa and placed it in the middle of the floor. He kicked off his shoes, sat on the pillow, and struck a meditation posture. Back straight, hands on his knees, head held high. *Breathe in through the nose. Breathe out through the mouth...*

A buzz punctured Robbie's peace. "Shit," he muttered, startled by the intercom.

"Mr. Crowe," Winnie said, "Mr. Hope is here to see you."

He stood and gathered himself, tossing the pillow back on the sofa, and hit the intercom switch. "In a minute. Just finishing up a call." A few more deep breaths and he hit the button on his desk to open the door. And there, in a moment, was Walker, standing at the threshold, a looming shadow backlit by the bright lights from the outer office.

"Okay to come in?"

Robbie nodded. "Of course," he said tersely.

Robbie retreated to the sanctuary of his paper fortress, the massive piles of reports and folders that rimmed his desk. Walker took one of the two chairs in front of the desk. For the first time, he noted that Robbie's desk was on a slightly elevated platform, which forced visitors to look up at him.

Walker crossed his legs and sat calmly, holding a lightbulb in his lap.

"What have you got there?" Robbie asked. "Is that supposed to represent some big idea? Pretty hackneyed cliché, if you ask me."

"This? Nah," Walker said, holding up the lightbulb. "It's my response to your Code Blue."

"Code Blue?"

"You know, the note you sent me saying we have the wrong blue in our presentation materials. With all those exclamation points, I was afraid someone might be having a heart attack down here."

Robbie harrumphed. "Maybe it's not a priority to you. But it's pretty important to me. That color has been part of my life since the day I was born."

"Understood. That's why I want to try somethin' here."

He stood and pulled a handkerchief from his pocket to remove the lightbulb in the lamp on Robbie's desk, casting the chairman in an even darker humor. Then he inserted the new lightbulb into the lamp.

"I think you'll see our Progress Reports differently from now on."

God, Robbie hated this guy. "And why is that?"

"After extensive study—and I mean with the top engineers in our company, workin' 'round the clock—we determined that the Broad Street Blue in our reports was *exactly* the right formulation of RGB and, for that matter, CMYK," Walker said, triumphantly. "It's your LED lightbulb that made it appear to be out of compliance."

Robbie reddened, bristling at Walker's gloating. "Okay. Fine. But I don't understand why we can't produce it in such a way that it looks right in *any* light."

Walker ran his tongue around his cheek. "Sounds like an interestin' challenge, Robbie."

"Just figure it out, will you?"

"We'll do our best," Walker said. He held up the old lightbulb. "What would you like me to do with this?"

Robbie bit his lip. "I'll stick it somewhere." He put his palms on the desk. "Is that it? Is that all you wanted to see me about?"

"No," Walker said, turning icy. "I'd like to know where things stand."

"Things?"

"Between you and me. I read—like everyone else around here—that the board is questionin' my leadership. In the past forty-eight hours, I've talked to every board member but one. And they've all reiterated their support not only for me, but for our plan and our leadership team. You're the only director

I haven't spoken to, so I'm wonderin' if this is comin' from you. Is there somethin' I should know?"

Robbie fidgeted, looking around the room. *Was that a fruit fly?* How could he get out of this? Where was Digby when he needed him? He desperately wanted to step on the pedal for the bat phone, but then what?

"Let me think," Robbie said, folding his arms over his chest and scanning the ceiling. "Nothing in particular..."

"There seemed to be some concern about my long-term plan."

"Oh. Well, yeah. There's that. Maybe some board members aren't being entirely straight with you, like they are with me. But what they're asking me is where we are on the vision thing."

Walker nodded. "Ah, right. That vision thingy."

"The *vision*."

"And what exactly is the vision?"

Robbie flushed. "You don't know? I've only given a hundred speeches on it. I mean, it's about doing good and doing well. Christ. Just look at my letter in our Corporate Sustainability Report, will ya? There's a bunch of crap in there about it."

"Well, I do recall that before I got here, I'd seen lots of pretty pictures of cows munchin' grass around solar panels. And dolphins swimmin' 'round offshore windmills, as if they were somehow additive to the aquatic environment." Walker scratched his head. "I just don't know how that translates into business. How does that make money?"

Robbie leaned forward and glared at Walker. "Short answer: I don't know. Long answer: We need to figure it out. Everyone else in our industry seems to be making progress. Hell, I look at the talk shows on Sunday morning, and they have nothing but commercials about companies saving the world. Where are we? Nowhere. The only reason Windacious and Sungod didn't work out was because they were ahead of their time. But that doesn't mean we should abandon our efforts in renewable energy."

"I couldn't agree more. And the fact is, we haven't. I promise you: we're always on the lookout for investments in that area."

"Well, who the hell knows it? Everywhere I go, all I get is crap about our carbon footprint. What are we? Like, Number 8 in the world for carbon emissions? It's *embarrassing*."

Walker nodded sympathetically. "Perhaps you haven't noticed this in our Progress Reports—I know you were distracted by the blue—but we're tryin' hard to reduce that carbon footprint by convertin' our coal plants to natural gas. Some of our friends in the environmental movement won't allow it and they're blockin' our pipeline permits in court. That includes opposition from the Planetistas, which I understand is a group supported by the Crowe Foundation."

"That's right," Robbie said, raising his chin defiantly.

"I don't understand that, Robbie. Why would we support anyone who's actively working against us?"

Robbie pounded the desktop with his index finger. "Because, Walker, there are bigger issues here. I want Crowe Power to be supportive of environmental and social issues that benefit *everyone* on our planet. Sometimes that's means going against our own short-term interests. And you know what? So be it. We need to be big enough to take it, to do the right thing, regardless of our own selfish concerns."

"I hear you, Robbie. But just so you know, that's why our plant conversions are goin' slower than we'd like."

"Fine. I can accept that. What about solar energy? Wind? I don't see why this company, that's doing *soooo* well, according to *everything* I read, can't place a few bets on renewables. We have to start somewhere."

Walker stood. "You're absolutely right. We can do that. And I promise you, we will. In fact, I'm goin' to get on it right away."

"Great," Robbie said, hitting the button on his desk and twirling around in his chair.

"We good?" Walker said to the back of Robbie's head.

"Oh yeah. We're fine," Robbie said, typing away. *Just get the fuck out of my office.*

Walker barely squeezed through the fast-closing door as it hit him in the ass.

"We need to get that door fixed," Winnie said with a shake of the head.

"I don't know," Walker said with a smile. "It seems to be workin' exactly the way he wants it."

Walker nodded absently to Natalia, who was working on her computer, then walked briskly out of the office, through the outer suite, and into the hallway, where he pulled out his phone and called Marty.

Walker spoke quietly. "Hook. Line. Sinker."

"He bit?"

"On all the bait I had in the bucket."

"Excellent."

"From Code Blue to green," Walker said. "Let's move."

45. FAMILY AFFAIR

Per tradition, the annual gathering of Homer Crowe's many heirs occurred on the founder's birthday in May at his magnificent former estate, Grandview, on a bluff overlooking the Hudson River in Dutchess County. The 34,000-square-foot stone mansion, a glowering Gothic Revival masterpiece, was conveniently situated a half-mile upriver from the cottage of Homer's longtime secretary and paramour, Agnes Ludlow. Homer kept fit by rowing to Agnes's home while her cuckolded husband, a Crowe Power mechanic, was away on various missions for the company, usually to repair a boiler or turbine in some far-flung part of the country. While rumors of Homer's exceedingly close relationship with Agnes were largely confirmed by the birth of twin girls who looked suspiciously like the hawk-faced Homer, his wife, Mary, chose to ignore the gossipmongers. She lived at Grandview and they did not. Or, as she once observed in her salty way, "The only advantage they have over me is they can kiss my ass and I can't."

After Homer died in 1955 and Mary followed in 1966, the property was donated to a non-profit foundation that managed its upkeep and gave tours to the public, while the Crowe family retained perpetual rights to use it as needed. Aside from an occasional wedding, the main family usage was the annual meeting, which attracted generations of Crowes from around the world to discuss matters pertaining to the company, their trusts and their income.

Robbie looked gloomily out the window from the back seat of an Escalade as it snaked up the winding road toward the mansion. "God, I hate this event," he muttered.

Digby looked up from the papers on his lap. "Grin and bear it," he said. "These are your peeps, bro."

"Why can't we just do a conference call or something? I can't stand all the fucking glad-handing and chit-chat."

"Seriously. What's the big deal?"

"They all *want* something from me."

Digby put his papers away. "All they want is to see you in the flesh. Hear the inside dope from the inside dope. It's something to talk about back home—social currency in Beverly Hills and Bar Harbor whenever people are talking about the family businesses. They can say, 'Robbie told me this... Robbie told me that.' Just don't tell them anything consequential. It'll end up on Page Six."

"Oh hell. How can they possibly understand anything I'm telling them, anyway? They're all living off their trust funds and dividends. I'm the only one who has a real job."

"If you want to call it that."

Robbie cast a stink-eye at Digby. "Really, Digs? What would *you* call it?"

"C'mon. I'm yanking your chain, which seems particularly short these days. Lighten up. Until we get this Walker issue settled, you need to keep everyone in the family on your good side."

"Stop, already. I get it. I just hate acting so... goddamn *nice*."

"I'm sure that's difficult for you. But you have to try." Digby glanced back at the Lincoln Navigator behind them, then turned back to Robbie. "Why did you ask Lindsey and Bits to ride separately?"

"I told them we had work to do on the way."

"I must have missed the memo. What work?"

"It was bullshit, alright? Lindsey's driving me nuts. Ever since Chase went off to school, she's had no one else in the house to focus on but me. Now I'm living under a microscope. 'Where *were* you?' 'When are you coming *home*?' 'Who *called*?' It's more than I can take. Now she wants to go out to the beach house this weekend. Just the two of us."

"She loves you."

"Yeah, yeah, yeah."

"You know that can't be bad."

"Oh please, Digs. Just her and me? What are we going to do? A 'romantic' weekend? There's nothing more boring than fucking your wife."

Digby scratched his chin. "I don't think so."

Robbie stared hard at Digby. "You trying to tell me something?"

"I'm trying to get you to loosen up. Settle down, will you? It's showtime. Turn on that famous charm. I know you have it in there somewhere."

+++

Boris parked under the mansion's porte cochère and hustled out of the car to open the door for Robbie. He and Digby waited for the car behind them to drop off Lindsey and Bits, Digby's wife, and together they walked through the mansion to the veranda, where the family gathered on a patio offering a commanding view of the valley and the Homer & Mary Crowe Nature Preserve, a thick forest of red oak, sugar maple, beech and tulip trees. Upon arrival, guests were offered organic sparkling organic wine from Ollie Crowe Vineyards in Healdsburg, California, and hors d'oeuvres from Understory, a "sustainable" new restaurant in Chappaqua featuring foods foraged from the local woods. The celebrated chef, wearing a cape around his bony shoulders, demonstrated to the delighted guests how they should dig into a massive pile of pine branches to find weeds and snails. He provided safety glasses for those concerned about getting pine needles in their eyes.

"You just *have* to try the nettles," gushed Morgan Frontenac, Robbie's third cousin, as she greeted him with air kisses. "They're *amazing*."

"I will, for sure," Robbie told her, cheerfully.

Digby shrugged and turned back to Robbie. "Haven't had a decent pile of nettles all day."

"I'd prefer some deadly nightshade about now," Robbie said.

Robbie strolled the veranda with Digby in tow while Lindsey and Bits high-tailed it to a high-top table in the corner, where they huddled with a bottle of rosé. As the adults milled about with their drinks, children played among the statuary and fountains, and tumbled around in the grass.

Robbie smiled, nodded, and shook hands with his cousins, offering seemingly sincere questions about their lives and making comments about how good they looked and how delighted he was to see them, leaving one and all feeling that he was truly one of their best friends in the world and a wonderful human being. He appeared to be genuinely interested in their remarks about their work with civic boards, failed business ventures, world travels, and troubled offspring with prescription-drug addictions. Wishing his ancient Aunt Lizzie the best of health and bidding her a lovely summer, he spotted the approach of a fortyish man with sandy hair parted at the side, dressed in gray slacks, a blue blazer and sockless brown loafers. Robbie turned away and whispered to Digby. "Who is this dork? He's like a fourth cousin or something, twice removed, but not removed far enough..."

Digby looked around Robbie's head, then whispered back. "Trey?"

"That's it. *Trey.* Homer Crowe the Third. Aunt Mimi's kid," Robbie said, before turning to greet him. "Trey! Great to see you. Where you been, man?"

"Hey Robbie," Trey said, offering a limp handshake. "Digby."

"You're looking fantastic. What are you up to these days?"

"Not a lot actually," he shrugged. "Playing some guitar. Learning Chinese... *slowly.* A little tennis. A little golf. You know the drill."

"Well, you're certainly keeping busy. You know, for a working stiff like me, that sounds like the life. I'm jealous. How's your golf game?"

"Okay, I suppose. No danger of joining the tour anytime soon."

"Who is?" Robbie said with a forced chuckle. "I've got a 13-handicap at the putt-putt in Montauk."

"Funny," Trey said with a yawn. "Robbie, I've been thinking I'd like to join the battle over there at the company. I'd really like something to do with my life that feels more, you know, *substantial.* I mean, I'm educated. It's probably time I do something with that, considering I'm pushing forty. And if I could help in some way—"

"Really interesting thought there, Trey. What brought this on?"

"Oh, Dede's been after me to get out of the house. You know, 'for better or for worse, but not for lunch?'"

"Of course. Linz feels the same way. What did you have in mind?"

"First off, I should say, don't worry. I have absolutely *no* designs on a job like yours."

"That's a relief, I suppose."

"I'm thinking I could start small, like a vice president or something. Even if the title's more of an honorary sort of thing."

Robbie nodded. "A vice president. That's an idea. But you know, we don't really have honorary titles in the company. You'd have to take charge of a particular area."

"I was always pretty good with numbers. So… finance, maybe?"

"Was that your degree?"

"No. I was art history at Williams. But I took a few courses, just so I could understand my investments. Knocked down mostly A's, well, one A, and a couple B's. Pretty sure I could have gotten into grad school, but you may recall I went to live in an ashram for a couple years."

"Right, right," Robbie said. "I love your new enthusiasm for our company, Trey. We need all the great resources we can get, and no doubt, you have a lot to offer." He slapped Digby on the back. "Why don't you and Digs talk this through and see if there's something that aligns our needs with your talents and experience."

Trey brightened. "I stand ready to serve."

"And I thank you," Robbie said. "Sincerely."

Robbie turned away to find Uncle Chuck replacing his empty tumbler of scotch with a fresh one from a silver tray. "Sheez," Robbie muttered. "What a moron."

"Trey?" Chuck said. "He just wants to help."

"Any way we can get him a job at a competitor?" Robbie said, looking over the horizon at the setting sun that cast a warm glow on the gathering. "I'd like to get this show on the road. I've got to get back to the city."

Chuck sipped his drink. "Hot date?"

"Meeting of the Communist Party," Robbie said.

"You'll feel right at home." Chuck picked up a spoon from a high-top and clinked his glass, prompting heads to turn his way as he set down his drink. "Good evening, everyone," he said, as the conversational din subsided. "Welcome to our annual gathering. This is, I believe, the 47th family meeting here at the estate of our splendid forbearers."

Family members turned to Chuck and quieted down as he continued. "It's always a joy for me to come back each year and remember all the good times

I've had here, going back to my childhood. Riding my tricycle through my Great-Grandma's rose garden, much to her dismay. Tumbling down that hill, just like the kids are doing now. Tinkering with dynamos in the garage with Great-Grandpa. Coming here is also a reminder of how lucky we all were to have had such a giant of business in our family. Without him, where would we all be?"

There was applause and shouts of "Hear, hear."

"No doubt, Homer Crowe was a singular genius in American history. A man of remarkable vision, industry, and capacity for hard work. As history has proven, God broke the mold and didn't make another. But, in his infinite wisdom and grace and beneficence, he did give us... Robbie."

Robbie winced as the family applauded. Was that a *shot?* Uncle Chuck couldn't say, "Fortunately, he gave us Robbie?" Or, "Thank God he gave us Robbie?" *What the hell.* Robbie stepped forward and cast a sidelong look at Uncle Chuck, who was picking up his drink and taking a seat on a tall stool. Well, Robbie thought, *fuck him and the Bentley he rode in on.*

"Thank you so much, Uncle Chuck," Robbie said as the applause simmered down. "I honestly don't know where I'd be without that kind of support."

Chuck raised his glass and smiled.

"Alright. Let's start with the good news." Robbie plunged ahead with a summary of the company's progress over the past year: staggering profits, record-high dividends, and share buybacks that cranked up the value of their stock. Everyone he looked at over the grounds of his great-great-grandparents' estate was considerably richer this lovely evening than they were the year before. No wonder they were getting crooked-faced on cases of Ollie Crowe's grape juice. Just a few miles downriver from FDR's estate, happy days were here again.

"And yet," Robbie said somberly, pausing for dramatic effect, "I wish I could say that all is well on Broad Street. It's not." He went on to detail the looming threat to the family's reputation because of its lack of significant progress on environmental and social issues that could impede their license to operate facilities in various communities around the world. Despite Walker Hope's glittering reviews from Wall Street, Robbie confided that he did not believe Walker had the family's best interests at heart. "At the end of the day, he's not one of us."

There were nods of agreement, as Robbie pressed on.

"Frankly, I blame myself," he said. "I let Walker wander a bit off the leash, thinking he'd pursue the ambitious ideas we laid out years ago. And the sad truth is, he has not. He's strictly a bottom-line guy, at the expense of everything else. And it could get much, much worse. I happen to believe — and I know many of you share this view — that we must think beyond the next quarter's results. We need to consider the future for our children and our grandchildren. How will they be viewed by society? As good people? People who did the right thing? Or will they be thought of as part of a family that had a chance to lead on some of the biggest issues of our time but blew it? It may seem hard to believe, but those kids having fun over there on the hill could become pariahs."

There was a low murmur of assent, a somber nodding of heads, a pouring of more wine and cordials, as Robbie asked for questions and comments. He nodded to Jack Dillworth, a forty-something first cousin on his mother's side, who owned a bed-and-breakfast in Kennebunkport with his estranged wife and operated it with his twenty-one-year-old girlfriend, who was hugging his arm with her left hand and a brandy snifter with her right.

"Robbie, I certainly hear where you're coming from. I think we all share your concern," Jack said. "But, you know, another worry I have for our future generations is their financial security. Since the rumor circulated this week that Walker might be leaving, our shares are down almost ten percent."

"That's right," Robbie said. "And you know what? I'm fine with that. Really. Let the shorts and the hedges and the other people who don't believe in us get out. We want people buying our stock because they *believe* in us. They know we're a good company and that we're going to do the right thing. That's because we're the people with our name over the door. Nobody cares about this more than we do. The people who know us know we're in this for the long haul."

More nods of agreement, but less vigorous. Topher Crowe, a millennial first cousin wearing a black t-shirt with an unbuttoned plaid shirt over the top, raised his hand.

"Robbie, I think saving the world is cool. I mean, we all want that, right?" Topher said. "But I kind of wonder: if we, like, change all our plants to more sustainable power, does that mean the company makes less money? And all of us would, too?"

"No. Not at all," Robbie said, looking to a deeply skeptical Uncle Chuck, who had his arms folded across his chest. "Not if you look at it over the long run."

"That's nice, dear," Aunt Lizzie said. "But I don't have a long run."

Robbie acknowledged the laughter with an uneasy smile. "I understand, Aunt Lizzie. I'm not sure I do either. But this isn't about us. This is about them," he said, pointing to the kids playing on the hill. "I'm absolutely determined to help make the next century of Crowe even better than the first. That's why I think we need to look at things differently. You know, research shows that companies that lead on environmental and social issues have much better performance than the S&P 500."

Uncle Chuck said, "What research is that, Robbie?"

"Well," Robbie said, "I don't have it right in front of me, but I know I read it somewhere."

"Send it along when you find it, will you?"

"Of course." Robbie noted his audience shifting on their feet, anxiously. "Look. Nobody loves this company or this family more than I do. And let me tell you, it makes me uncomfortable when people are pounding the hood of my car when I'm going into work, shouting that I—and by extension, all of you—am a greedy monster. If I'm greedy about anything, it's this: I want it all. A sustainable company *and* a profitable company. A company that does what it takes, but also does it the right way. A company we can all be proud of—this year, next year and for many, many years to come. All I ask is that you continue to have my back, just as you always have, and I'll have yours. Walker Hope has done a fine job, to a point. But he's taken this as far as he can go, given his background and his capability. Now we need to reassess, and that's what I intend to do. And I guarantee you, this won't be taken lightly. It will be fair and objective, just as you would expect."

The applause was tepid as Robbie nodded his thanks and stepped off to the side to meet Digby. "How'd I do?"

"You want an honest answer?"

"Not particularly."

"You were fabulous."

46. DRINKIN' BUDDIES

Marty was at his desk, wading through the job postings on LinkedIn and ZipRecruiter.com when Carly appeared in the doorway.

"You've been summoned," she said.

Marty slumped. "Can't you come in here just once and say, 'Walker would like you to take the rest of the day off?'"

"Your wish may have come true."

"How's that?"

"Walker wants to see you. At a bar."

"That hardly qualifies as a day off. Why does he want to meet in a bar?"

"Maybe he wanted to talk to you in a place that isn't bugged."

"Well," he said, slapping his knees with both hands and hunching forward. "I suppose that makes sense. When would he like to meet?"

"Now."

"*Alone?*"

"I don't *know*, Marty. Would you like me to call and find out if he has another date?"

"No. Sorry. *Shit.* I'll just go. I'm sure it will be... fine. It's just that—"

"I know. You hate the guy."

"*No.* Not at all. I don't *hate* the guy. I just don't find him to be a barrel of laughs."

"Well, don't feel guilty about it. He doesn't seem wild about you either," Carly shrugged. "So I guess you're even."

Marty's heart raced as he walked a short block down Beaver Street. What did Walker want now? Nothing good could come from a loosened tongue with the boss. Marty would have to drink very slowly, lest he venture anywhere near the truth regarding his thoughts about the job, Walker, Robbie or his own pathetic financial circumstances. He rounded the corner on Hanover Square and stepped warily down the stairs to Harry's, where a crowd of male office workers from nearby buildings gathered in boisterous clusters at the bar, and waitresses navigated around them with trays of drinks. Marty found his CEO alone at a dark counter along the windows finishing a bourbon on the rocks, handing the empty glass to a waitress, and asking for another. It was clear Walker had a running start. Marty was skilled at catching up but reminded himself to go slowly. This was treacherous territory.

"Marty, my friend," Walker said, extending a hand. "You look like a man who could use a drink."

"I'll say. What are you having?"

"A little ice. A lotta Maker's."

"Make mine with a splash of soda," Marty said. Yeah, sure. *Soda will slow things down.*

As the waitress moved off, Walker appraised Marty with an expression that looked almost like affection. "You know, Marty, I don't think I fully appreciated until yesterday what a connivin' son-of-a-gun you are," Walker said. "Gotta say, I'm impressed."

"This is a street fight," Marty said with a shrug. "Robbie brings a knife. We bring a windmill."

"I like that," Walker said, with a laugh. "And I must say I was surprised by that, too. I always thought you were a Robbie guy."

As they clinked glasses together and sipped their drinks, Marty considered his headhunter's advice. *At some point, you're going to have to pick sides.* "Up until recently, I've never really looked at it that way," Marty said. "I've always considered myself a Crowe Power guy—an advocate for what's best for the company."

"Good answer," Walker said. "So, in that vein, you think this BlowCo project out in the Hamptons will be good for the company?"

"Of course. It builds our green credentials. Gives us some talking points with the NGOs. And," Marty paused and sipped his drink. *Should he say it?*

"And what?" Walker said.

"It will drive our chairman fucking *crazy.*"

Walker burst out laughing, slapping his knee. "Oh man. I would *love* to see his face when he hears."

"You're not going to tell him?"

"Heavens, no. I'd rather he heard it elsewhere. Why should I get all the glory?"

They clinked glasses again. "Show me where this BlowCo project is, exactly," Walker said.

Marty called up a map on his phone and ran his fingers across the screen to show the shoreline of East Hampton. "That's where it would be. Right about here," Marty said, pointing to a spot three miles off the coast. "Robbie should be able to see our project right from his front porch, which is here. He can track the progress every time he looks out his window, runs on the beach, or picnics in the dunes."

Walker clapped his hands together in glee. "Well, here's the deal. We hammered out an agreement with BlowCo this afternoon. They've agreed we can publicize it any way we want. So I'd like you to get the word out tomorrow. Robbie's headin' out to his beach house for the weekend. Let's be sure that everyone out there knows about this. Blanket the Hamptons. Do interviews on local radio. Whatever it takes. A significant commitment to renewable resources on the part of Crowe Power should get the attention it deserves."

"Consider it done," Marty said, as they clinked their glasses together. And clinked again with a fresh round. And again, and again. Thank God Marty ordered a splash in each drink. Compared to the people around him, he could barely feel a buzz at all, even if the speech he was thinking in his head wasn't entirely in sync with the words coming out of his mouth. And yet, his attitude had changed considerably since he walked in the door. Why, he wasn't finding Walker such a pedantic prick after all. Pop a few drinks in him and he could be almost *fun*. He was kicking back and laughing, telling stories about his awkward meetings with Robbie, and offering caustic assessments of the people in his leadership team. So-and-so was terrible in their job; so-and-so was going to get an assignment offer that would make them quit. Okay, *fun* might be an overstatement, but Walker was certainly more tolerable when viewed through the bottom of a tumbler. Walker was bringing him into his thinking, treating him almost like a respected colleague. Marty took a healthy swig of his bourbon—*don't forget the soda!*—and relaxed his posture, smiling easily with his new buddy.

"So tell me," Walker said, "how do you like your job?"

"Oh, man, it's great." *Graaaaaate.*

"What do you like about it?"

Marty rolled his eyes back in his head, thinking. There had to be something he liked. *Oh.* "Well, of course, at the top of the list is working with great people. I mean—and this sounds like sucking up, but it's really not—it's just such a privilege working with you. I learn so much every day."

"Go on," Walker said, eagerly. "Tell me."

Marty was confused. "Tell you?"

"What you've learned from me."

Think, Marty. There had to be something. How much had he had to drink? And *when had Walker stopped drinking?* "I think it's just the whole approach, you know? The discipline. The processes. The fact that you hold people accountable."

"Even when it's you?"

"Yes, sir. Absolutely. Can't say it doesn't sting. But, at the end of the day, I know you're right and that it's for my own good. That's why you are where you are."

"I've heard some people think I make too much money."

Marty winced in an exaggerated way, as if it were pained by the suggestion. "Who? Bernie Sanders?"

"People in the company."

"Oh, come on. You make, what, 780 times the average Crowe Power worker? That's... fair."

"You think so?"

"It's like I tell the press all the time. Your comp reflects your market value. Simple as that. It's the capitalist system. Can't squawk about that unless you're... I don't know. Some sort of commie or something." *Jeezus. Did he just stay that?* Okay. Stop drinking.

"Seven-hundred-eighty to one, huh?" Walker said. "How much more do I make than you?"

Marty blinked hard several times, trying to do the math in his fuzzy head. "Well, let me think. I guess your comp's about, oh, fifty times what I make, which is, you know…"

Walker stared at him, unblinking. "No. What?"

"*Appropriate*, right? I mean, I certainly didn't drive the stock up a thousand percent. That's on you as the leader. I just do what I can to help."

Walker nodded. "*Soooo* glad you feel that way, Marty. You're a good, loyal soldier."

Marty nodded. "Sir, yes, sir." They were pals now, bonding, a mini band of brothers, working arm-in-arm to battle the evil emperor, Robbie Crowe.

Walker leaned over and looked Marty in the eye. "And that's really, really important, because I need you to trust me when I tell you something."

Marty nodded eagerly. "Of course."

"I'm going to have to let you go."

Marty wobbled on his chair. "You're… *what?*"

"It's going to be okay. But I'm giving you notice now."

Marty couldn't speak.

"Don't worry. You still have two weeks, and I need you to work as hard as ever. You'll get a full severance package—including vesting in your stocks, your pension, the whole thing. But then you're done at Crowe."

"I don't understand, Walker. *Why?*"

"You'll understand soon enough. This is actually a good thing for you," he said. "Wish I could say more right now. Just trust me on this."

With that, Marty's new pal stood and signaled for the waitress. "And just so you know, we had to cancel your company credit card as part of the separation process."

"Of course," Marty said.

"But hey," Walker said, patting him on the shoulder. "Don't worry about the drinks. I've got these."

47. EBB TIDE

The sun had risen over the Eastern horizon but there was still a morning chill in the air as Robbie finished his run on the beach. Sweating and catching his breath, he trudged through the sand toward his beach house. There he found Lindsey, snuggled under a blanket with a cup of Irish coffee in a woven barrel chair on the 100-foot-long veranda.

"The view is so calming," she said, as Robbie climbed up the stairs. "Nothing but sun and sand and water as far as the eye can see."

"Yeah," Robbie said, glancing over his shoulder toward the Atlantic. "I guess."

"Occasionally a seagull flies by or a flock of plovers skitters across the dune. I like to look out at the horizon and think about what lies beyond. I wonder: what are they doing over there in Portugal and Spain right now?"

Robbie rolled his eyes. *Seriously? Who the hell cares? What was she talking about anyway?* "Hadn't given that a lot of thought."

"Did you hear about that windfarm they want to build out there? They might start on it this summer if they get a permit. It would be right in the middle of our view."

Robbie sat on the wooden swing chained to the ceiling and pushed off the floor. "I wouldn't worry about it. They'll never get it past the homeowners out here. They're going to sue them until the company goes out of business. From what I hear that should be any day now."

"They were gathering signatures outside Citarella to oppose it. I signed for both of us."

Robbie stopped. "You *what?* No, no, no. You can't put my name on anything like that. Are you out of your mind? Do you know how many statements I've made in support of wind energy? I can't turn around and oppose it when it's in my own backyard. I'd look like a damn NIMBY."

"It's not *exactly* in your backyard."

"It may as well be. Just leave me out of it. Please. I can't be involved in any way."

Lindsey shrugged and scanned the horizon. "We should come here more often," she said.

"Of course," he said. "We should also go more often to Palm Beach and London and Tuscany and Montecito, too. It feels like a waste to have all these homes and never use them. But I don't see that changing any time soon. If Tim takes over as CEO, he's going to need a lot of help."

"So... what does that mean exactly?"

"It means I'm going to be very busy showing him the ropes."

She sat up in her seat and faced him. "Oh, lord. I don't want to go through that again."

"Through *what?*"

"When you were running Strategy, the job was a terrible strain on you. I don't think you understand that all that stress took a toll on your home life, too. The children never saw you. And neither did I."

Robbie sighed. "Oh God. *Again?* How many times do we have to go over that?"

"Okay," she said, curtly. "If my concerns aren't important—"

"Look," he said, sitting up. "It's not going to be like that. Yes, a new CEO would require more of my time. I can't avoid that. Tim would need some hand-holding to get up and running. But, it won't require the time commitment I had when I was running the brains of our business. Things would be different."

Lindsey took a sip of her Irish coffee and leaned a little closer. "They'd have to be. I won't go through that again."

Robbie twitched, and his eyes widened. Was she saying she'd divorce him? He envisioned a series of dominoes falling and landing on him like a ton of bricks, leaving him with a vastly diminished portfolio—financially, socially and every other way he could think of.

"Listen, Maria..."

"*Maria?*"

"Sorry," Robbie said, recoiling. "What'd I say?"

"Maria. Who's that?"

"I don't know. Sorry. I just had an email from work."

"See. This is exactly the problem. You're already so distracted you don't even know who you're talking to."

"I hear you," he said, patting the back of her hand. "And I promise, I'm not going to let work consume me."

She relaxed at last and smiled. "Seriously?"

"Yes. Absolutely."

"You would do that? For us?"

He offered his most humble, guilty dog face. "Consider it a promise."

48. HOWIE DID IT

Howie-Do-It grabbed the 6 a.m. Delta flight out of LaGuardia to Detroit Metropolitan Airport, arriving six hours ahead of Walker's scheduled landing. He killed time on a metal bench in the baggage area, eating jelly donuts and watching old gladiator movies on his iPad, before taking a shuttle bus to the Hertz lot to retrieve his surveillance vehicle. He searched for the most menacing car he could get for his company-approved expense level, only to settle for a red Toyota Corolla, and parked outside the Signature terminal, tracking Crowe Bird II from Teterboro through the FlightAware app on his phone. Walker, per usual, landed precisely on time, and Howie vigorously snapped pictures of him hopping into the back seat of an Escalade. *Evidence!*

Howie followed close behind the Escalade on I-94 toward downtown Detroit, slaloming around the speeding semis and pickup trucks. When the caravan reached the stately Neo-Renaissance-style Book Cadillac, Howie pulled in behind Walker's car and snapped a photo of him entering the building. *More evidence!* Then Howie left his own car to the valet and followed Walker inside, discreetly taking shots of Walker on the escalator to the second-floor lobby, and again as he disappeared around a corner toward the elevator bank. As Howie quickly scanned the shots on his phone, he was startled by a voice behind him.

"Hello there," Walker said.

Howie, ashen, turned around.

"Howie-Do-It, right?" Walker said.

Howie cleared his throat and summoned what little bravado he could. "Who's askin'?" he said with a squeak in his voice.

Walker laughed. "You know who I am. You *do* work at Crowe Power?"

"So?"

"What brings you to town, Howie?"

"I'm... visiting a friend."

"Funny," Walker said, putting his hands casually in his pockets. "So am I."

"That's cool. I gotta get going. He's expecting me."

Walker took a step closer to Howie, until he was less than a foot away, crowding him, and his smile vanished. "What exactly do you do at Crowe, Howie?"

"I... really can't say."

"Yes, you can."

"You're not my boss."

"Should we get your boss on the phone? We can call Robbie Crowe right now."

"He wouldn't know nothin'."

"No, probably not. He doesn't seem to know much about a lot of things once they go kablooey." Walker put his hand on Howie's shoulder, and squeezed it firmly. "What, exactly, are you lookin' for here, Howie? Maybe I can help you."

Howie rolled his eyes, thinking.

"Come on now," Walker said. "I hate for you to come all this way for nothin'. You can do this."

"Well. Truth be told, I'm actually here to *protect* you."

"Is that right?"

"Well, yeah. As you know, there's a lot of concern about the use of company resources. We've had anonymous reports that you are using the company plane to see a woman who happens to not be your wife. If that got out, it could be a scandal for the company."

Walker nodded. "I totally get that. And let me tell you something. You're absolutely right. I am seeing a woman who is not my wife. Want to meet my girl?"

"I... uh..."

"Aw, come on up. You don't want to go back to your boss empty-handed. He'd be disappointed."

Walker guided Howie with a gentle shove to the elevator, which took them to the 29th floor. There they entered a two-story penthouse and were met by Malaya Mendoza, who greeted Walker with a warm embrace and a kiss on the cheek.

"Mr. Hope, I did not know you were bringing a friend," she said, puzzled.

"Howie's our new friend, Malaya. He's got a tough job at our company and I want to help him do it."

Howie couldn't believe his good luck. His adrenaline surged as he moved in for the kill. "Do you mind if I get a picture?"

"Mind? Heavens no," Walker said, grandly. He put his arm around Malaya and smiled as Howie snapped away.

"Great," Howie said. "I think I'm finished here. I can leave you two alone."

"Don't go yet," Walker said, slapping his hands together. "I want you to meet Mamaw."

"Who's that?"

"You can't be much of a detective, Howie, if you don't know Mamaw's my grandmother. She raised me after my momma died. Ninety-seven years old next week and sharp as a tack. How's she doing today, Malaya?"

"Feisty as ever."

"Excellent," Walker said. "Let's go see her."

Walker bounded up the staircase two steps at a time, with Howie trailing. At a doorway to a bedroom, Walker paused and knocked on the open door. "Mamaw, are you decent?"

"No, but I'll see you anyhow," she said.

Howie braced himself. Was this going to be a *Psycho* moment? A wizened old granny in a rocker and Walker in a gray wig with a big knife? They entered the room to find Walker's grandmother sitting in an easy chair in the corner by the windows, her lap covered with a crocheted blanket, reading the *Wall Street Journal*. Walker bent over and kissed her on the forehead, and she reached up to pat his arm.

"Hello sweetie," she said, smiling. "You're lookin' good." She leaned over to see Howie. "Who's that?"

Walker stepped aside, then brought Howie forward by the arm. "This is Howie, Mamaw. He's spyin' on me for the chairman."

"Pleased to meet you," Howie said, weakly.

"I don't understand," Mamaw said, eying Howie. "Your *company* is spying on you?"

"Yessum," Walker said.

"Well, that don't make a lick of sense."

"No, it doesn't. But, for some reason or another, they have me under surveillance. They bug my office. Go through my files. They—he—even followed me here from New York."

Mamaw was puzzled. She glared at Howie, who was staring at his shoes, then looked back to Walker. "I don't get this at all. Did you do something wrong, honey?"

"No, no, no. They're just hopin' I did."

Mamaw chuckled. "They don't know you, do they?" She peered at Howie through her rimless glasses. "You there. You're what? A company goon?"

Howie shook his head. "Not exactly."

"The mill used to send people snoopin' around my house after my husband was involved in a strike," Mamaw said. "He put a lickin' on them with a crowbar and that was that. But I never heard tell of a company spyin' on the boss."

"As you may remember, Mamaw," Walker said, "I report to a board of directors. And someone on that board apparently wants me to leave."

"Walker, I think you need to work somewhere else. A company that behaves like that doesn't deserve you. But," she said, looking Howie up and down, "I'm pretty sure it deserves him."

"Aw, he's alright, Mamaw. Just doin' his job." Walker turned to Howie. "As long as you got your camera, Howie, what do you say we take some selfies?"

Howie shrugged and Walker put his arm around Howie's shoulder and snapped a few shots with Howie's phone. "Let's do one with Mamaw," Walker said.

"Oh, stop it," she barked. "I don't want my picture taken."

"Come on, Mamaw," Walker said. "A souvenir for our new friend, Howie."

Howie sighed. This was a disaster. What the hell was he going to tell Robbie?

49. AN ILL WIND DOTH BLOW

Boris pulled his gleaming black car fifty yards short of the entrance to the elegant restaurant Le Bilboquet, situated at the foot of the Long Wharf Village Pier on the waterfront in Sag Harbor, the quaint bayside town where Robbie's neighbors parked their yachts.

"What the hell, Boris?" Robbie yelped from the back seat. "Should we take a bus the rest of the way?"

"You shouldn't get out," Boris said, looking at Robbie in the rear-view mirror. "There's some sort of problem out there."

Robbie peered out the window to see Eva, the restaurant's notoriously implacable hostess, holding a clipboard and facing down an angry trio of mothers with a small legion of children clad in beach gear. Eva examined the array of cut-offs, flip-flops, and t-shirts with a whiff of disgust, and told them to come back another day when they were properly dressed, prompting hoots and cat-calls and shouts of "go to hell" and "fuck off."

"We're afraid of moms with strollers?" Robbie said. "How bad can it be?"

Lindsey, alarmed, clutched his upper arm. "You don't know. They could have guns."

"If I can take on protesters in the middle of Broad Street," Robbie said, "I can certainly handle this."

Boris parked the Escalade and jumped out of the driver's seat to open the door for Robbie, who emerged wearing white jeans and a blue linen coat, and Lindsey, in slim-fitting black leather pants, with a white silk blouse and gray gabardine jacket, and one of her many pairs of high-heeled Louboutins. Together, they tiptoed their way around the restaurant's reject pile, trying to avoid being noticed.

One of the mothers spotted them and wheeled around. "Yeah, that's right," she shouted. "Go on in, *assholes*. Join the other millionaires and billionaires." That elicited laughter and hoots from the others as Robbie nodded, smiled tightly, and mumbled, "Thank you."

Lindsey looked at him as if he were insane. "*Thank* you? For *what?*"

"I don't know. What the hell am I supposed to say?" he said, holding her by the arm and escorting her safely inside the restaurant, where they were met immediately by Pierre, the beaming host. "Bonsoir, mon amis," he said grandly.

"What the hell, Pierre. It's like the French Revolution out there," Robbie said, shaking his head. "You could really use a private entrance."

Robbie and Lindsey were ushered out to the peaceful deck overlooking the harbor and were seated along the water at a table with a vase holding a freshly cut sunflower at its center. Two servers arrived instantly to pour champagne. "So sorry about the commotion," Pierre said. "This is on me."

As they looked over the menus, Robbie sensed a bad vibe. He glanced around him at the deck crowded with wealthy New Yorkers and their families, the U.S. Secretary of Commerce, and an array of celebrities and runway models. Was it his imagination, or were other diners regarding him with disdain? Were they blaming him for the hubbub at the gate? His question was answered with the appearance of neighbor Mack Ack, a hedge fund manager, who rushed over to their table, looking deeply distressed.

"Excuse me, Linz," he said. "Wondering if I can borrow Captain Planet for a minute."

"I wish you would," she said, signaling the waiter for a stronger drink.

Mack pushed Robbie past a wall of aquamarine tiles into a corner of the bar. "What's up?" Robbie said. "You seem a bit frazzled."

"I am, because of you and your stupid fucking company," Mack said.

"What did I do?"

"You know I'm trying to sell my place, right?"

"Yeah. You bought some monster house further down the shore. I read it's twenty-thousand square feet?"

"A teardown, but that's not the point. How the hell am I supposed to sell this allegedly *prime* real estate overlooking the ocean when you're going to build a fucking windfarm right off the shore."

"I don't know what you're talking about."

Mack flushed red, and his voice rose. "Bullshit. I just heard it on the radio. Crowe Power announced it was investing in BlowCo, those cocksuckers behind the Atlantica project that we've been trying to kill for the past year."

Robbie sagged. "Honest to God, Mack. I had no idea."

"How can that be? You are the chairman, right? The report I heard said this investment reflected your 'green vision,' whatever the hell that means."

"Mack. Seriously. Nobody told me anything about this."

"Well, let me tell you something about *my* vision: it's an unobstructed view of the ocean from the house I'm trying to sell, *and* from the one I just bought. I don't need any goddamned whirlygigs on the horizon. And I don't think anyone else here wants to see that either."

Suddenly, Robbie understood the strange vibe in the dining room, just as his phone dinged with a company alert. He pulled it out of his pocket to see the notification: "CRO: Crowe Power Invests $20 million in BlowCo."

"Look, Mack. I don't like this any better than you do. But I've got to tell you. If we're going to have a more sustainable future, we're all going to have to sacrifice a little bit."

Mack laughed bitterly. "Oh we are, are we? Well, let me tell you something. You can sacrifice all you want," Mack said, jabbing a finger in Robbie's chest. "But it's not up to *you* to sign *me* up for your crusade. Jesus, man. You couldn't think of something more popular to support? Like clubbing baby seals? You know, it's one thing for you to refuse to join our lawsuit against these BlowCo assholes. You've taken a public position on this green crap. I get that. What I don't get is why you've just financed their fight against us, your friends and neighbors. Now I've got to dig into my pocket to contribute even *more* to our legal fund. What the hell, man. You've screwed me every which way."

"Believe me, I had no intention of doing that."

"No. I'm sure you're full of good intentions. You always are, Robbie. That's what I like about you—and what I find so infuriating. So yeah, go ahead. Build some windmills. Just put 'em in fucking Jersey, where all that other shit is, alright?"

"Let me look into this, Mack. Maybe there's a way to fix this."

"I hope so. You know, I've got more than a few shares in your company."

"I appreciate that. Thank you."

"And I've held on, even while others bailed when the news broke about your CEO being on the way out. Everyone said, 'Robbie's screwing this up.' I said, 'Give him a chance.' I mean, how much damage can one man do? But you know what? I'm done."

Mack turned on his heel and walked away. Robbie took a deep breath and walked slowly back to the table, feeling all eyes in the room upon him. That included Lindsey, who greeted him with an icy stare.

"I heard," she said, coldly. "I thought you couldn't be involved in any way."

Robbie shook his head. "Let's get out of here."

50. PLAN B

A bad evening turned worse when Howie texted Robbie a selfie of himself and Walker, followed by another shot of Walker and some gnarly old bag. *Who the hell was that?* Robbie, riding to the beach house with a sullen Lindsey in the back of the Escalade, stared in disbelief at the shot of his loyal subject and his arch-nemesis smiling like long lost pals.

Robbie punched in a response.

ROBBIE
WTF??

HOWIE
Dude. Sorry. Long story.

Robbie punched in Howie's number.

"I don't need pictures of you, dipshit. I know what you look like. I want photos of Walker's girlfriend."

"He doesn't have one," Howie said sadly. "He goes to Detroit to see his grandmother."

"Is *that* who's in the photo? She's gotta be a hundred-and-forty!"

"Ninety-seven, almost," Howie said. "Tough old broad."

"Well, hell, man. What am I supposed to do with this?"

"Nothing."

"I don't get it. Why can't he be normal like everyone else and just have a girlfriend? What's *wrong* with him?"

"You know, he's actually kind of a nice guy," Howie said. "He asked me to stay for lunch."

"Are you out of your *mind*? I want this guy gone."

"He said nice things about you."

"I don't give a rat's ass. I *hate* him. Do you not understand that?"

"I guess I got carried away, especially after a few beers."

"You were drinking with him? Good lord, Howie."

"Guess I let you down, huh?"

"I don't know what you were thinking. What am I supposed to do now? Board meeting's Monday and I've got nothing. I'm going to have to build a case from scratch." Robbie shook his head, pondering this cruel twist of fate. "Now I hate that guy *even more* for making me go through all this shit just to get rid of him."

"I understand your frustration."

"Do you? Cause I guess it's *all* up to me again. As usual."

+++

Arriving at the beach house, Lindsey walked silently to the stairs while Robbie headed straight out to the veranda to dial Digby. "Can you believe that asshole?" he said, pacing and biting a fingernail.

"By 'that asshole,' you mean Walker?"

"You are quick, Digby."

"What's the report out of Detroit?"

"Dead end. I should have known. Who keeps a love nest in Detroit?"

"I don't know. The Four Tops?"

"It was rhetorical, Digby. I'm not looking for an answer. I'm looking for a way to whack this guy. What about the BlowCo investment? That *must* be a fireable offense. Easily."

"Actually, no," Digby said, with a sigh. "Our governance bylaws say he's totally within his budget authority. The spend is only $20 million—well below the level he needs for board approval."

"Then he should be fired for insubordination."

"For making progress on your green vision? How does that work?"

"Well, goddamn it, Digby, find *something*."

"What?"

"*Anything.* You're the fucking lawyer here. Do I have to think of everything? What is wrong with you? I need some help here."

Digby took a deep breath. "Alright, Robbie. Let's step back for a minute. It's obvious that he's putting his thumb in your eye with this BlowCo deal."

"Clearly."

"It's a deliberate provocation, which makes me wonder why."

"Who gives a crap?"

"Hold on there a second. Before we react, ask yourself: does he *want* to get fired?"

"You don't get it, Digs. *I don't care.* He needs to just *go*."

Digby was quiet a moment. At last, he said, "Alright. When?"

"Monday. At the board meeting."

"I don't see how you're going to pull that off."

"Maybe we get one of directors to call for an emergency meeting of the Executive Committee because of all the rumors floating around. We could have a PowerPoint presentation for them, laying out all the reasons why he's got to go."

"What reasons are those?"

"It was all there in the Buzzniss story, Digby. What more do we need?"

"Wait a second. You want *me* to do this?"

"*Yes*, I want you to do this. You think I've got time to do it? Do you have any idea how much I have on my plate?"

"I have a pretty good idea."

Silence on the line, then: "If you think you're being funny, you're not."

"I'll have it for you first thing Monday."

"Make it tomorrow night. Come Monday morning, we need to be locked and loaded. I want to take that guy down."

PART THREE

51. SAND IN THE GEARS

Robbie's morning run along the beach turned into a slow jog, and finally a walk. *God, he was tired.* He had run as far as the house where a woman in a wide-brim straw hat often liked to sunbathe nude in the dunes, only to find her beach deserted. Now, on his way back, he sat down on the sand, out of the path of joggers and walkers, and considered the many ways that everyone was letting him down. Maybe he should just head into the sea and swim out as far as he could, never to be heard from again. How would they all feel then? Would they think the world was a better place without him, or would they regret how badly they treated him? They'd be *soooo* sorry.

How about that jerk neighbor, Mack Ack? How *dare* he get in Robbie's face and scold him like an unruly child. Would Mack be any better off with a truly inconsiderate neighbor—like a hip-hop mogul, or a movie star throwing wild parties, or somebody running an Airbnb rental? *No.* And what about Lindsey? All she does these days is pout, while all he does is provide the most comfortable life possible for her. Does she appreciate it? *No.* And his stupid board of directors. *God!* Do they understand he's trying to protect their good names as well as his own? That he's really, when you think about it, going after Walker on their behalf? Do they even get how selfless he can be? *No.* It's just so goddamned *unfair.*

As he began to feel a chill, he pushed himself up, knocked the sand off his shorts, and headed back toward the house. Would it be so bad to see windmills on the horizon? Maybe not. In fact, it might be a good example for the rest of the world. But renewable energy wasn't really the point of Walker's move, which Robbie understood very well. It was a provocation—exactly the kind of move Robbie would make on an adversary.

He trudged toward the house, hoping to avoid Lindsey. Alas, she was on the veranda again with another Irish coffee, her eyes fixed on the horizon as he came up the steps.

"I hope we can still see the sunrise through all the windmills," she said.

"It's not a brick wall, Linz. It's windmills. Very graceful. They're still most of the time. And when they move, it's a 'synchronous dance with nature.' At least, that's what it says in the brochure."

"Great," she snapped. "I'll invite friends over to watch the BlowCo Bolshoi."

"Don't worry. It's not going to happen."

A phone rang and Robbie pulled it out of his pocket, looked at it, and shoved it back in his shorts.

Lindsey looked puzzled. "I saw your phone on the kitchen counter," she said. "I didn't know you had a second one."

"This?" he said with a shrug. "It's one I keep for emergencies."

"Like what?" she said, sitting up.

"You know, if something blows up at one of our plants."

"So... you're not going to answer it?"

He shrugged. "Nah."

"Why not?"

"It's probably nothing."

"You just said it was for *emergencies*."

"Okay. Fine. *Fine.*" He pulled the phone out of his shorts and punched a button. "Hello? Hello?" He looked at Lindsey and shook his head. "Happy now? Nobody was even on the line. Probably a wrong number."

Lindsey glared at Robbie. "I don't know what's going on with you, but I really don't like it."

"You know what?" he said testily. "I don't like what's going on with me, either. I've got a major showdown with our CEO next week. I'm an outcast out here because of this stupid fucking BlowCo project that I had nothing to do with but everyone attributes to me. I'm besieged by radical protesters every morning who'd love nothing more than to beat me within an inch of my life.

So, yeah. There's a lot of crap in my life right now. And, frankly, I don't need you to add to the pile."

"You know damn well that's not what I'm talking about. So don't deflect."

"What *are* you talking about?"

"I'm talking about *you*."

"Stop, Lindsey. Just stop. I really can't have this conversation right now. I've got a lot on my mind."

"So do I. Ever think of that?"

He stepped closer to her, his tone more conciliatory. "Look. Until I get this Walker situation settled, I need all the focus I can get. If I've been less than attentive, forgive me, please. My mind has been 100 percent on my work. It has to be. But it's only temporary."

She nodded in a way that was accepting, if not forgiving. "Do what you have to do."

"First thing I have to do is shower and clear my head," Robbie said. "Then I've got to pull the blinds in the study and dig down to prepare for next week."

He patted her arm as he walked past her. When she heard him climb the stairs toward the master suite, she followed quietly into the house and waited at the foot of the stairs until she heard the water running. Then she tiptoed up the steps and down the hallway into Robbie's dressing room, where his running shorts had been tossed on a chair. There, she found his "emergency" phone, an iPhone X.

She typed in the code from their security system at home, which happily unlocked the device, then quickly searched through the recent phone calls and voicemails, all of which were from someone named "Maria." As she heard the shower water stop, she hit the top text string, also from Maria. The most recent message:

Today 9:25 AM
MARIA
Call me, asshole.

That's funny, Lindsey thought, as she shut off the phone and put it back in Robbie's shorts. *I call him asshole all the time.* She would like to meet this Maria, sooner rather than later. They might have a lot in common.

52. PLAN C

Robbie hovered over his laptop in the study in the east wing of the house, looking at Digby's case for the removal of Walker B. Hope as CEO of Crowe Power Company for the Executive Committee of the Board of Directors. The first slide was brief and to the point: Walker Hope had done the job he was hired to do and it was time for him to go—simple as that. The company needed a new kind of Chief Executive Officer who could take the company to the next level and fulfill Robbie's grand vision. While the details behind such a course were a little fuzzy, it would be up to the next CEO, working hand in hand with the chairman, to formulate a strategy and execute. Fortunately, as the last page showed, they had the perfect candidate already in the building: Timothy J. Padden, unsung hero of the company's recent successes, and a far more compatible figure.

Robbie flipped through the slides before calling Digby. "You didn't quite nail everything, but I guess it's serviceable," Robbie said.

"What did I miss?"

"I think we could use more on what a sustainable future looks like," Robbie said, testily. "There are just a bunch of X's in here."

"I didn't fill that part out because, frankly, I don't know."

"What the hell, Digby. You couldn't pull up one of my speeches?"

"I did. They're a little light on the details."

"C'mon," Robbie said. "I could rattle them off in my sleep. It's all about being more inclusive. More caring. More environmentally friendly. Blah, blah, blah."

"I got the blah, blah, blah part."

"Throw in some stuff about 'less pollution.'"

"You know, if we shut down all of our plants," Digby said, "they won't pollute at all."

"And maybe if I fire you right now, you won't have to worry about helping me anymore."

"Not the worst idea I've heard this weekend."

"Look," Robbie, said, "let's just leave that sustainability stuff at a high level. Tim can figure it out once he's in the chair. He's a smart guy."

"I'm okay with that."

"So here's what I'm thinking about how this goes down. First, I hit Walker right after he delivers the CEO Report."

"How in the world are you going to do that?" Digby asked. "He's going to get up there and say everything's peachy. And he'll have the numbers to back him up."

"That's right. And then I'll blitz him with a bunch of questions that will make him squirm."

"Like what?"

"I don't know," Robbie said. "Maybe something like where we stand with diversity hires. You know, how many women and minorities we have in the company. How many in the management ranks. Stuff like that."

"Do you know the answer?"

"No. But I'm sure he won't either, which is the point. Then I'm going to press him on our carbon emissions. Why are the trend lines so awful? And why hasn't he done something about it?"

"Okay," Digby said. "So you throw a few jabs at him. That doesn't sound like a knock-out."

"No. It doesn't have to be. All I need to do is to wobble him, get him leaning on the ropes. The Executive Committee can finish him off."

"Who on the committee would do that?"

Robbie said, "I'm thinking Carlton."

"I don't see that at all," Digby replied. "Didn't he lecture you about fiduciary responsibility?"

"Yes, he did," Robbie said. "But that also applies to all the business we do with his nice little firm. Shame if something were to happen to it."

53. HARDBALL

Robbie collected himself with deep cleansing breaths—inhale deeply through the nose, exhale through the mouth—before calling Carlton at 6 p.m., when he was known to be served his daily "tonic," on the rocks, in the study of his apartment on Park Avenue. Hitting him at the precise time that he was decompressing couldn't hurt. At the very least, it could make the medicine he was about to administer a little easier to swallow.

"Carlton, I'm calling to say thank you for our meeting the other day. Your counsel and advice have always been so helpful to me."

"It's quite alright, Robbie," Carlton said, sipping his drink. "That's why you have independent directors. Always good to get a little outside perspective."

"Absolutely," Robbie said. "You made me think a lot about fiduciary responsibility."

"Excellent. Glad to be helpful."

"Of course, I was thinking about it in terms of Rothstein Lucas," Robbie said. "It's incredible how many ties there are between my company and my family and your firm and your family going back decades. It's amazing, really, all the interlocking relationships."

"I've always been proud of our association, Robbie. I want to it to stay that way."

"Of course," Robbie said. "You know the feeling is mutual. And I speak not just for myself, but for my entire family. We've been pleased to assist all the grandchildren and nieces and nephews of yours that we've had working at Crowe. We've also been incredibly blessed with the professionalism shown by everyone at your firm for all the contract and litigation work we've awarded you over the years. And, at the center of it all, your terrific work with the Crowe Family Trust, which I know is a significant annuity for your firm."

Carlton paused for a moment before responding. "Yes, and it's deeply appreciated, as I've said many times to you and your uncle. Is there something you're getting at, Robbie? I'm about to leave for dinner."

"Yes, unfortunately," Robbie said, somberly. "I wanted to give you a heads-up on something that's bothering me. There's a bit of agitation from some of the younger family members to consider bidding out the family business." Robbie listened for a response, but heard silence, then continued. "Of course, I've said we can't possibly do that because Carlton is our guy. He's always looked out for the family's best interests as if they were his own. Sure, he may push back a bit at times. That's his job. But when I let it be known that we need to move on an issue because it is for the clear benefit of our family, he *always* defers to our judgment. Always. And it's because of him that Rothstein Lucas & Pratt has kept our family business for so long. It's been what? Forty-two years? Carlton knows when it's time to speak, and when it's time to listen. And when it's time to act. Like now."

Carlton said flatly, "Let's get it on the table, Robbie."

"I can't defend you any longer if you don't have my back."

"And the only way to demonstrate my allegiance is to give you my vote?"

"That's a start," Robbie said.

"You want more?" Carlton asked.

"Following the CEO Report to the Board tomorrow, I plan to raise a number of questions about areas that I think Walker has neglected against my express wishes. Afterward, I want you to offer a motion for an emergency meeting of the Executive Committee."

"Where you want a vote of no confidence."

"If that's the judgment of the committee, as I assume it will be after they see the presentation you'll give them. Aside from Jayne and Harvey, all the other outside directors will follow your lead. And I'm confident you'll vote your conscience."

"And the crown will be restored."

"Board willing."

Robbie could hear Carlton's ice cubes clinking in his glass. *He had him.* "When exactly do you want me to do this, Robbie?"

"Wait until I've gone through my questions," Robbie said. "When I feel the time is right, I'll give you a sign."

54. THE AUDITION

A butler ushered Tim Padden into the dining room of Chuck and Sylvia Crowe's plush apartment on Park Avenue, where he was met by Chuck, with his ever-present crystal glass of Johnnie Walker Blue, and Robbie, holding a glass of Chateau Margaux.

"Thank you, boys, for coming out on a Sunday night," Chuck said, as he indicated Tim should take a chair in the middle of the dining table, where he encountered a befuddling array of stemware, china and utensils.

"I'm very glad to be here," Tim said, looking around at the elegant space, with spotlighted paintings by Picasso and Modigliani. "Beautiful room."

"I had a little help from Ralph Lauren."

"Ah, of course," Tim said with a knowing smile. "The store on Madison?"

"No. Ralph."

"I see."

"Longtime friend of the family," Chuck said with a shrug as he reached for his scotch. "Would you like a drink?"

Tim looked up to the uniformed waiter who suddenly appeared at his arm. "I'd like a Coke, please."

Chuck cast an arched eyebrow to Robbie, which Tim noticed. *This guy doesn't drink?*

"School night," Tim said.

"You have homework?" Chuck asked.

"I think this is it," Robbie said with a laugh, trying to lighten the mood.

Tim tried to shift the subject. "I love the music," he offered.

"If I'm not mistaken, that's The Four Seasons," Robbie said.

"Really?" Tim said, with surprise. "From *Jersey Boys*?"

"Vivaldi," Chuck said.

"Ah. Right," Tim said, sheepishly.

"Frankie Vivaldi," Chuck said, drily. "Remember him? Lead singer, I think."

Tim laughed uneasily. "*I'm Working My Way Back to You.*"

"Let's see how close you get," Chuck said with a sinister smile.

Robbie reached over and patted Tim's arm. If he didn't rescue him soon, Tim would be tossed before the salad.

"Uncle Chuck, I think it would be interesting for you to hear a bit about Tim's background. The ties he has with our family are incredible."

Tim nodded. "That's right. Thanks, Robbie. My family history goes way back with your company. In fact, my great-great-grandfather worked in the Ohio River power plant in Steubenville back in the 1930s."

"You don't say," said Chuck, taking a drag on a cigarette.

"And the funny thing is, he actually met Homer Crowe."

"No kidding," Chuck said. "So did I."

"He was working on a boiler when Homer Crowe came by on a tour of the plant. Mr. Crowe stopped and asked him what he was doing. They even talked briefly about the boiler and its mechanics, which seemed to delight Mr. Crowe. Great-Granddad was so impressed by his interest not only in the machine but in him. It was quite remarkable. And it made a lasting impression."

"That's very touching," Chuck said flatly.

"He never forgot it."

Chuck shrugged. "I'm sure Homer did. But that was him, alright—a lot more interested in boilers than anything else, including his kids. My grandfather barely knew him. I think he saw him about as often as your great-grandfather did."

Tim knitted his brow in concern. "That doesn't sound very good."

"No. It wasn't. Then again, we come from a long line of people who didn't know how to be parents."

"I'm genuinely sorry to hear that. I mean, the love of a strong parent—"

Chuck cut him off. "Yeah, right. So tell me, Tim. You've talked with Robbie about the possibility of becoming CEO. Why would you want a job like that?"

"Well, first of all, I have to say it's an honor to even be considered," Tim said. "To follow in the footsteps of giants such as Homer Crowe, your brother Les, and so many others would be very, very humbling."

"Uh-huh," Chuck said.

"But, quite honestly, the thing that intrigues me most is the opportunity to help Robbie fulfill his remarkable vision," Tim said, casting a glance toward Robbie, who nodded eagerly. "We've talked an awful lot about the direction of the company, and I have to say there's absolutely no daylight between us. Robbie, as chairman, has laid out a very compelling vision for the company's future. As the Chief Executive, my job would be, quite simply, to execute."

Chuck exhaled a stream of blue smoke and nodded. "And what, exactly, is your interpretation of that vision?"

"As Robbie has said many times, I think we have to be responsible citizens," Tim said. "We have to consider more than our shareholders and think about the communities where we operate, the welfare of our employees, and the impact we make on this planet we call home."

"Well, I suppose it's home for me at least a little while longer. What I'd like to know is how all that stakeholder stuff makes money. A lot of us in the family have grown rather fond of our income."

"With all due respect, sir, I don't think doing well and doing good are mutually exclusive," Tim said. "It can be done in a smart, thoughtful way. We can't cling to the old ways. We need to embrace the future and anticipate where society's going. Fact is, I don't believe we can expect the same levels of profitability from our traditional plants that we've had in the recent past. We need to diversify our portfolio and get ahead in areas like renewable energy."

"Like BlowCo?"

"That was ill-considered," Tim said, casting another glance toward Robbie. "Notwithstanding the difficulties of getting a permit, there was no line of sight into profitability there."

Robbie interjected. "Uncle Chuck, you know Walker was just trying to stick it up my ass."

"Yes, and his aim was pretty good."

"Not from my end," Robbie said.

"No," Chuck conceded. "It must hurt to sit down."

Robbie winced. "Walker has no real interest in BlowCo or anything like it. Never has and never will."

Chuck turned to Tim. "Would you agree with that assessment?"

"Walker's all about the plan," Tim said. "If it's not in the plan, he just doesn't care."

"That's why he's got to go," Robbie said, "and why Tim needs to take over."

"The bottom line," Tim said, "is exactly what Robbie said when we first started talking about this. He doesn't need the best CEO in America. That's very narrow thinking. He needs the best CEO for the *planet.*"

Chuck burst out laughing. "And what planet would that be?"

Tim looked puzzled. "Why, Earth, of course."

Chuck sighed and pushed himself up from the chair. "I should be relieved, I suppose, you didn't name somewhere else, like Pluto."

"That's technically not a planet," Tim said.

"No," Chuck said. "And you're technically not the CEO, either."

55. THE REVIEW

When dinner was over, Tim shook hands with Robbie and Chuck and was guided out by the butler, leaving the Crowe scions alone in the dining room. Chuck lit a cigarette with his silver lighter, leaned against a chair and looked at Robbie with a squint.

"Really, Robbie?" he said, blowing smoke out his nose.

"What?"

"You think this guy's better than Walker?" Chuck asked. "He's been carrying Walker's bags the past 10 years."

"He's been the power behind the throne."

"Maybe there's a reason he's *behind* the throne," Chuck said. "I gotta tell you: I'm not impressed. He's got the sense of a walnut."

"I think he was nervous."

"He wasn't too nervous to pucker his lips. Good lord. He sounds like a man whose primary skill is butt-smooching. Now, sensing an opportunity to move up, he's decided to kiss your ass instead of Walker's. Not the worst call on his part, but fairly obvious. I mean, c'mon. 'Best CEO for the planet?' Who's he trying to kid?"

"Look, Uncle Chuck," Robbie said, "I need someone who gets the vision. Someone who can execute it. Walker is very limited."

"Walker turned the damn company around," Chuck said. "I don't see what's so limiting about that."

"That's great. But his bag of tricks is empty. Tim," Robbie said, indicating the door with his thumb, "has another whole bag."

"He didn't bring it with him tonight. Maybe he checked it with the doorman."

"Uncle Chuck, I'm with these guys every day. I see them in action. Tim's the real deal. He's been living in Walker's shadow for so long. He's bursting to prove himself."

Chuck turned away, pacing at the table, his hands plunged into his pockets. "I wish I could say I see what enthralls you. I don't."

Robbie followed Chuck around the table, pleading. "We don't have to make this decision tonight. All I ask is that you keep an open mind. You know I want nothing more than to do the right thing for this company and for our family. That's all."

"Your motives are pure?" Chuck said, his tongue in his cheek.

"Take me out of the equation, alright? Because this isn't about me. It is about our company's long-term sustainability. About our children and our grandchildren and our great-grandchildren—"

Chuck interjected. "Right. And their cats and dogs and pet turtles. I've heard all this before. What happens when you get sick of this new guy in a couple years?"

"Honestly?" Robbie said. "I don't see that happening."

"I do. I've seen it plenty of times already. And I'm not picking on you, Robbie. It's part of our family tradition. Crowe executives have been as disposable as the garbage. Although, I could see Walker getting recycled somewhere. He's a man of considerable talent."

"And you know what? I don't really care. He can go wherever the hell he wants to go. I just want him to go. Period."

"Alright," Chuck said, stubbing out his cigarette. "I tell you what. I believe that a chairman has to have his team around him, people he or she believes in. So how about this? You put this issue in front of the Executive Committee tomorrow. See what they think. If they're on board, I won't stand in your way."

56. BITS AND PIECES

L indsey parted the curtains in the second-floor study and watched the taillights of Robbie's chauffeur-driven Escalade disappear to the west on 67th Street toward Fifth Avenue, then picked up her phone and dialed her sister-in-law, Bits.

"You free for brunch this morning?"

"C'mon, honey. I'm *always* free for brunch. You know that," Bits said. "I have my physical therapist coming over at 9, and he is totally hot, so I don't intend to miss it. But I'm clear by 10:30 or so. What's your pleasure? Breakfast at Tiffany's?"

"Depends. Is their bar open?"

"Oh dear."

"Oh yeah," Lindsey said. "How about the Carlyle? Might take a while to get bombed on mimosas, but I'm fairly determined."

Mid-morning, they slid into a corner banquette and ordered the basic Carlyle American Breakfast for $42 each, along with a round of mimosas. As the waiter theatrically fluttered white linen napkins in the air and draped them over their laps, Bits leaned over and put her hand on the back of Lindsey's. "So your weekend in the Hamptons didn't turn out like you planned."

"Not at all," Lindsey said sadly. "My marriage is hanging by a thread. And, I think, so is my sanity."

Bits sighed. "I don't know what to suggest now," she said. "I'm out of tricks."

"Robbie isn't. I found out he's been having an affair with a woman named Maria, a lawyer at the company. She works for Digby."

"*No.*"

"Yes," Lindsey said. "Funny thing is—except I'm not laughing—she doesn't seem to be any happier with him than I am. I saw a text on his phone where she called him an asshole."

"Sounds like you have something in common."

"That's what I'm thinking."

The drinks were brought on a silver tray and placed on the tabletop. "Bottoms up," Lindsey said, before downing the beverage and swirling her index finger in the air to signal another round.

"Wow," Bits said, watching Lindsey dab her mouth with the napkin. "That was impressive."

"Lots of practice lately."

"I don't think I've ever seen you like this," Bits observed.

"Get used to it," Lindsey said, flatly.

"Lindsey. I am so sorry. I know you're in real pain. But, please, *please*, don't torture yourself."

"I don't consider champagne torture exactly. But I would like to torture somebody."

"Fine," Bits said. "Torture *him.* It's not that hard, you know. When we were growing up, I beat the daylights out of Robbie on a regular basis. He was so scared around me that he put a special lock on his bedroom door. He's quite the wimp if you press him. And he's especially afraid of girls. Mother. Nanny Esther. Me. Maybe that's why he tries so hard to be such a puffed-up alpha dog."

"Overcompensating?" Lindsey asked.

"I suppose. There's a little man inside him."

"Well, there's a little man on the outside, too."

"Oh, I know," Bits said with a laugh. "I've seen the original equipment. I was relieved to grow up and see they weren't all like that."

They clinked glasses.

"So," Lindsey said, "here's the question that kept me up all night. How should I confront him?"

Bits laughed. "Oh, *no, no, no,* dear. That's not your job. Crowe women don't do the dirty work. That's for someone else."

"Like?"

"Let *her* do it."

"Her?" Lindsey asked.

"The other woman," Bits said. "Marie, Maria. Whatever her name is. Let her know, in your own civilized way, that you're on to her and to him. Tell her you've had enough of Robbie and she can have ol' 'asshole' for herself. I'm sure she'd take it from there. Then he can decide whether he truly wants to stay married or not."

Lindsey nodded, pointedly picking up her mimosa and placing it across the table, out of reach. "I wonder if Maria would like to join me for tea today."

"Do you have her number?"

"You bet I do," Lindsey said. "And I have his number, too."

57. MAKING AN ENTRANCE

W ith protests continuing in front of Crowe World Headquarters on Broad Street, board directors were diverted to the service entrance on New Street, a narrow alley between Wall Street and Beaver that was typically the province of delivery trucks, dumpsters, and service workers and students taking smoke breaks. The morning air carried the aroma of wet pavement, garbage, cigarettes, and weed.

Tom Michaels' security crew swept the area of the homeless and their bags and shopping carts as soon as the sun came up. Now Tom and half his team stood sentry at the company's back door, overseeing the line of black limousines squeezing through the alley to drop off the stiff, elderly directors. The other half kept an eye on the protests out front and scanned the sidewalks, doorways, and windows of New Street for signs of disruption.

The arriving board members represented a veritable *Who's Who in America*, circa 1993. At one time, they were among the foremost leaders of American business, government, academia, and philanthropy. There were former cabinet secretaries and senators, retired CEOs from celebrated companies, a university president and the current chairman of the Africa Electrification Project. Most of the directors had transitioned out of their leadership roles a decade or more earlier and were now battling the infirmities of old age, but they were loyal and well-compensated friends of the family, and exceedingly wealthy thanks to their accumulations of Crowe stock, which appreciated smartly under Walker's leadership.

Natalia, at Robbie's request, was helping Winnie guide the directors through the back entrance of the building to the express elevator that would take them to the 24th floor and the Gertrude H. Crowe Board Room, named for Homer Crowe's sainted mother.

"It's a wonderful board," Winnie noted in reverent tones. "You're about to meet some of the world's most distinguished people."

"I hear 'extinguished' is more like it," Natalia said.

"Don't let Mr. Crowe hear you say that," Winnie said sharply.

"He's the one who told me."

"Well, he should know better. These are very, very fine people. They go back a long way with the company, and many of them are personal friends of the family. They deserve Mr. Crowe's respect—and, I would think, yours."

Natalia shrugged. "I suppose they're kind of cute, in a way. But, honestly, it looks like most of them are well past their prime."

On cue, a black Lincoln Town Car pulled up to the curb with Carlton Lucas sunken into the back seat. His dead weight required the muscle of three security guards to extract him. With a "one-two-three" and a heave-ho, they pushed from behind and pulled from the front to remove him from the car. Tom steadied Carlton on the sidewalk while Winnie greeted him like a long-lost friend.

"Mr. Lucas," she said, sweetly. "What a pleasure to see you."

"Whew," Carlton wheezed, as the driver rushed around the car and handed him his brass-handle cane. "Wasn't sure I was going to make it. Let me just... stand here... a, a second... catch... my... breath."

Tom said. "Take your time, sir."

Winnie squeezed Tom's forearm and talked close to his ear. "Robbie wants to make sure Carlton is handled with extra care. Take him up, will you? Don't put him through the revolving door. You remember what happened last time. And make sure he gets all the way up into the Board Room. If he needs to go the bathroom, please go in with him and make sure he comes out—and that he's cleaned up, if you know what I mean."

Tom nodded and took Carlton by the arm. Behind him, Willard Clark, the 91-year old former Secretary of the Interior under Reagan, who had been exceedingly helpful in suspending regulations to secure pollution permits for Crowe plants in the West, exited the front seat of a Lincoln Navigator. Willard was helped down to the sidewalk, while the driver retrieved a walker from the back and snapped it into place on the curb. Winnie then helped steady him.

"Mr. Clark, we are so glad you could be here," Winnie said.

"I'm glad to be anywhere," he said, before stopping suddenly and looking around the street. "Where the hell am I?"

"This is the back entrance to our building," Winnie said. "We have protesters out front."

He dismissed them with a wave of his hand. "I don't need to see those rascals. And they sure as hell don't need to see me."

Winnie whispered to Natalia. "Stay with him. He always wants to go off to the cafeteria. He can't. Tell him there are bagels in the Board Room. That will get him moving in the right direction." Natalia nodded and walked over to meet Willard. "Good morning, Mr. Clark. I'm Natalia and I work with Mr. Crowe."

Willard looked up in foggy surprise. "Homer?"

"No," she said. "Robbie Crowe, our chairman."

"You don't have to tell me," Willard said, with a laugh. "The young fella. I knew him when he was in short pants."

Virtually all the "independent" directors in the funeral-like procession of black cars down New Street were deeply dependent on the good graces of the company and the family, which had much to do with their wealth, status and power. There was Melvyn Somers, the former CEO and current stockholder of Appalachian Coal Corp, a major supplier to Crowe Power; Tommy MacDonald, once the head of Bear Stearns, but who now served as a trustee of the charitable Crowe Family Foundation at a generous stipend; Virginia Einholz, the former governor of Delaware, whose support for a power plant on the Delaware River earned her a seat on the board when she was defeated for re-election; and Waylon Frazier, Chairman of the Africa Electrification Project, whose principal financial benefactor was the Crowe Corporate Fund. As Robbie's father once told him: "They all know where their buns are buttered."

When the directors emerged from the elevator upstairs, they made their way slowly through the Hall of Fam toward the double-door entrance to the Board Room, where Robbie and Chuck were having a last-minute confab.

"Whatever happens," Chuck said, "you can't let this look like some sort of personal vendetta against Walker."

"Of course not," Robbie said, biting a nail. "I totally get that. It's like *The Godfather*. This isn't personal. It's business."

"Don't lose your cool."

"Why would I? There's nothing to get emotional about. It's all about the facts."

58. SHOWDOWN

The Board Room, built in 1927 to the specifications of the illustrious founder, was a meticulously maintained mahogany-paneled sanctuary overlooking Lower Manhattan, the East River, Brooklyn, and the Rockaways, with the Atlantic Ocean reflecting a sparkling morning sun in the distance. Opposite the windows was a gallery of black-and-white historic photographs representing the company's lines of business: power plants, pipelines, refineries, trucks, and tankers. A massive screen with a giant logo of Crowe Power in certified Broad Street Blue dominated one end of the long room. At the other end was a buffet with uniformed servers, where Natalia directed Willard, who was greeted by Chuck and Robbie.

"Willard, my old friend," Chuck said, warmly.

"Not *too* old, Chuck," Willard said, before peering quizzically at Robbie. *Who the hell was that guy?*

Chuck noticed Willard's puzzlement. "Willard, you remember Robbie."

"Oh, yes. Of course, I do," he said, expansively. "My knees are gone, not my mind."

"That's the spirit," Chuck said. "How was your flight?"

Willard's head snapped back and he eyed Chuck suspiciously. "From where?"

"Weren't you coming from West Palm?" Chuck suggested.

"By golly," Willard said with a wink, "I bet you're right."

"We're just very glad you could make it," Robbie said. "We have a very full agenda and we'll definitely need your perspective."

"Glad to do my part. When's lunch?"

"One o'clock, as usual," Robbie said.

Willard nodded. "Well then, I guess we better get going."

Now Robbie was confused. "Where?"

"To *lunch*," Willard said incredulously. "What the hell do you *think* I'm talking about?"

"It's only 10 o'clock, Willard," Chuck said.

"Alright. I give up," he said with a laugh. "You New Yorkers and your late lunches." He looked to Robbie. "Can you help me find my seat, young man?"

Robbie rolled his eyes and whispered to his uncle. "He has no idea what I do here."

"Why should he be any different than the rest of us?" Chuck said. He turned to greet Barbara Butler, the former CEO of the old Mid-Atlantic Power & Light. Barbara had earned her lifetime seat on the board by approving Crowe Power's takeover of her company in 1991 at a very favorable price. She'd been collecting dividends from Crowe ever since.

"I hope to God this isn't a long one today," she said in a whisper. "My flight to Scottsdale's at 5."

Chuck looked at his watch. "That might be cutting it close. We'll do what we can to move things along."

"Please do," she said. "I'm in a golf tournament tomorrow morning."

Willard clutched Robbie's upper arm and Robbie took baby steps as they made their way toward his seat in the back of the room next to Carlton. "Don't walk so damn fast," Willard said.

Robbie, exasperated, caught Natalia's eye and motioned her over. She took Willard from Robbie and eased him into a large leather swivel chair. As she helped lift his legs and swing them around under the table, he steadied himself with a shaky hand on her lower back, which he then slid south to her ass, where he felt her left cheek.

"Mr. Clark," she said firmly. "I believe you've misplaced something."

"What?" he said, concerned.

"Your sense of propriety," she said, grabbing his wrist and placing it on the armrest.

"It was worth it," he said, with a leer.

"It won't be if you do it again," Natalia said before leaning over and whispering in his ear. "I don't give a damn who you are or how old you are. You try that again and I'll break your fingers. Got it?"

Willard shrunk into his seat like a turtle. "That's pretty clear," he said.

"Good," she said. "Now. May I get you some water or coffee?"

Robbie slid over to Carlton, who was settled into a plush leather chair. Robbie gently patted him on the shoulder. "Good morning, Carlton."

"Robbie," Carlton said quietly.

"So glad we had a chance to catch up yesterday," Robbie said. "I really appreciate your support."

Carlton nodded solemnly as he looked up. "I owe a lot to you and your family, Robbie," he said. "I'm not an ungrateful man."

Robbie patted him like a good doggie and walked to the front of the room, where Tim Padden, Anna Pachulski, and other senior executives were taking their place on the smaller, stiff-backed chairs along the windows, where they could be seen but not heard, unless absolutely necessary. Natalia was accorded a chair, as well, per Robbie's instruction, so that she could bear witness to Robbie's masterful leadership.

Robbie took his place at the head of the table, with his Uncle Chuck seated at his right, and Walker on his left. Walker sat up ramrod straight and methodically leafed through his three-inch thick binder, with a special focus on the Appendix, refreshing his memory on every conceivable fact that might be asked of him. Today, Walker knew, was far less about the directors' satisfaction with the company's performance; the desired outcome would depend more on his *own* performance. Satisfied that he was as ready as he'd ever be, he closed the binder, folded his hands on his lap, and took long deep breaths.

Robbie waited for delivery of his Bolivian Jungle Roast coffee from Café Che before bringing the meeting to order a few minutes after 10. He offered a welcome to the directors and guests, with a discreet nod to Natalia, who sat impassively next to Digby. He then provided the room with an overview of the agenda: Walker on the company's progress against its plan; CFO Anna Pachulski on the financial forecast, international tax issues and the prospect of an upgrade in the company's credit rating; Digby on a variety of legal matters, including the stalled New Jersey pipeline; and Human Resources Vice-President Jasmine Holmes previewing an employee video on the company's newly adopted Core Values of "Teamwork" and "Collaboration," along with a rundown on the next three rounds of job cuts.

"With that, I'd like to turn it over to our CEO. Walker?" Robbie said.

"Thank you, Robbie and good morning, everyone," Walker said, jovially, as he stood at the lectern next to the screen and clicked on the first of forty-six PowerPoint slides. "So excited to see everyone here again. I'm very happy to share with you today our team's excellent progress against our plan."

Robbie abandoned his chair in front of the screen and walked toward the back, where he leaned against the buffet while Walker led the directors through an exhaustive but impressive litany of achievements. Virtually every objective for the year was on track, save the stalled pipeline in New Jersey, and much of the forecasted results exceeded the initial goals. Revenues and profits were predicted to come in twenty percent higher for the year, and costs were projected to land four percent lower if they could wrench some concessions from the steelworkers' union.

"If we can continue to avoid unscheduled downtime at our refineries, we expect to significantly exceed the Street's estimates for earnings. So much so, in fact, that I would recommend we update our guidance for the year," Walker said. "And, given the strong macroeconomy, we see no reason why these positive trends can't continue into next year."

All the directors except Robbie applauded as Walker laid down the clicker and stepped off to the side.

"Really impressive, Walker," Chuck said, casting an I-told-you-so glance toward Robbie in the back.

"Thank you, Chuck," Walker said, before noting Robbie's gloomy puss. "I'm happy to answer any questions."

Robbie caught Natalia's eye, then stepped up toward the table and put a hand on the back of Carlton's chair, where Carlton appeared to be in deep slumber. "Walker, it's clear we're hitting our milestones, but I can't help wondering: Are these the *right* milestones?"

"Not sure what you mean, Robbie," Walker said politely. "This is the plan approved by this board in December."

"Right. And this board represents our shareholders. But what about all the people who have an interest in our environmental and social performance? I didn't see anything in there about ESG."

At the back of the room, Willard looked past the napping Carlton to Barbara, and asked, "What's he talking about? Is that the stuff in Chinese food?"

Barbara shook her head, annoyed, and whispered back. "I have no idea, and frankly, I don't care. If we don't get moving, I'm going to miss my flight."

Walker stepped behind the lectern. "We cover Environment, Social and Governance in our Corporate Sustainability Report," he said, picking up the most recent copy from his briefing materials and holding it aloft.

"I'm aware, but I'm not persuaded that's nearly enough," Robbie said, tartly, as he began to pace. "We pat ourselves on the back for printing this catalogue of facts and figures on recycled paper that we put on coffee tables in the lobby of Headquarters. Then we call it a day and that's it until next year. Nobody reads it."

Walker took a deep breath to maintain his composure. "Is that our fault?"

"No. But it's our problem. I don't think issuing a report no one reads is enough anymore. Not when people expect so much more out of us. We need to be thinking about these issues *every day*. They need to be integrated into the way we do business. Our vision has got to be bigger than quarterly profitability."

Waylon Frazier, head of the African Electrification Project, raised his hand and Walker nodded toward him. "I just want to say I'm proud to be associated with this company, which is a pretty damn good corporate citizen. We write out all kinds of checks for education and infrastructure projects in communities where we operate—and I mean all over the world. What did we spend last year? Forty million dollars?"

"Forty-three," Walker said.

"I think the problem is we don't get enough credit for that," Waylon said. "If we do, I sure don't see it."

"I appreciate that, Waylon, but it's not just about getting credit," Robbie said, walking along the bank of windows, closer to Natalia, who was leaning forward, engrossed. "It's not about writing checks. It's about doing the *right thing*. That doesn't seem to be part of our vocabulary."

Jayne Willson, one of Moe's proxies, cleared her throat before speaking. "I'm not sure I understand the threat here, Robbie. Are we really worried about making that scruffy crowd of protesters happy? Because I don't think we can. We're much more useful to them as an enemy. They raise money by making us out to be the bad guys."

"And we give them the ammo to shoot us. Half of our power plants still burn coal."

"Right—*clean* coal," Jayne said.

"Let's not kid ourselves, Jayne," Robbie said. "There's no such thing."

"Fine. Clean-*er*. How's that?" Jayne said. "It's all relative."

"Yes, I suppose, like clean Agent Orange," Robbie said.

"I've seen a number of companies set a target for when they won't use coal any longer," said Melvyn Somers. "Why don't we set a deadline for ourselves? Armstrong Power just announced they set a target for 2050. That sounds about right to me."

"We should do the same damn thing," Chuck said. "If we fall short, hell, they can reach me at Forest Lawn."

There was laughter around the room—except from Robbie. "Walker, I'd like to know your view," Robbie said.

Walker looked up at the ceiling for a moment. Then he turned back to the room. "Here's what I would suggest," he said. "Let's consider setting some goals in this area for next year in our business plan. Robbie, we'd be honored to have you participate in the planning process. You clearly have a lot of passion around this issue. Your leadership would be most welcome."

"We can't *wait* until next year," Robbie said. "The world is in crisis *right now*. Angry mobs are protesting outside our office every single day. They want to know what we're going to do about it and when we're going to do it. We can't throw them a Corporate Sustainability Report and say that's it."

"What would you like us to do?" asked Harvey Mandelbaum, Moe's other proxy. "Bring the protesters inside? Have a chai and a chat?"

Robbie looked to Natalia, who appeared to be hanging on every word, then back to Harvey. "In a word: yes. I think we should be talking to them."

"You can't negotiate with those people," Harvey said. "They're savages."

"We can and we should," Robbie said. "It's important to find out what they want." *Was Natalia smiling?* It sure looked like it. He was becoming a… genuine hero! The People's Champion!

Jayne scoffed. "Robbie, I hope you're kidding. We know what they want: money. Once they stick that needle in your arm, you'll never get it out again."

Robbie was tiring of the argument. It was time to get moving. He looked to Carlton to give him the high sign to call for an emergency meeting of the Executive Committee, but the old coot was still snoozing. *The senile old fuck!*

"I'd like to know something, Robbie," Harvey said. "Exactly where do you think we're coming up short?"

Robbie, face reddening, was now officially agitated, first by the discussion, second by the unflappable Walker, and third by Rip van Carlton. *Wake up, you double-crossing bastard!* "I think we're coming up short everywhere," Robbie said. "Take a look at the back of the Sustainability Report where we bury all the numbers."

"The numbers aren't buried, Robbie," Walker said. "They're printed, for the whole wide world to see. We're as transparent as can be."

Robbie walked toward the front of the room, standing on the other side of the screen from Walker.

"Really. What do the numbers tell *you?*"

"Why, they indicate to me that we're makin' steady progress. We're not perfect, but our performance is constantly improvin'."

"*Improving?* We're at bottom of our industry. Our SOx sucks. Our NOx is noxious. We're putting enough carbon into the air to warm several planets."

Walker remained calm—was that a *smirk?* —pissing off Robbie even more. Said Walker, "We're gettin' *better*, Robbie, which is the goal. It's all part of our plan."

"*Screw* the plan! Better isn't good enough. Don't you get it? How many times do I have to say this?" Robbie, exasperated, turned to the directors. "Don't you see what's going on here? It's all about deferring the tough decisions. And you can do that when you're a short-timer, like him. I can't. I'm here for the long haul. That's my name on all that crap that's coming out of our stacks out there."

"Yes," Walker said. "And all that money that's coming in, too."

Now Robbie was seething. "I don't give a good goddamn about the money. I care about making a commitment to change. And that starts at the top."

"You mean, with you?" Walker said.

The fucking troll! "No," Robbie said. "You."

"I don't follow. What is it, exactly, that's botherin' you?"

Robbie leaned over and balled his fists onto the table, scowling at Walker. "THIS is what's bothering me," he said. "*I can't... fucking... STAND YOU!*"

Though he knew Robbie harbored animosity, to hear it expressed so vehemently made Walker feel like he'd been punched in the mouth. There was a shuffling of chairs and Chuck quickly got to his feet, pulling Robbie away. "Maybe we should take a break."

Robbie looked up and gathered himself. "Hold on. Sorry. It's okay. I, uh... I think I saw Carlton raise his hand back there. Let's hear what he has to say."

He looked to the back of the room, where Carlton's head drooped onto his chest. Robbie nodded to Barbara, who turned to Carlton and gently shook him by the shoulder, which sent Carlton tumbling into the conference table, his forehead slamming into the wood. *Whomp!*

"Oh my *God!*" she shrieked.

Suddenly, everyone was up and rushing to the back of the room. Digby thrust open the door and shouted, *"We need help in here!"* In the hallway, a medical crew on standby for just such an emergency came rushing down the hall with resuscitation equipment, with orderlies pushing a gurney.

Inside the Board Room, the directors made way as the leader of the medical team, Dr. Deevey, rushed to Carlton's side. He felt Carlton's temple, which was ice cold, and his right wrist, which was extended across the table, and the carotid arteries in his neck. He reached a stethoscope under the table and pushed it up to his chest. Digby and Robbie stood nearby, watching anxiously, as the doctor stood and put his stethoscope slowly back into his coat pocket.

"I'm sorry. He's gone."

"Gone?" Chuck said. "Are you sure?"

"I would say he's been dead for approximately an hour."

"Oh, lord. We thought he was asleep," Barbara said.

"I take it he doesn't usually say a lot in meetings?" the doctor said.

"He was definitely more quiet than usual," she said.

"Understandable," the doctor said. "Considering that, you know, he's dead."

"Yes. That certainly explains a lot," Barbara said.

Willard shook his head. "I bet it was that damn PowerPoint presentation. Could have killed anybody."

Robbie pulled Digby off to the corner near the window, where they spoke with hands over their mouths. "Okay, Mr. Board Secretary. What the hell do we do now?"

Digby shrugged. "I have no freaking clue. Want me to check my *Robert's Rules of Order*?"

"I can't believe this," Robbie said, biting a nail. "He couldn't live long enough to make the motion I wanted? He died just to pimp me."

"Of course," Digby said. "It's amazing the lengths people will go to disappoint you."

"Well, you tell me. How the hell do I get them into an Executive Committee now?"

Digby looked over at the prostrate Carlton and cocked his head to the side. "I suppose we could consider the way his arm was going up. Kind of looks like he was about to raise his hand."

Robbie looked over. "Oh my god. You're *right!* It does look like that. Maybe we should make a chalk outline and take a picture?"

"Stop it, Robbie. I was joking."

"Can't we just say Carlton was about to make a motion?"

"When he's *dead?* Don't be ridiculous," Digby said.

"Well, we've got to do something. I can't take this anymore."

"Forget it. It can't happen now. You're stuck with Walker, at least for now."

They were interrupted by a voice at their back. "Not necessarily," Walker said.

59. PEACE IN OUR TIME

Walker followed Robbie and Digby into the pantry next to the Board Room and closed the door. Robbie leaned against a counter loaded with extra trays of fruits, muffins and bagels, while Digby sat on a steel chair and Walker closed the door behind them.

"I'll go," Walker said, "under the right terms."

Robbie exhaled deeply. *Thank you, sweet Jesus.* "Look, I'm sorry it got a little ugly in there," he said. "I don't know what got into me."

"No apologies needed. I'm a big boy," Walker said. "Last thing I want to do is stay at a company where I'm no longer welcome. And it's clear I'm not welcome here anymore. We all have a 'sell-by' date. Looks like I'm past mine. Time to move on."

Digby said, "What did you mean by 'right terms?'"

"Let's keep it simple. I want this to be an amicable parting of ways, just as you do," Walker said. "We'll call it a resignation, not a termination. But I want a package akin to what I would get if I were fired without cause. Full salary, bonus, and benefits for the next two years. A pension that begins immediately. Complete vesting of all my shares. A press release announcing my departure that I get to approve."

Robbie nodded with relief and looked to Digby. "Check, check, check," Robbie said. "I'd call that a deal."

"Not quite," Walker said. "I also want a release from my non-compete agreement."

"Hold on," Digby said, standing up. "Does that mean you're going to a competitor?"

"With all due respect, Digby," he said with a smile that looked more like a snarl, "it's none of your business what I do once I leave this building. Now, if you don't want me to leave…"

Robbie, alarmed, pulled on Digby's arm. "I don't think that's a big deal."

Digby shook his head. "Robbie, I think we should discuss this."

"No," Robbie said emphatically. "I've had enough discussion. I think, for the good of all concerned, we just need to move ahead quickly and get this behind us. If that's what Walker needs, then I say give it to him."

Walker approached Robbie and extended his hand. Robbie regarded it as if he had just been offered a dead hamster, but he took it nevertheless.

"I just want to say thank you," Walker said. "It's been a good run."

"Good luck," Robbie said. "Seriously."

"Hope you get that color thing straightened out."

Robbie sniffed. "I'm sure Tim will handle it."

"He's got the skills for it, no doubt."

"He probably gives a shit, too," Robbie said. "Which is something I value even more."

"I'll be watching you guys," Walker said, as he opened the door. "I'm still a shareholder, you know."

A triumphant smile spread across Robbie's face. "As am I."

Walker nodded, wistfully. "Don't I know it."

60. COME ON AND CELEBRATE

Robbie found a bottle of Dom Perignon in his office wine cooler and some dusty champagne flutes in the pantry cupboard. He held one up for Natalia to see. "Apparently, we haven't had reason to celebrate around here for some time," he said, jovially.

"I'll rinse those if you want to pop the cork," Natalia said.

Robbie removed the wire and the crumbling foil and pushed the cork off with his thumbs, sending it into the ceiling as champagne gushed out of the bottle. Natalia caught as much as she could in their two glasses and gave one to Robbie.

"Congratulations," she said. "May this be the start of a new era for Crowe Power."

"With your help, it will be," Robbie said, as they clinked glasses. "From here on, we're going to take a very different path. It may get rough at times, but I think we can do some serious good here."

The intercom buzzed, prompting Robbie to shake his head wearily. *It's always something.* "Mr. Crowe," Winnie said, "Maria Territo is on her way up to see you."

"Oh, for God's sake," Robbie said in disgust before pressing the button. "Tell her she can't see me now. I'm in a meeting. I'll call her later."

"Yes, sir," Winnie said.

"Who's that?" Natalia asked.

"Maria? Nobody. Just a lawyer downstairs. She's handled some of my personal things, and I guess she feels that gives her the right to just drop by anytime. And the fact is, she can't. There are protocols that we have to follow around here to keep order. Otherwise, what would we have? Chaos, right?"

Robbie grabbed the champagne bottle, walked over to the sofa, and sat down, throwing his head back. Natalia followed and sat in the chair next to him.

"Let's not worry about her," Robbie said. "How do you think I did?"

"You got the result you wanted. Can't get better than that."

"Right. But I mean me. How do you think I handled it? I stood up for the protesters. You saw that for yourself."

"I did. And I must say, I was impressed. That was not the kind of dialogue I would ever expect to see in the boardroom of a company like Crowe Power."

Robbie smiled. "Isn't that *exactly* what I promised the crowd out there on Broad Street?" he said, pointing vaguely toward the east. "They probably thought I was kidding. Now you know. I mean what I say."

"Witness," she said, raising her right hand.

"Cheers to that," he said, clinking glasses again and drinking before pouring them each some more and reflecting. "I almost felt sorry for Walker. Poor bastard didn't know what hit him. He probably thought he was just going to sail through the meeting as usual, getting no resistance at all. Then, *wham!* A shot to the ribs. *Wham!* A sock to the jaw. *Boom!* An uppercut, right to the chin. Oh *man*. I laid him out like a blanket, don't you think? I mean, figuratively speaking. Guy like him has probably never been in a street fight before."

"You have?"

"Well, not exactly. But you know, back in the eighth grade, I got into a scuffle in the dining hall."

"I see," she said.

"Yeah. And I've got to tell you: I just took this guy out."

"Really. Why?"

"He cut in front of me in the lunch line. So I just, *boom.* One punch in the gut. Bent him over and that was it. Think I knocked the wind out of him. After that, nobody wanted to fight me."

"I'm sure," she said.

"You've seen prison movies, right?"

"Not my preferred genre, but yes."

"People don't believe this, but life inside a prep school can be like that. You have a million little cliques in there. Kids from the old-money families. Kids from nouveau-riche families. Kids from other countries. You have to establish your turf in there, just like I do in here. It was a great life lesson. Let people know right up front what you'll tolerate and what you won't. And, you know, the good thing is that Tim Padden witnessed this meeting. He'll *definitely* know better than to step on my toes. Because now he knows: I refuse to take crap from anybody."

Loud voices coming from the outer office caused both Robbie and Natalia to look toward the door. "What the hell's going on out there now?" he grumbled.

The door creaked open, revealing Winnie, standing with her back to Robbie's office, holding her arms akimbo, trying to block the portal. On the other side was an enraged Maria.

"I told you, Maria," Winnie shouted. "You can't go in there. He's in a meeting."

Maria peered over Winnie's shoulder. "Winnie. Get out of my way."

"I'm going to call security if you don't leave right this minute," Winnie said.

"Call 'em after you get up," Maria said. With that, Maria shoved Winnie backward, sending her tumbling to the floor. Maria then stepped over her and charged into the office, holding rolled up papers in her hand.

She walked over to Robbie on the sofa. "After two years," she said, "you think you can just buy me off with a promotion—on the other side of the ocean?"

"What?" Robbie cried.

"You're dumping me. Is that the idea?" she said.

Robbie glanced to Natalia, then back to Maria. "I have no idea what you're talking about."

"I know exactly how you operate," she said, before looking over to Natalia. "You better pay attention, honey. You might be next."

"I don't think so," Natalia said.

"Don't kid yourself. You're probably the reason he's pushing me out."

Natalia was too stunned to move. Behind Maria, Winnie had risen unsteadily to her feet and wobbled to the phone, holding her arm.

"It's like this, sweetie," Maria said, moving in closer. "He groomed me just the way he's grooming you. A little wine in the office. Private meetings. Special attention. It's the beginning of your seduction. And that's fine. You're a big girl. You can decide for yourself what you want to do. But know this: all his girlfriends—and there's a long line of them—get bought off once he's had his fill. And he won't even have the balls to tell you himself. He'll send his limp dick brother-in-law, Digby, to give you the word and hand you the papers to sign," she said, holding the papers up. "Keep your mouth shut and you'll get a big check or a big promotion. You make the call as to whether it's worth it or not. But as for me: I'm not buying the bullshit he's selling."

Robbie, heart racing, shook his head. "Maria, you've got this all wrong. How would I know you're offered a promotion? That's totally up to management, not me. I have *nothing* to do with that. And I certainly wouldn't send you overseas."

"Oh really," she said, putting her hands on her hips.

"Besides, what's so bad about Italy? Don't you have family back there?"

"I didn't say anything about Italy."

"Well, no. But I... I... just assumed. I mean, you said it was across the ocean."

"Right. Like there's only one ocean. And only one country on the other side. Why, it must be Italy! Of course. You're a fucking soothsayer." She pushed aside the coffee table, sending the glasses and the bottle of Dom Perignon to the floor, then stood over him, balling up the papers in her hand. "Enough of your crap, Robbie. Seriously. Time to plug your pie hole," she said, shoving the papers in his mouth, as he thrashed about, fending her off as best he could. "How do you like this? Taste like chicken?"

"Stop it. You're hurting me," he wailed. "Maria. Please. *Winnie! I need you in here now!*"

Tom Michaels and another security agent rushed into the office and pulled Maria off Robbie. "So sorry, Mr. Crowe," Tom said. "We'll handle it."

"Let go," Maria said, shaking their grip off her arms. "I can walk on my own."

Tom looked to Robbie for approval to release her. "Fine," Robbie said, rubbing his jaw. "Let her go."

Maria looked back as they crossed the threshold. "By the way," she called out, "I had tea with your wife this afternoon. She was asking whether I knew of a good locksmith on the Upper East Side."

Robbie sat up, shaking his head, his eyes teary and his face reddened, a small blot of blood on his lip. Then he looked up to Natalia, who could barely contain her laughter. She stood and looked down on him. "I think *she's* been in a street fight before."

61. GOODBYE AND GOOD LUCK

At 6:45 p.m., Walker made one last bed-check on the 24th floor, partly to see who was around when they didn't care what the boss thought anymore. Unlike every other day since he'd arrived four years earlier, everyone on his leadership team had departed, except Tim. Walker found him pulling files from a cabinet, preparing to move on up.

"Just want to say good luck, Tim," Walker said, popping his head in.

"That's very gracious of you, Walker. Thank you." Tim walked over to shake hands with Walker and savor his moment of triumph. He had been carrying Walker's bags for so long, it was a relief to unburden himself. The apprentice was at last the master. *Damn,* that felt good. As they shook hands, Tim turned his hand over to underscore his new dominance.

If Walker noticed, it didn't show. "You were a great help to me over the years," Walker said. "I know you'll do well."

Tim considered a last bit of flattery about how much he'd learned from Walker but decided against. Such butt-kissing was no longer necessary, at least with Walker's particular rear end. "I'm looking forward to it," he said. "Do you know what you're going to do next?"

"I suspect there will be an opportunity out there for me somewhere," Walker said. "Who knows? We may have an opportunity to work together again."

Tim smirked. *Yeah, right.* "I'm pretty sure our run is over," he said. "But never say never, right? Stranger things have happened."

"Stranger things *do* happen," Walker said. "Especially when it comes to Crowe."

62. BEST LAID PLANS

As the cleaning crew picked up broken glass from the oriental rugs, Robbie slumped behind his desk, staring at the reports that he might now have to read. His faithful servant Howie-Do-It sat in one of the wingback chairs in front of his desk, offering solace.

"Dude," Howie said, "You can stay at my place if you have to. I've got, like, a sofa bed in my living room."

Robbie waved that off. "Thanks, Howie. I can always stay here if I need to. I'll be fine."

"If you change your mind, let me know. I don't have much food in the house right now, but there's a place next door that sells killer slices for a buck."

"Thanks. Seriously."

"Just sayin'," he said, thumping his chest with a fist. "I'm here for you, man."

Robbie leaned back in his chair, putting his hands behind his head, reflecting. "You know, for a while there, I was having a really good day. Everything was going so well."

"Yeah, except for the dude dying," Howie said.

"There was that, I suppose. But everything else was great." The office door creaked open, and Digby entered. "Somehow, I have a feeling it's about to get worse again."

"Not at all," Digby said, beaming. "I actually have some good news."

Robbie perked up. "Lay it on me."

"First of all, Maria is gone."

"Thank *God!*" Robbie exclaimed.

"Thank me, actually," Digby said. "She has resigned and signed an agreement not to sue, in return for a check and a release from her non-compete."

"How much?"

"Three million dollars."

"Okay. I can live with that," Robbie agreed.

"It's our going rate, so to speak."

"Digs, I'm starting to think you might actually be competent."

"There's more," Digby said. "Jayne and Harvey are resigning from the board. We're thinking that means Moe is pulling out of our shares. Apparently, dumping Walker was the last straw. We wore him out."

"No Moe headaches?"

"No Moe tears," Digby said with a smile.

Robbie laughed and fist bumped Digby and Howie. "Hot *damn*. That'll teach that prick. He never should have messed with me in the first place. Who did he think he was? Coming in here and telling me how to run my business. Pushing that ridiculous goober on me as CEO. *God.* I am so done with the whole lot of them."

"The timing is very, very lucky," Digby said. "If Lindsey were to go through with a divorce, your stock holdings will be cut in half. And she'll have the third largest share of Crowe Power stock in the family bloc."

"I can't worry about that now."

"You might have to."

Robbie asked, "Why? What are you getting at, Digby?"

"Meaning, she could potentially swing a vote—and in a way you might not like."

"Oh, come on," Robbie said. "What does she know about the business?"

"Enough to know how to piss you off."

A light knock on the door frame prompted Robbie to look around Digby to see Marty. Beleaguered, he looked to Digby. "Where the *hell* is Winnie?"

"I believe she's at NYU Langone getting treatment for a broken arm."

"And, what," he said, looking at his watch, "she couldn't be back here by now?"

Digby shrugged.

"Robbie?" asked Marty, still standing in the threshold.

"What," Robbie said, irritated. "*What?*"

"I wanted to show you a draft of the press release."

"Fine," Robbie snorted. "Leave it here on the desk. I'm in a meeting."

Marty placed the release on the closest pile of papers on the desk. "Walker's already approved it. We would like to get it out before the market opens tomorrow."

"Are you *deaf*, Marty? I'm in a *meeting.* I'll let you know when I let you know. This will be on my timetable, not yours." First order of business for Tim tomorrow morning would be to fire this asshole.

"Understood," Marty said. "I also left you a print-out of a piece that just popped on the *Fortune* website that I think you'll want to see."

"Fine, Marty. *Fine.* Now will you please just get the fuck out of here?"

"I am leaving," Marty said, with a smile.

Marty walked out and Digby picked up the release, glanced at it and shrugged. "Looks okay to me," he said, tossing it onto a pile on Robbie's desk. Then he looked at the *Fortune* piece and plopped down in the other wingback chair as he read.

"Oh, poo," he said, handing the print-out to Robbie.

FORTUNE.COM EXCLUSIVE

CROWE POWERLESS

Walker B. Hope Leads Exodus to Staminum
Source: Takeover Bid for Crowe in the Works

By Sarah Hudson
Senior Editor

In a stunning turn in fortune, Crowe Power Co. on Monday lost its star CEO, Walker B. Hope, its leading outside investor, Maurice "Moe" Klinger, two members of its

Board of Directors, Jayne Willson and Harvey Mandelbaum, and two senior executives—all of whom are moving to Staminum, a rival energy firm seeking rejuvenation and a possible takeover of Crowe.

While neither company would comment Monday afternoon, sources familiar with the shakeup say that a recent effort by Crowe Power Chairman L. Robertson "Robbie" Crowe III to oust Hope created an opportunity for Staminum to import vital new leadership, which critics complained that it has lacked for many years. With Hope suddenly at the helm, Staminum regains credibility as a player in the industry.

"Robbie Crowe better look in the rear-view mirror," said an investor with knowledge of the situation. "His family has eighteen percent of the stock, but that's a long way from fifty-one. And who knows how others in the family bloc will react when Staminum starts waving money under their noses. Do they still have the heart to fight for the company? Maybe some of them have had enough."

Hope, who led Crowe Power to record profits and a spectacular rise in the company's share price, will have the backing of hedge fund manager Klinger, who filed a notice late Monday that he has acquired at least five percent of Staminum's outstanding shares. He will also have the advice of new General Counsel Maria Territo, who is said to have intimate knowledge of Crowe family workings, and Marty McGarry, who is leaving Crowe Power to become the new Chief Communications Officer for Staminum.

McGarry, reached at Crowe Power headquarters while cleaning out his office late Monday, said Robbie Crowe was in meetings and could not be reached for comment.

Robbie looked up from the report, slack-jawed, a bit of saliva beading on the side of his mouth, his eyes hazy.

"Walker's coming after me," Robbie said. "Isn't he?"

Digby nodded. "Sure looks like it."

Robbie stared at his desk. "That fucking hillbilly…"

"… just played you like a banjo," Digby added. "What are you going to do?"

Robbie shook his head. "First thing is I probably ought to do is send flowers to Lindsey. How do you even do that?"

Howie held up his hand. "You want me to handle it, boss?"

"Yeah. If you would," Robbie said. "Pick something nice."

"What does she like?"

"I don't know. Anything. Something that says I care."

Digby folded his arms across his chest. "Do you?"

Robbie looked up, dazed. "Does she?"

"Well," Digby said. "I guess you'll find out soon enough."

ABOUT THE AUTHOR

JON PEPPER is a novelist, consultant and entrepreneur based in New York City. His company, Indelable, advises leaders on how to define, promote, and define their businesses. He was previously an executive for two Fortune 100 companies, a business columnist and national writer for The Detroit News, a reporter for the Detroit Free Press, a magazine publisher, a radio talk show host and an advertising copywriter. He and his wife, Diane, who designed this book cover, reside in Manhattan.

More about Jon and his novels is available at www.jonpepperbooks.com

The first book in this series, A Turn in Fortune, is available on Amazon

You can learn about Jon's consulting firm at www.indelable.com

Made in the USA
Coppell, TX
12 November 2022

86249006R00146